RUPTURED

A NOVEL

RUPTURED

A NOVEL

BY

RON SINGERTON

www.penmorepress.com

APPRECIATION

I wish to thank my wife, Darla, for her insight, contribution and unstinting assistance in writing and preparation of *Ruptured*. This book would not have been possible without her motivation, patience, and editing. I owe her my deepest gratitude.

I also want to acknowledge the assistance given to me by my esteemed publisher, Michael James, CEO of Penmore Press. His encouragement and support for this work and my five historical novels has been invaluable.

PROLOGUE
Election Day

Washington. D.C.

The bars of Capitol Hill, Georgetown and Alexandria were filled on that frigid night, but not by revelers. Speculation, conjecture and rumor floated like phantom wisps in a horror film.

Steven Whitinghill was sitting at the wooden bar of The Bottom Line with his closest friend, Eli Barett, and staring into his Black Russian. He was hoping the caffeine would keep him alert in the hours ahead, but God! he needed the alcohol to file down the edges. A strange vision came to him: Vikings in silent boats crowned with dragon heads slinking up a river to a slumbering village in the dead of night. All too vividly, he could imagine the carnage and terror that followed.

Eli broke Steven's thoughts with an elbow nudge. "Have you considered moving back home? Not that you can't stay at my place — as long as you buy the beer."

Steven snorted. "Can't go back. Janice is there when she's not sleeping with Goodwin. Gotta wait until she completely moves out."

"How long have you two been separated, six weeks?"

"That long?" Steven took a gulp of his drink.

"At least. Hell, she's been working for him for five months," responded Eli.

"She's a smart woman. I didn't think she would fall for him," said Steven, downing the rest of his Black Russian.

"What's not to fall for? The senator has southern charm, charisma, and money. He gives her attention and lots of affection, be it love or lust. And you, all work and no play, had your head in the sand."

Steven shook his head. "I was trying to balance it all: marriage, work and country. You know that."

"Sure, Director, but you lost her. That's a fact."

They fell silent, their eyes on the bar's TV, watching scenes of the chaos in the House and Senate. Eli didn't bother to use a glass, drinking straight from the bottle of IPA. Pointing to the TV, he said, "You gonna watch the swearing in? I hear it's gonna be quite colorful down there in Alabama. Period uniforms and all." He grimaced, then set the beer bottle to spin, teetering on its base as it rotated.

"Scary stuff, treason," Eli remarked. "Arrests and lockups, or worse—war."

"You really think *she's* into all that stuff?"

"Maybe not all of it, but she'll cling to Goodwin, and he's a True Believer."

"Yep. Seduced her quite nicely, in and out of bed," replied Steven, eyes turned away, not wishing Barett to see his anguish.

"Think she'll get charged? If it comes to that?"

Steven shrugged. "Have to see how it shakes out. But Goodwin? At some point I'll deal with him." He didn't know how, but he knew in his gut there would be a reckoning.

A pall fell over the city. At the closing hour, patrons drifted away, some to cars, some to taxis, some to walk the short distance to their homes on nearby streets, all of them wishing that the day's events had been a freakish nightmare of some sci-fi fantasy, and the next day would be ordinary and calm, sunny and bright—a fine day to be alive.

CHAPTER 1

ALARMS

Washington D.C.; Studio of Freedom America

"If I am not inaugurated as President of the United States within two weeks from this date, I will announce the establishment of an independent and sovereign nation," declared Mississippi Senator Jefferson Calhoun Lee. "A nation delivered from liberal domination of this country by the current government."

Urbane, with white, shoulder-length hair and an imposing demeanor, he stared into the TV lens and pronounced his words with the authority of one well-versed in speaking into cameras, projecting his appeal directly to the viewers.

"Indeed, the sacred ground of decent, God-fearing people will be conceived and dedicated as the Nationalist Christian Republic of America."

In resonant, measured tones, his forefinger pointing upward, he continued. "The secession of twenty-five states— or more!—will be the beginning of freedom, of a holy era. Freedom, my friends, is before us. Freedom! This is my pledge, so help me God!"

The camera panned to talk show host Danny Von Hoffmann, who, despite his rapturous approval, attempted to appear balanced and professional.

"Senator, I'm certain that your pronouncements will be gratefully received by countless millions. But since November, there have been numerous counts and re-counts of popular and electoral college votes. Even a few individuals in right-wing media claim that the incumbent, Ms. Edith Barnes, has won re-election by a substantial margin. What do you have to say to these naysayers?"

The senator steepled his fingers and adopted a judicious pose. With thoughtful concern, he tilted his head, smiled graciously, and responded. "It is common knowledge that the Supreme Court handed the matter of the electoral count back to the state of North Carolina. Their electors determined that the winning count belongs to me and me alone. Thus it is my firm conviction, backed by legal and constitutional experts, that the presidency is mine."

"Of course," said Von Hoffmann deferentially, "But what if . . ."

"There are no 'what ifs'!" Lips pressed firmly together, face flushed, Lee leaned forward, hands pressed against the fabric of the Kiton cashmere suit he wore. "The travesties of the past will no longer be tolerated. Not by me, not by the millions of God-fearing, righteous voters who determined that I am the legitimate leader of the United States. The woman occupying the White House is an imposter!"

Regaining his composure and in a mellifluous tone, he continued, "I want to make it abundantly clear that this election was stolen from me. And if that crime is not rectified, in two weeks' time there will be an inauguration in Montgomery, Alabama, where I shall become the president of a new nation. So is the will of the people, and that is a promise I solemnly make!"

"Is there a particular reason for choosing that date, February 18th?" asked Von Hoffman eagerly.

"Yes. On that day, in 1861, my hero, Mister Jefferson Davis, was inaugurated as president of the Confederacy. It will be the day I will be sworn in as president of a new and glorious nation."

"You can turn it off," said President Edith Barnes. A lengthy moment passed in the Situation Room before she stood and said, "We will deal with this. We most certainly will."

*****

Janice Whitinghill, wife of the FBI Director, descended from the gallery to the Senate floor to stand beside Alabama senator James Goodwin. "This is a historic moment," she said, smiling up at him.

He took her hand in his. "Yes, and it's really happening. Just like a thunderstorm, it's been building. Now for the flood."

Pleased with his behind the scenes role in orchestrating events, he contemplated the chaos in the Senate as numerous office holders tried in vain to stave off the catastrophe. The exasperated Sergeant at Arms was shouting for order, but the admonishment went ignored, lost in the din of belligerent voices.

"It's over!" came the sharp baritone voice of the Senate minority leader. There was a sudden silence as all eyes turned toward him. "We are going; we've heard enough," he said, his arm sweeping toward the rear door.

"No, you can't go!" implored the senior senator from New York. "All your demands are negotiable. This cannot happen!"

Senator Lee gave him a reproachful look and said, "But it has. It is the time of winnowing, and the wheat shall be separated from the chaff."

Senators watched in varying degrees of chagrin and despair as nearly all the opposition exited the chamber. Dozens of House members standing in the gallery followed their senate colleagues.

"The buses for Dulles are waiting," said James Goodwin, turning to Janice. "We'll all take the flight from here to Montgomery. I do hope you're coming."

"Of course I'm coming along! I won't stay here without you," she replied, her hand clutching his. "Are we going to the old Capitol when we get there?"

"We'll go there for the inauguration, but that's still days away. We'll go to my place first, relax a bit, and I'll show you around town. Then we'll see my friend take the oath as the President of the NCRA."

"I still have to get used to the acronym," said Janice.

"Nationalist Christian Republic of America. A new country, and one that lets businesses operate without interference. Now let's get to those buses. Have your phone ready. This will be magnificent."

"I imagine the whole world will be watching," said Janice as they queued up in line.

"They'll be watching and sitting on their hands while our compatriots are creating a new order. And you and I shall have a front row seat."

February 18, Inauguration Day
Montgomery, Alabama

Janice sat beside Goodwin at the front of a flower-bedecked dais, alongside several dozen other politicians and wealthy donors to President Lee's political campaigns. Goodwin had been offered a post as foreign secretary but had turned it down, preferring that of senior advisor to Lee.

"But foreign secretary would have been a wonderful position," Janice had said. "We would have been able to travel all over the world, and I've always wanted to do that."

"No, love, I'd rather be the one to put ideas in Lee's head. And I have a hunch that people in the NCRA may not be doing much traveling, at least not at first. Too much to do at home! And there is this to consider: foreign nations might not be handing out many invitations."

"No?" said Janice, her brow wrinkled.

Goodwin had smiled at her and said, "I imagine that soon, very soon, Edith Barnes will try to restrict our citizens gallivanting around. It was called the Anaconda Plan during the Civil War. Closed our borders and crippled Confederate commerce."

"You think Edith will do that? An embargo?"

"I suspect so. And then foreign nations will have to choose between the old, failed government and recognizing the NCRA for what it is: a sovereign nation in its own right. Some foreign powers will immediately see the advantage of aligning with us, but others will dither."

The Cabinet members of the NCRA began to take their seats as the inauguration began.

Janice looked about and, suddenly alarmed, turned to Goodwin "What's *he* doing here?" She jerked her head ever so slightly towards the taciturn man standing next to Lee.

Goodwin turned and eyed the cadaverous figure. "Stanley Palmer? He's Secretary of Internal Security. Lee chose him personally."

"That's impossible! He's a known white sup—."

"Decorum, my dear. Our President is very fond of Palmer's views, has been for a long time. Lee favors like-minded people from the media."

"But he's a bigot and . . ."

"And a scapegoat if things go awry," Goodwin said smoothy. "It's about deflection, avoidance of blame."

"I detest the man."

"Of course you do."

"I don't want to be anywhere near him."

"You're my aide, not his. Just ignore him. Now let's watch the proceedings."

Hundreds of people had been given a copy of the NCRA Constitution, a slender document encased in a black leather binder printed with gold letters which, except for the title, looked much like a Bible. The resemblance was intentional. Not wishing to discuss Palmer any further, Janice opened the cover and began to read the document for the first time.

She noted that all NCRA laws were essentially in the hands of President Lee and his Supreme Court appointees, to be determined and changed at their will.

Article One maintained that freedom of speech would be guaranteed as long as it did not violate the spirit and religious beliefs of the new nation.

The second Article stated that all white citizens would be allowed to carry firearms, and that each state would organize armed militias for the purpose of defusing any opposition to governmental requirements.

Article Three gave the president emergency powers over the high court and congressional body. This was followed by a ban on gays and transgender people from holding office, as well as non-Christians and non-white ethnicities.

The Fourth Article required the government to gain possession of lands owned and inhabited by minorities if these lands were deemed essential to the economic well-being of the NCRA. Moreover, said populations might be detained in specially designated environments if there was unruly opposition.

The fifth Article stated that no white women shall be allowed to undergo an abortion. Any violation of the destruction of an embryo shall have the offending party subject to a charge of homicide.

Janice frowned and showed this to Goodwin.

"The vast majority of the population here are evangelicals. They've wanted that to be law for decades. The same with the law regarding school prayer. This is simply the will of the people, my dear. That is what democracy means."

Janice closed the slim volume and studied the row of dignitaries. One couple seemed out of place.

She turned to Goodwin. "Who are they?"

He followed her eyes and focused on a man of very dark complexion. Beside him was seated a beautiful Hispanic woman in a bright dress.

"Ralph Prescott and his wife, Maria. He's got huge farms in the state, along with various hotel chains. Very well off, very conservative, and hates government regulation. I told Lee that it would look good to have a man of color as a member in his cabinet. Prescott was given the post of Secretary of Agriculture, since he knows farming."

"I wonder how he will be treated," Janice said, watching the man in pleasant conversation with his fellow appointees.

"You may be surprised by the baggage people carry with them," murmured Goodwin. "Before the Civil War, his great-great-grand-daddy was one of several black men who owned slaves. But he'd never talk about that. The important thing to know is that he has some dealings with Jeff Lee, but that's all kind of murky and they don't pry into each other's business affairs. It's not a comfortable thing to do."

"What about his wife?"

"Maria Gonzales Estavo Prescott. She has ties to the President of Mexico and was a TV host for *El Mundo* in Mexico City. They've been together a long time, and she has a good life here. I've heard they've had disputes over the status of migrants in the NCRA. But she's in very nice digs, not some hovel in Mexico City, and the secret to getting ahead is to take care of yourself and not look back."

There were sounds of a disturbance off to one side. Palmer's security detail had halted a contingent of marchers wearing white robes and pointed hoods who had been approaching the inauguration. Goodwin rose to watch and Janice asked, "What's happening?"

"Klan members, all decked out. We knew they'd be here, supporters of Lee. He's not opposed to them, but he doesn't want them on TV. Palmer's people were tasked with keeping them off camera."

The former speaker of the House, a thickly set congressman from North Carolina, tapped the microphone and announced, "Ladies and gentlemen, on this fine day, we have the privilege of presenting the oath of office to the first president of the Nationalist Christian Republic of America."

There was wild and sustained applause as Jefferson Calhoun Lee approached the podium, his fourth wife standing beside him holding his family Bible.

In solemn tones, the oath was administered by a Baptist minister, and then Lee addressed his audience in his stentorian voice.

"On this momentous occasion, we celebrate the beginning of a new nation, conceived with God's blessing. It is a true Christian nation, harking back to the original concept of belief in the Supreme Deity which was paramount with our founding fathers. With humility and righteousness in sight of the Lord, we will adhere to the dictates of our sacred Constitution and the liberties it grants to our citizens of this nation."

Janice's eyes drifted to the ancient Capitol dome, the pillars and portico where Jefferson Davis had taken his oath of office on that February day so long ago.

With fervor and determination, Lee grasped the podium and said, "Let me assure the world that we will staunchly oppose any intimidation, aggression and opposing forces, foreign or domestic, that threaten the sanctity of this nation. I know that there will be difficulties and challenges, we must expect that, but we will not be cowed, nor will we falter. We, the people, will persevere in all that is holy, and we shall triumph! So help us, God!"

Another thunderous applause filled the air. Lee moved about, shaking hands with cabinet members and elite citizens. Beyond the open area, thousands of newly designated NCRA citizens occupied viewing stands that bordered the parade route. As the sounds of approval died down, Lee returned to the microphone. With an encompassing gesture, he addressed his audience once more. "And now, we will turn to the festivities that celebrate this historic event. Here comes the parade!"

Everyone turned their attention to the road and the first contingent of marchers: the Montgomery High School band. Drums rattled out a quick-time march accompanied by Sousa tunes. Those were interspersed with "Dixie" and other numbers associated with the Confederacy.

A cheer went up as two dozen re-enactment cavalry, the Sussex Light Dragoons in splendid grey uniforms, trotted before the reviewing stand. An order was given and, with expert precision, sabers were drawn from scabbards, hilts raised to eye level, and faces turned to President Lee. He stood, saluting in return as the riders spun their mounts in unison before returning sabers and forming columns of four.

They were followed by the First Louisiana Zouaves wearing red fezzes, embroidered red vests and baggy striped pants, all based on a style worn by the French Foreign Legion during their nineteenth century wars in North Africa. Shouldering five-foot long muskets with glistening bayonets affixed, they marched in front of a contingent of South Carolina field artillery with accompanying caissons. The heavy muzzle-loading cannons were pulled by plow horses and rumbled past the stands as riders raised their hats amid the din of sustained cheers.

The re-enactor units were followed by an assortment of floats representing various industries and universities. Spectators cheered each contingent as they passed, and a sense of merriment pervaded the densely packed crowd. The NCRA flags — white with a blue cross, and the Confederate stars and bars in the upper left corner — were waved as shouts of approval filled the air.

Influential captains of industry as well as governors and wealthy supporters filed onto the dais to congratulate Lee. After twenty minutes of glad-handing and mutual congratulations, Lee glanced toward well-wishers in the first row of seats, then made his way over to Goodwin and Janice. Smiling approvingly, he said, "Cabinet meeting first thing in the morning, and I want both of you there. Lots of important legislation to be done. Got to get everything off on the right foot. And, young lady, I have a very important job for you. I'll tell you about it tomorrow."

On the drive home to Goodwin's estate, James looked over at Janice. "You look rather pensive. What's on your mind, babe?"

"Just musing. I'm sure everything is going to be fine, and I'm really impressed by Lee. He was extremely gracious, and I know how greatly he will value your assistance."

"But?"

"It's just that I have been to dozens of inaugurations and parades, and I've always proud to see the Marines, Army and other services march by. But none of them were here today."

"No, they wouldn't be. That's all U.S., and they have a little problem with us, darling. I'm sure that we will eventually have our own forces, besides the militias: armored, naval, and air and space contingents. Don't worry your pretty head about it. We'll be a world power, and unlike other nations there will not be any internal hostilities. None whatsoever. As the poem goes, 'God's in his heaven and all's right with the world.'"

"I presume you are right," replied Janice, smiling. She loved that Goodwin could quote poetry as well as apposite passages from the Bible; so few men bothered to read these days. She squeezed his arm and added, "I adore you."

"And I you, babe."

She stared out the window, watching the wind gusting through the Magnolia trees.

CHAPTER 2

A MATTER OF RETRIBUTION

Montgomery, Alabama, 18 months earlier

Stanley Palmer pulled his mic closer and proudly said, "Well, y'all, I have just been informed that my good friend, our very own Jefferson Calhoun Lee, has confirmed his decision to run for the office of President of the United States of America, and has told me in confidence his plans for our nation. Great things are about to happen, so spread the word and vote for the right man! Yes, I promise that great things are on the horizon. So farewell, and God bless us."

The radio show Palmer had run for the past five years was located in a small station inside a strip mall. Palmer had argued for a better location, but management said revenues would not allow it. He knew that he had at least a million followers, locally and nationally, but management wanted to keep their profit margin high, and a bigger studio would be an exorbitant cost. And, as they pointed out, this was just a talk show.

Stanley Palmer was a dour man, nearly skeletal, with a bald head a face with wrinkles so deep they resembled crevasses in a mountain range. He glanced at the large clock on the wall. *Alice will be calling at twelve,* he reminded himself. He and his wife Alice were supposed to meet for lunch with Danny Von Hoffmann, the on-camera face of the nationally syndicated program *Freedom America*.

Pen in hand, he looked over his notes for the midday show. He wanted to add at least one more dig at his favorite target, Edith Barnes, President of the United States. He added several rhetorical questions, some accusations and innuendo, and sat back, pleased with himself. Then he checked the clock again and frowned. It was already twelve-twenty. *What could Alice possibly be doing?* She knew he had to be back on the air by one forty-five.

Just as he was starting to worry, his phone rang. He glanced at the screen, surprised to see Danny Von Hoffmann's number instead of his wife's. He answered it quickly.

"Palmer, there's been an accident on Third," said Von Hoffmann. I'm heading down there; you want to come?"

"Yeah. If Alice calls, I'll just tell her that we'll do lunch tomorrow. Any details?"

"Hit and run, I think. Cops, ambulance. We'll take my car; I'll swing by to pick you up."

A crowd had gathered on the sidewalk beside the wreck. A Volkswagen had been slammed into a tree and was nearly bent in half. There was no sign of the car that struck it. Two fire engines had arrived with the jaws of life to remove the driver, who lay motionless across what remained of the front seat.

Police cars blocked the road, but Von Hoffmann flashed his press badge and his car was allowed to snake past. Two firemen managed to tear off the driver's side door as Von Hoffmann and Palmer approached the scene.

Palmer abruptly stopped. Though the vehicle was mangled almost beyond recognition, the rear license plate was clearly visible.

"Oh my God! Oh my God!" said Palmer, suddenly pushing a policeman out of the way and dashing toward the wreck.

"Alice! Alice!" he cried, as her lifeless body was slowly extricated; firemen laid her gently on a gurney. Tears streamed down Palmer's face as he crumpled beside her.

A priest who had accompanied the ambulance driver laid his hand on Palmer's shoulder and said, "She's with God. I'm sure she felt no pain. It was instantaneous, according to the police."

"Someone else is in there!" shouted a fireman.

Palmer looked up as a dark-haired teenage girl was lifted from the back seat.

"She's alive! Careful, careful. Get that gurney over here," said a cop. He and a fireman pulled Palmer's daughter Shelley from the wreck.

"Is she going to live?" asked Palmer, as the girl was placed in the ambulance.

"Let's pray that she does," said the attendant as he closed the vehicle's doors. "She's unconscious, and she has a broken arm, so we're taking her straight to the ER."

Sirens wailing, the ambulance and a patrol car raced to the emergency room, followed by Von Hoffmann and Palmer. Two hours later, the coroner's assistant found Palmer sitting in the waiting room.

"Are you Mr. Palmer, the husband of the deceased?"

"Yes. Can I see her later? I don't want her cut up. No autopsy. She never drank, never did drugs, nothing like that. No autopsy, you hear?"

"I'll tell that to the coroner. He will contact you and arrange a time for you to come in."

Palmer, stunned by the morning's tragedy, sat anxiously in the hospital waiting room, Von Hoffmann in the chair next to him. Two more long hours passed before a doctor entered, removed his mask and said, "Mr. Palmer, Shelley is awake. She is doing well and should have a full recovery. You can see her now."

"I've got to interview the police," said Von Hoffmann. "We'll find out who did this. But Palmer, take a week off, comfort your daughter. I'll cover for you."

"Thanks," said Palmer. "I hope they find the son of a bitch. If they don't, I will, and I'm going to kill the bastard. Whoever did this is going to be pulp. There won't be enough left to cremate."

The driver responsible for yesterday's hit and run accident, which resulted in one death and one injury, was nineteen-year-old Douglas Atherman. He was apprehended two miles from the scene of the crime.

ran the column in the *Montgomery Star* the next morning. A few days later, a follow up article reported:

Mr. Atherman, who is a student at the University of Alabama, ran a red light and struck the car containing Alice Palmer, wife of radio announcer Stanley Palmer, and their daughter, Shelley Palmer. Mrs. Palmer sustained fatal injuries. The Palmer's daughter survived but is still hospitalized.

Douglas Atherman has been arraigned and bail has been set at two hundred and fifty thousand dollars. His father, U.S. Senator Eland Atherman of Colorado, was seen at court and has hired an attorney.

A card arrived at Palmer's home, a modest house on the edge of town with an extensive garden, lovingly maintained by Alice. Palmer opened the envelope, took out the card and read,

Dear Mr. Palmer,

I wish to tender my condolences upon the passing of your wife. I know that she is in heaven with the Lord and surely smiles upon you and your daughter each and every day. I want you to know that I am a great fan of yours and listen to your splendid program as often as I can, since I am in absolute agreement with your sentiments and proposals. I wish you the very best and look forward to speaking with you in the not too distant future.

Most sincerely,

Jefferson Calhoun Lee

*****

A capital crime case can take years to resolve, but the death of Alice Palmer never even went to trial. There was one very simple reason: diplomatic immunity. As a family member of a sitting senator, Douglas Atherman was eventually deemed exempt, despite Lee's efforts to exert influence on his friend's behalf.

Four months following the accident, Danny Von Hoffmann stood outside the Montgomery courthouse, microphone in hand. Senator Atherman stood on the courthouse steps, along with the defense attorney. Approaching the Senator, Von Hofmann said, "We understand that you refused to post bail, Senator. Is that because you anticipated the release of your son?"

"My son is very remorseful and had no prior violations. I think his time in jail has made a deep impression on him, as will the one hundred hours of community service he has volunteered to undertake. I have no further comment."

That very afternoon, Palmer made this interview the subject of his radio show.

"A miscarriage of justice and most assuredly a backroom deal!" Palmer shouted into the mic. "The kid was on drugs, ran the red light, slammed into my wife's car and killed her! And what does he get? A slap on the wrist! I say this to you, my friends, the justice system is riddled with corruption, run by liberal judges on the take. And it will be so until they are voted out, disbarred, and left twisting in the wind! And the same goes for the administration of Edith Barnes, whose minions enable these spineless miscreants, who wring their hands and cringe at the thought of putting away drug-crazed minors.

"The senator claims his son was 'remorseful'. The hell he was! He didn't say a word to me. No apology, not the slightest sign of regret. Just a smug look. That son of a bitch should be spending the rest of his life in prison! Not community service, but hard time in the worst penal colony in Alabama. Failing that, he should be taken out and shot! Yes, in sensible nations, the relatives of the slain have the right to execute the perp. Give me the gun, and I will pull the trigger. Damn right I will, and Lord help anyone who gets in my way!"

*****

Sheets of rain descended on the street as Douglas Atherman left a raucous frat party. It was good to be out of jail, enjoying college life again in a part of the country what wasn't covered with snow for one-fourth of the year. Only a few street lights glowed as he pulled the hood of his jacket up over his cap and walked unsteadily to his car, two blocks away. He pulled a flask from his pocket and took a long swig. The scotch gave him temporary warmth.

Having been drinking heavily for the last three hours, Douglas's vision was blurry, the pavement shimmering beneath the sallow street lights. He barely noticed a tall, gaunt man, hat pulled low as he passed. Nor did he see him suddenly turn three steps behind him and, with a swift, angry stroke, slam the heavy wooden bat into his spine.

Douglas screamed, reached back, and then toppled to the ground, passing out from the pain. Unconscious, he was unaware of the removal of his wallet and the theft of his money.

Thirty minutes later, he came to his senses and tried to stand up, but his legs didn't respond. Terrified, he realized he could not feel them. He never would again.

Two days later, an article in the *Montgomery Tribune* read:

> *Douglas Atherman was found near the intersection of Mission Hills and Pleasanton, the apparent victim of a robbery. Sources report that he was in a state of extreme intoxication. He was taken to Montgomery General Hospital.*

A month later, Stanley Palmer parked a block away from the hospital's front doors as two orderlies wheeled Douglas to his father's waiting limo. Palmer watched as Senator Atherman arranged his son's limp legs inside the vehicle. As the limo was driven away, Palmer scowled. *It was supposed to be a life for a life*. He started the engine, turned on country music, and drove home.

*****

It was the winter PTA meeting of the year at Shelley Palmer's high school. Her father gave Gracie Edelstein, Shelley's history teacher, an almost imperceptible nod as he wandered about the classroom. An American flag was displayed in the corner; world maps of various historical periods covered one wall. Another wall displayed grade A compositions by students, one of which was Shelley's. A third wall exhibited photographs of famous people, including Frederick Douglass, John F. Kennedy, Sojourner Truth and Dr. Jonas Salk, the inventor of the polio vaccine.

Along with the American figures were pictures of Nelson Mandela, Oppenheimer, Anne Frank, David Ben-Gurion—the first president of Israel—and photos of World War II Nazi concentration camps, with commentary regarding the murder of Jews and non-Jews.

These attracted the attention of Palmer, whose eyes narrowed as he pursed his lips. Abruptly turning to his daughter, he said, "Shelley, we're leaving here. Right now."

"But I want to introduce you to Mrs. Edelstein," Shelley said plaintively.

"I said we're going. I don't want to have to tell you again."

Shelley followed her father out of the class and across the campus.

"She's a really nice teacher," said Shelley, as Palmer peevishly drove home.

"I'm taking you out of that woman's class tomorrow morning. And that Mexican language teacher's class, too."

"But I need those credits to graduate, Dad. You can't do that!"

"I can do whatever I want. I didn't know that you had a Jew teacher for history. That stuff on the wall about concentration camps is bullshit. It's all made up to denigrate

Germans. Those camps never existed! You hear? And you wrote a *paper* about it?"

"I did the research, we saw the actual film footage. Mrs. Edelstein isn't lying, Dad. Her grandfather fought the Nazis at Bastogne, and then was with General Patton when he visited the camps. *American* soldiers liberated them, they took the pictures!"

Palmer shook his head but remained silent for the next ten minutes. Finally, he said, "No, I'm not taking you out of those classes. I'm taking you out of that school. You can get your diploma from home. I'll find you a suitable teacher for home schooling. That's how it's going to be."

The previous year, despite her dad's objections, her mom had insisted that Shelley be allowed to travel with members of her high school class to Washington D.C. for meetings with representatives of numerous community development organizations.

It had been an exciting excursion for Shelley, who had never adventured beyond Montgomery. She'd had a front row seat when Janice Whitinghill had addressed the students about organizational techniques. A luncheon had followed in which Shelley found herself sitting at a table between Mrs. Whitinghill and her daughter, Evelyn. Terribly shy, Shelley had been in awe of being spoken to as if she was truly an adult. During the conversation, Shelley had mentioned that after graduation she would love to work in Washington, perhaps for an organization like the one to which Janice belonged.

Mrs. Whitinghill had agreed that it would be a very fine experience and even mentioned that there might be a project that Shelley and Evelyn could work on together. She'd handed Shelley a business card, telling her to call her and she would be glad to assist her in finding a position to begin her career. Just how much her parents would approve, Shelley had no idea, but the very thought of it had filled her with joy. A whole new world had seemed possible.

Now here she was, close to graduating. Would Mrs. Whitinghill remember her? Would she even be able to travel? Things we getting weird, now that Georgia was no longer going to be part of The United States. Her father seemed about as happy as it was possible for him to be about the prospect of succession, but Shelley wasn't so sure. Well, she'd leave a phone message for Mrs. Whitinghill. Maybe she could reconnect with that world of possibilities.

*****

Shelley saw the incoming phone call and recognized the caller ID. Relieved that she was alone and, for a change, unsupervised, she answered the phone with an eager, "Hello?"

"Hello, Shelley. This is Janice. Thank you for your very kind message; I'm so pleased you remember me. I find myself in Montgomery, so I thought I would phone to see how you are doing."

"Oh, thank you for calling, Mrs. Whitinghill! So much has changed since I met you. Everything has turned upside down."

"Please, call me Janice. Upside down? Is there a problem?"

"Yes, a terrible one. My mother was killed in an automobile accident last year, and my father has changed completely, especially towards me."

"Oh, dear God!" I'm so sorry to hear about your mother. And what's happening with your dad?"

"He's always been very protective. He even objected to me going on that school trip where I met you. Now he wants total control of everything I do: where I go, who I meet, even

21

what I wear. And worse, when he's gone, he has a woman watch me. I as much of my time in my room just so I don't have to see her."

"Shelley, I won't be going back to D.C. Things have changed for me, too. I know that we haven't had a lot of time to get to know each other very well, but I see you as a second daughter. So I don't feel strange telling you that I'm with another man, a very important one."

There was a moment of silence before Shelley asked, "Is Evelyn with you?"

"No, she's in Baltimore, at college."

"Oh, I see. Janice, do you think you can help me? I would really like to see you. I don't know of anybody else I can talk to."

"Of course, I would be glad to help. Are things that bad between you and your father? Have you tried talking to him?"

"It's impossible. He's become a tyrant, and I absolutely detest him and that woman," said Shelley between sobs.

"What woman?" asked Janice.

"The one he found to teach me, as part of home-schooling. Her name is Elsa Kessel, and I can barely understand her. When she gets impatient, she yells in German at me. And she doesn't even have a college degree!"

"She's German?"

"Austrian, according to my father. She's sixty-three, skinny, never smiles, and she's paid to follow me everywhere. She's like one of those North Korean minders. I'm not allowed to talk to anybody, especially any boy, not even my old friends from school. Janice, I can't stand this anymore, and I really want to meet with you. Alone."

"How can you do that if she's always with you?"

"I can sneak away at night. She sleeps in the old guest house. The one that was once a carriage barn. She retires at seven and spends nearly an hour in prayer, then makes tea and watches television. I can get out and meet you at the coffee shop on Clay."

"Tomorrow night at nine, would that be okay?"

"Yes, oh yes. Nothing's the same. My father's not the same since my mom died. She used to keep him from hitting me or keeping me in the house but now—"

"How old are you?"

"I'll be eighteen in three weeks."

"Then you'll legally be an adult. You don't have to stay with him, and even now you can report him for child abuse if he hits you."

"I... I'm afraid of what he might do to me."

"I'll press charges if you don't. Tomorrow, we'll talk. But Shelley, I just think he's being overly protective of you."

"Maybe, but it's like he's demented. He shouts a lot, sometimes at me, sometimes at what he calls 'the system.'"

"Yes, I've heard his radio program. Some of his views are quite extreme."

"I've heard them, too. Very scary.

Shelley was quiet for a moment then said, "Is Evelyn going to be visiting you?"

"No, she won't be coming to Alabama. She is living on campus. At least I think so. Unfortunately, we've had a rather serious disagreement, and we're not really on speaking terms right now."

"That's too bad. I really like her. She seems determined and so independent. She wouldn't put up with somebody like my dad."

"A bit too independent, I'm afraid, Shelley. And she won't come to me for any advice."

"Well anyway, now you have another daughter, and I do need your advice. Okay, I'll see you tomorrow. And I'll call if I have any problem."

But the next morning, Shelley awoke a virtual prisoner. While sleeping, a latch had been screwed on to the outside of her bedroom door and she was locked inside.

Shelley pounded on the door and yelled, "Mrs. Kessel, let me out!"

"*Nein, nein.* Your father told me that I must watch you very closely and I should not allow you to leave. I know that you will run off, and I can't allow that to happen. I will let you out when he returns."

This is terrible, thought Shelley as she slumped on her bed. She knew it would be useless to try to change Mrs. Kessel's mind. Tears rolled down her cheeks and she felt totally helpless.

Janice will know what to do, she thought. She suddenly jumped off the bed, searched in her purse for her phone, and made the call. "Mrs. Whitinghill, this is Shelley. I'm imprisoned in my room. Mrs. Kessel, has locked me in. Can you help me?"

"Is your father coming home soon?"

"No, he's gone with Von Hoffmann to some sort of rally. But she's here."

"I'm coming over and I won't be alone."

"What can you do?"

"Break in if I have to. But my boyfriend knows people. See you soon."

CHAPTER 3

SEDUCTION

Arms crossed, a police officer stood behind Janice and a social worker from the Children's Defense, Safety and Health Administration. The woman handed Frau Kessel an official paper and said, "Under Alabama state law, it is illegal to lock a minor in a room under any circumstances. You can ask her to stay in a particular place, but you cannot imprison or restrain her. Any future action of this type will result in suspension of license or arrest. Is that clear?"

"I was only doing what I was told. I had no idea it was some sort of violation. In Vienna we—"

"This is not Austria, Frau Kessel," said the social worker. "Release Shelley immediately, and I advise you to keep your distance. We will be in touch with Mr. Palmer."

Janice bought coffee and a bag of donuts and sat on a park bench with Shelley.

"I don't know what I would have done if you hadn't shown up with that woman and the cop. I think Mrs. Kessel was scared. She seemed very apologetic when she let me out."

"Facing police and a social worker in Austria may not be a pleasant thing. She won't bother you anymore."

"I saw her packing. I think she'll be gone by the time I get home."

They sipped their coffee and had polished off four donuts when Shelley said, "I can't tell you how much I miss Mom, even if we didn't always agree on things. She was very traditional. She hated it when I wore pants and plaid shirts. She said I look like a homeless girl. But it hides my tummy." She looked down at the donut in her hand. "And she would not have approved of these. I look like a plum already. I see other girls, shapely girls, and I just want to run and hide."

"You don't look like a plum, Shelley, and there's no need to hide. I shouldn't have bought the donuts, but I thought we needed a lift."

"Yeah, I guess so." There was a moment of silence, then she said, "I haven't done anything exciting in my entire life. I've only been out of Montgomery once, and that's when I met you in D.C. My mom arranged it in my junior year. My dad was totally against it. And then he really embarrassed me the night of the PTA event. I didn't even have an opportunity to say goodbye to Mrs. Edelstein. She must be wondering what happened."

"You can call her. She should know it was not your decision to drop her class or leave the school."

Shelley nodded and said, "You know, some of the kids were saying things about my dad. Some liked what he had to say, but others began to stay away from me. And to be honest, I only had a few friends anyway. I don't make friends easily, Janice. People don't like being around a plump girl."

"Being overweight isn't a prison sentence, Shelley. A lot of men like women with a few extra pounds."

"I haven't met any. Do you know what? I haven't even kissed a boy. My two best friends have had sex with their boyfriends, and they really enjoyed it. But they're pretty and have no problem attracting boys."

"Shelley, you should know that for boys sex is all about fun, but it can be dangerous for girls unless they know what they're doing. Boys may become fathers, perhaps by accident, but its girls who get pregnant, and that's serious. I hope your friends took precautions."

"They didn't say anything about that."

"Well, I hope for their sakes they did. And there's something else you should understand. Beauty is not just about good looks. It's what's inside. Yeah, sex is fun, but eventually you'll find someone nice, someone who cares for and deserves you. Don't worry about the sex, that will come. You need to focus more on furthering your education and choosing a good career. The more diverse and interesting you are, the more men will find you."

Shelley frowned and kicked her feet against the bench. "My father won't pay for a college education. He didn't even allow me to finish high school." Shelley stared at her hands in her lap. "That's all good advice, but my life is so damn dull. I would love to go to a dance or a party, something *really* wild. I dream of losing myself in some debauched fantasy like in the magazines I stole from my dad. He hides them from me, but I know where they are. I found one of his DVDs, too. Real sex stuff, and very exciting."

"So, you watched it?"

"I did, yes. They were doing things I never even imagined."

"You know that's all staged, choreographed, the exaggerated sighs, the moans and all."

"But the men's things are hard and go in real deep. That's not faked."

Janice sighed and softly said, "I can't help you there, Shelley. But soon it will be possible for you to meet boys if you wish. And I have a few suggestions."

Shelley looked at Janice expectantly.

"First, change your hairstyle. It needs some flair. Put on some lipstick, but not too much. And your mom was right: get out of those clothes—no ripped pants and baggy shirts. You don't have to look like you're on display, but wear something nice. And if you need money, I will give it to you."

"Really, you'll do that?"

"I will. You can be the daughter I no longer have. We can go shopping. I think that will be fun."

"Great! What else?"

"Hang out in places where you can have conversations, where you can find intelligent boys who will listen to you, and where you can get a sense of what they're like."

"I won't know what to say."

"Read some books, go to the library, bookstores, see what guys read. Plan out a strategy. It doesn't have to be complicated. Smile, ask questions. Most guys want to talk about themselves. Let them. If you meet someone you like, stroke his ego."

"It sounds cunning, deceiving even."

"Life is often like that, Shelley. Dating is a game, and it's good to know what's on—or off—the chessboard."

*****

Montgomery, two weeks later

Leland Galway II zipped through traffic at forty-five miles per hour, cutting between cars until he arrived at the frat house. At twenty-three, he felt on top of the world. Tearing into the drive, he parked and goosed the engine of the silver MX-6 Miata, a gift from his wealthy father.

At six-foot-two with a thicket of bright blond shoulder-length hair, Leland exuded supreme confidence. Seeing his fraternity brothers staring down from the second story Victorian, he gave the "V" sign as he slid out of the convertible and pointed to the magnificent car. From under the seat, he snatched a bottle of Jack Daniels and strode into the house.

Leland had graduated in June with a Bachelor of Arts but bragged that he never read a single textbook, or any other book for that matter. With a handsome bribe that few would refuse, he borrowed class notes the day before the exam, crammed and got a grade of "C" every time.

His intense concentration was devoted to another subject, one that that was much more enjoyable and one in which he never got less than an "A." Being one of the wealthiest and best-looking students, he was singularly adept at bedding virtually any girl he picked up. Once finished with her, he enhanced his popularity with his frat brothers by threatening blackmail against any girl who refused to be laid by them in turn. Their appreciation knew no bounds and rarely would any woman in the Bible Belt admit the disgrace, least of all to her parents.

"Goddamn! Another score," blurted Vincent Drake, seeing the grin on Leland's face. "How many does that make?" he asked approvingly.

Leland shrugged, a sly smile on his lips. "Lost count years ago, but this one was a sweet piece of cake." Then correcting himself, he said, "No, Vincent, a very, very fine piece of ass. Moaned to high heaven and begged for every inch."

"Then come in, master. Reggie's in the den."

Leland followed his best friend and saw Reggie, a bespeckled junior with a chubby face and double chin, sprawled out on a giant bean bag. Leland was once again reminded that it was only Reggie's brilliant mind and his father's donations to the fraternity that gave this geeky loser any sort of status.

"Gonna tell us about it? What was she like?" asked Reggie as Leland sank into a sofa after pouring three glasses of the world's finest whisky.

"Fantastic. Did her sister, too," Leland replied, stretching his legs on an ottoman.

"I assume that you're going to give her to us," said Vincent, an "A" student and the recipient of several hand-offs.

"Maybe. Yeah, the older one is a seven on the scale, the other a six, maybe a five."

"Use the potion?" asked Reggie.

"A few drops, didn't take much. They were ready."

The three of them downed their first glass when Vincent said, "With the car and your money, you can go for tens if you want. Why fives, sixes and sevens?"

Leland made a dismissive gesture and said, "Sure I can. Hell, I can just drive around and pick up cunt, married or single. But there's something about those lower numbers that's damn right thrilling. Don't get me wrong, I don't do dogs, never twos, threes or fours. No way. But fives and sixes are hungry for it. They don't get much and are usually desperate. And appreciative. Most of the eights, nines and tens are snotty bitches, think they're a gift from God."

"Yeah," said Reggie, who had never gotten within twenty yards of any eights, nines or tens. "Fives and sixes aren't too bad."

"Damn straight," chimed in Vincent. "Where did you find them, the one you had last night?"

"The bookstore on Second. So simple. I see them reading a book, pretend I'm interested, and strike up a conversation. It's so routine. They get excited, especially if I say something titillating. Get their phone number, maybe take them to a cheap dinner, hotel, then off go the clothes. And yeah, if they are a bit hesitant, a bit of wine, a discreet drop or two, and it's snatch time."

Reggie grinned and said, "Maybe we should tag along. What do you say?"

"Nope, can't divert their attention. I've worked out the perfect scenarios, each one tailored to a specific type. Sometimes I have to be serious, sometimes a clown, just depends. Have to do surveillance for a minute or two, read the body language with a sidelong glance. And then once she's the target you strike like a rattler. It's a science but also an art. But don't worry, I do favors for my buddies."

"So, you'll bring them over. I mean the ones last night?"

"I guess. Maybe I'll indulge, too."

"Roger that!" said Vincent.

"Wow!" shouted Reggie before downing another glass.

*****

A week passed after the shopping trip when Shelley phoned Janice. There was excitement in her voice as she said, "Janice, I tried on the new clothes, changed my hairstyle and put on the makeup you picked out. I look like a new person. But I think I should hide it all from my father."

"Yes, of course. But I can't wait to see you all dressed up."

"And do you know what else? I went to the bookstore and watched to see what the boys were reading. Mostly sci-fi, war magazines, sports and high-tech stuff. I bought three magazines on those subjects and read every word. And then I went back, found copies and pretended to read them."

"Okay, then what?"

"A few boys, well, young men, came by, and I tried to start a conversation. They were polite but didn't seem interested. I was kinda disappointed, having made all that effort. I was about to leave when this Adonis stopped and asked me what I was reading. I mean, this guy was beyond fantastic. He said that he had recently graduated from the university with a degree in history and was starting a master's and hoped to teach college."

"Interesting. What's his name?"

"He only gave me his first name, Leland. He's in one of those Greek fraternities, Delta Omega. He's really tall, has golden hair and the sweetest smile. He actually asked me questions and listened to me. And guess what? He said that they're going to have a party Saturday night and he wants to take me. I am beyond excited!"

"I'm happy for you, Shelley. But do be careful. People drink a lot at those parties, and they can get a bit wild."

"I hope it gets wild. This is the most fantastic thing that's ever happened to me. I'll tell you all about it afterwards. And I think Leland and I are going to get along really well."

"I hope so, too. You are now legal age and have a sensible head on your shoulders, but this will be your first experience in a totally different world. If you find it too stressful or dangerous, call me. I'll pick you up."

"Thanks, but I'll be okay," she said, hoping to sound confident.

Janice said nothing for a moment, then said, "Are you going to tell your dad?"

"Absolutely not! He wouldn't let me leave the house if he knew. And besides, he's going out of town to some Baptist convention."

"So, is Leland picking you up at your house?"

"I asked him not to. He said that I should wait for him at the bookstore. It's open till nine."

"Well, I hope you have a great time, Shelley. And yes, tell me all about it as soon as you can."

*****

Washington D. C.

FBI Director Steven Whitinghill sat despondently with Special Agent Eli Barett at their favorite watering hole in downtown D.C. Eli strode to the bar, ordered one scotch and a Black Russian, and returned to their table.

"Attitudinal adjustment," said Eli, plopping the glass of dark liquid in front of his boss.

"It's going to take a lot more than that," Steven said reluctantly.

"Brooding again?" asked Eli. "It's over, buddy, unless she gets an epiphany from God himself. And, I repeat, you were not there for her. Nose to the grindstone. Like a loaded truck with no working brakes and no off ramp, so you drove right into a steel girder. I warned you, and so did she."

"I'm not very good with warnings."

"Well, your lovely wife was bored to death, and Goodwin was simply biding his time, saw his opening and *voila*! And beyond that, you pissed him off."

"The committee hearings."

"Uh-huh. The good senator argued that federal money should go to halting illegal immigration, and you argued for funds to go to the apprehension of drug trafficking. He lost, but he gets sweet revenge: your wife, leaving you with a cold bed and distant memories."

"I think he's dirty. Can't prove it yet, but I suspect he's in with the cartels."

"Maybe, maybe not, but that's not going to get Janice back. And you may have other things to worry about."

*****

Montgomery, Alabama

Janice expected a call from Shelley the next day but there was none. She waited two days, then phoned, but all she got was the automated "leave a message."

Worried, she called the radio station, thinking that Palmer might have returned, but Von Hoffmann answered and said that Palmer had resigned.

"Do you want to call his cell? I can give you the number if you don't have it," said Hoffmann.

"Yes, please give it to me. I might have to phone him," she said, hoping that it wouldn't be necessary.

"If I hear from him, should I tell him that you want to speak to him?"

"No, it's rather personal."

"Sure, whatever you say. And by the way, I'd like to interview you on camera, since you seem to have the inside scoop on NCRA policies."

"Maybe some time, but not now. Have a nice day, talk to you later."

As Janice pulled up to Palmer's residence, Stanley's old Ford pickup was not in the driveway. *Fine*, she thought, *she didn't care to speak with him anyway*. She had only done so on one occasion, and it hadn't been pleasant. He was quite terse, nervous and brooding, with his turned down mouth and furtive glances. *Creepy*, she'd thought.

She parked at the curb then knocked on the door. A curtain opened a few inches, but Shelley didn't open the door.

"I've been trying to reach you," Janice said, peering into the window. "Are you okay?"

"I don't want to talk now. Go away, Janice, please go away. Maybe I'll call you later."

"What's wrong with now? You seem very upset. Tell me what happened. I might be able to help."

"There's nothing that can help. But thank you for coming, for checking on me." With no other choice, Janice left the Palmer home.

That night, she pondered what might have befallen the girl and assumed that she must have had a horrible experience. Rarely had she seen one so distraught. Eyes red, cheeks tear streaked, face blanched—an appearance of despair and something more. Dread. *It was her first date,* thought Janice, *and perhaps her last for a very long time.*

Janice was relieved when Shelley phoned a week later.

"My dad's at work. Can you come over?"

"I'm on my way," Janice replied.

The drapes were drawn and the house ghostly still when she entered. At the sight of Shelley, Janice wrapped her arms about the girl and said, "Don't you want some light in here? This is so terribly depressing."

Shelley shook her head. Turning from Janice, she sunk into the corner sofa and said, "I'm sorry for not letting you in before. I just couldn't."

"That's okay. You needed time. Now, if you can, tell me about Leland, the party."

Shelley sighed deeply, dabbed her eyes with a tissue, and said, "He picked me up and escorted me to his car. It was beautiful, all shiny with leather interior. He even opened the door for me. He was so dashing. I felt like a million bucks just being with him."

"And he took you to the party?"

"Yes, but not right away. It was already getting dark, and he said that we should get to know each other a bit more. Of course, I agreed, and he drove to a lookout just outside of town. He said that I probably had had a lot of dates and boyfriends because I am very pretty. Very, um, sensuous. Then he surprised me by asking me if I enjoyed sex, and I told him that I didn't have much experience with men."

"Go on, I'm getting the picture."

"He said that it's something I should learn about and perhaps he might be able to help. No, he said 'teach.' That's what he said. I was nervous but very excited, especially when he kissed me really deep. It was a wonderful kiss and lasted a long time. And then he reached behind the seat and pulled out a bottle of some kind of liquor. He said that a drink would calm me. He poured me a glass and I had some. And then we drove to the frat house."

"Did he drink any?"

"No, he said that he wouldn't drink and drive, and I thought that was very responsible."

"Sure, then what?"

"There were a lot of people at the party. It was loud and some were dancing, others making out. A few were practically naked, and one couple was already having sex. I thought we would dance along with the others and he might introduce me to his friends, but I started to get dizzy. Leland said that I might be coming down with something and I could get some rest upstairs and come down when I was feeling better."

"So, you went upstairs. To bed?"

"Uh-huh. I lay down and he lay next to me. I liked that; I thought it was very caring. He kissed me again, told me how sexy I looked and then. . ."

"Then what?" Janice asked, fearing the answer that she knew would come.

"I woke up about five hours later. Naked."

"Where was Leland?"

"Gone. Just gone. And so was everybody else. I'm not sure what happened but there was sticky stuff between my thighs, and I think he did it to me. But I'm not sure. I must have been half asleep. I really can't remember much of it at all."

"How did you get home?"

"I got dressed and just started walking. A police car stopped and when I told him who I was, he drove me home. And then I just collapsed."

"Dear Lord. Have you gone to a doctor?"

She shook her head. "Why should I?"

"Because Leland could have a disease. Or there could be other reasons."

"I don't want to go to a doctor. He will tell my father and. . ."

"You are of age. A doctor won't say anything. It's private and Palmer need never know."

Shelley sat with her head in her hands. "No, I don't want to. Other than you, I don't care to see anyone."

"Has Leland tried to get in touch?"

The girl shook her head. "I don't want anything to do with him. He was nothing like I thought he would be. And all those people, it was a nightmare. They all seemed so weird, so out of control. Drunk, practically ripping off clothes. I never saw anything like that before, not even in that film I told you about."

"I'm so sorry, Shelley. I feel responsible, having suggested how to meet boys. I never thought that. . ."

"It's not your fault. I wanted to meet some. I was so desperate."

"I should have told you not to go to the party."

Shelley shook her head. "If it didn't happen at the frat house it would have happened somewhere else. I think he had it all planned out. It could have been even worse."

Perhaps, thought Janice. *But worse may have only begun.*

CHAPTER 4

DESPERATION

"So, you defied me, went out behind my back and got yourself pregnant!" shouted Stanley Palmer eight weeks after the rape. "I went through your closet and saw those fancy clothes you got so you could lure some guy into fucking you. You're just a goddam whore. And where did you get the money for the clothes? Did you steal it?"

"No. A friend helped me. . ."

"Helped you? Who? You damn well better tell me who. I'll beat the shit out of him."

"It's a lady, a very kind lady," Shelley said, cringing as her father snarled inches from her face.

"Uh-huh. Now I want to know the truth. Did you seduce some guy? I know you're into sex stuff, dirty, filthy stuff. You fancied yourself up and got him into bed, didn't you?"

Shelley shook her head as Palmer stared at her with grey beady eyes.

"No, he raped me. I didn't seduce him, I was drugged. But you know what? I saw the magazines and the sex film you hid from Mother," Shelley said, suddenly defiant. You have dozens of them. After she got sick, you watched them incessantly. And I saw you go out late at night and come back before dawn. Who were you with? How much did it cost you?"

Shelley didn't have time to react as her father reared back and slapped her across the face, the sting instant as tears ran down her cheeks.

"I am a man, and whatever I do is none of your goddamn business. And don't you ever steal anything of mine again. You hear?"

"I hate you, and I'm not going to have the baby. And that's final. Just you watch."

He stood over her, looming. "What's his name? You tell me. The guy who did you."

"Leland Galway. He's in a fraternity called Delta Omega at the university. But he's really big, a lot bigger and stronger than you. I don't think you'll want to hit him. He can kill you."

"You said a frat boy. Is he white?"

"Yes."

Palmer headed for the door, turned and said, "You're gonna have that baby. No white girl gets an abortion around here."

*****

The pickup slid to the curb outside the Delta Kappa frat house at eleven in the morning. "None of this goes on the news, got it, Hoffmann?" said Palmer as he got out, removed a baseball bat from behind the seat and slipped a .38 into his overcoat pocket.

"I won't advise using the gun," said Von Hoffmann. "Might not be able to keep that quiet, especially if there are witnesses. This should have been a nighttime thing."

"Day, night, doesn't matter. You stay here unless I need you."

"Sure, but I'm not getting in trouble over this. It's your idea."

39

A gleaming Mazda sports car sat in the drive. Palmer gave it an appreciative glance, turned to Von Hoffmann, gestured back toward the car, and gave a little shake of the bat. Then, after looking into the windows of the house, he walked to the front door and rapped three times.

From a curtained window, several faces looked out. Leland spied the bat, gasped, turned to Vincent Drake and said, "I'm not here. Got that? Just don't let him in."

"Who is he?"

"I'm not sure, but got to be some girl's father."

That said, he bolted down the hall to a storage room where he closed and locked the door, propping a chair against it. Heart pounding in his chest, he waited.

"I'm looking for an asshole named Leland Galway. He belongs to this fraternity," said Palmer to Vincent, when he opened the door a crack.

"He's not here, sir," said Vincent, his eyes taking in the cadaverous man, baseball bat held low.

"That so?" said Palmer, kicking the door, which slammed into Vincent's head. The boy fell back, his hand pressed to a rising welt.

"I said, where the hell is he? You get him or I will."

"He's not here. Went shopping this morning. Probably at the mall."

"You don't fuck with me, sonny. My daughter tells me that he has a fancy car. Is that it, the one in the drive?"

Vincent nodded, then winced.

"Yes, sir, it is."

"Why didn't he drive it to the mall?"

"It's not far and he likes to walk."

"So, he likes to shop. You tell him to shop for a casket. He's gonna need it."

Palmer stopped by the Mazda and Von Hoffmann said, "One damn nice car. Too good for a kid."

"Yep," said Palmer, hefting the bat. He set to work, demolishing the convertible. He shattered the windows, smashed the headlights, and bashed in virtually every inch of the body. He popped the hood, slid a six-inch knife from his overcoat and cut every hose and wire, before slicing up the seats and ramming the blade into each tire. The Mazda sank to its rims.

"Looks different now, don't you think?" said Palmer.

"Yeah, worth about a hundred bucks, if that," said Von Hoffmann.

"But it's not over," said Palmer. "Not by a long shot."

*****

Another week had passed in which Shelley either remained in bed or sat in a rocker on the dilapidated front porch. Finally, out of desperation she made a call.

"I can't have the baby. I won't, I absolutely won't," said Shelley, when Janice picked up her phone.

"I understand why you feel that way, but I don't know what can be done. Not now, not the way things are here. It's not like we can hop on a plane or drive to Maryland."

"But you know people, important people," said Shelley.

"They won't help, can't help. Shelley, you can have the baby and put it up for adoption. I'm sure it will be an adorable child. You said that Leland was tall and handsome. People will want such a beautiful child."

"And what do I tell the adoption agency? That I was raped by a demented man and the child will likely inherit his genes? That he'll grow up to be a rapist or worse? Any takers?"

"You don't have to tell them anything like that, Shelley. You can even leave the infant on the steps of a church. Some priest or nun will take it in."

"Janice, I don't want to have the child. If you won't help me, I'll go and find someone who can."

"I didn't say I won't help; I just have to think of how, so we or some nurse or doctor won't be imprisoned. This is terribly serious. Give me a day or two. Don't do anything rash; don't run away. I'll call, I promise."

"Janice, I'm scared."

"Because of the abortion?"

"Not just that. It's my father. Did you ever listen to his show? He rants, real hateful stuff, mostly against foreigners and Jews. He said that they should be thrown out, expelled. I don't know much about history, but he mentions Himmler and Goebbels."

"They were Nazis during the Second World War. Goebbels was the propaganda minister and Himmler directed the extermination of the Jews and others opposed to Hitler's regime. Shelley, does your father belong to the neo-Nazis?"

"I don't know, but he's not said anything bad about them. I don't know any Jews, do you?"

"I have a good friend, a rabbi who lived next door to me when I was in D.C. He and his family moved here, to Montgomery."

"Do you think he can help?"

"I can phone him, but he might advise against an abortion."

"But call him, won't you? He might have some ideas."

"*I* have an idea, but it is going to require a journey. It may be a dangerous one. Be at the coffee shop at nine tomorrow morning," Janice said. It's a long drive, so wear something comfortable."

*****

"You found someone?" said Shelley, her voice hopeful, as Janice drove.

"I went to an emergency clinic after I sprained my ankle last year. There was a nurse there who helped women. That's where we're going."

"Does she know I'm coming?"

"No, I didn't call. Someone might ask questions, and I didn't want to leave a message. We'll just go and hope for the best."

The clinic was in a small town one hundred miles west of Montgomery. Shelley was pensive, and Janice was worried about how much time had passed. *If the nurse could not help, the only other possibility,* she thought, *is crossing into a right-to-quality-of-life state. But that would require driving hundreds of miles, and there might be road blocks as well as police and self-appointed vigilantes.*

The bounty for turning in those seeking abortions or their providers had risen astronomically. It was becoming a very profitable business, and violators of the law could be held at gunpoint because of the Alabama state law. She knew that a dozen other states were in the process of enacting that same statute. Her actions on this cold night would be considered a felony.

An hour into the drive, Janice remembered the gun. "Open the glove box," she said. "Don't touch the trigger; it's loaded."

Startled, Shelley said, "I didn't know you had that."

"My husband is in law enforcement, and we sometimes got death threats. He bought it for me."

"Do you think we'll need it?" Shelley asked as Janice slipped it into her purse.

"I hope not. I fired it at the range. He took me there, but I have never fired it anywhere else."

"But you know how to use it, right?"

"It's easy. Take off the safety, point it, and shoot. Don't tell anyone I have it, especially your dad."

They drove in silence for another twenty miles when Shelley said, "Can I ask you a question, a personal one?"

"You can ask but I might not want to answer."

"What happened between you and your daughter?"

"All I will say is that, until a year ago, when everything changed, we were very close. She became very upset when she learned that I left Steven, her father, whom she adores, and I fell in love with James Goodwin."

"Was there something else about Steven that made you leave him?"

"I'm not sure how I can put this, Shelley. Do you remember how excited you were when you first met Leland?"

"Yes, but I don't ever want to think about it."

"Of course, but that's the way I felt when I met Goodwin. But it was from the view and desires of a mature woman, a married woman escaping from a very dull relationship. Steven is a fine man, considerate, tenaciously honest but work is his driving force. We just..."

She hunted for the right word. "We drifted apart, Shelley. There was no breakup argument, no fight. That's not his way. And me? Well, the moment I saw Goodwin I knew that my life with Steven was over."

"What does Steven think of your boyfriend?"

"We haven't talked about it, but I know Steven detests him."

"Does he still love you?"

"I think so."

"Is he angry at you?"

"I'm sure he is."

"For being with Goodwin?"
"Yes," she said, hesitant to reveal anything more.
"But he can't do anything about it, can he?"
"I'm not so sure about that, Shelley."
"Why not?"
"Because he's the director of the FBI."

CHAPTER 5

SIX ROUNDS

There was a light drizzle as Janice drove slowly down the rural road, looking for the house that had been turned into a clinic. She pulled to the curb when she saw a sign that read "Emergency Services and Women's Assistance Center."

A lamp glowed in what she remembered to be the reception room, but she could see no figures inside.

"Those people are watching us," said Shelley.

Janice glanced toward the ancient house across the street. Three men, two in blue overalls, one wearing a tattered jacket, stood on the front porch.

"They look scary," Shelley said, an element of fear in her voice.

"Just ignore them," Janice said as she got out of the car.

"Should I come?" asked Shelley.

"Yes but let me do the talking."

Janice rang the doorbell and waited. Two minutes passed before a woman appeared.

"Hello," said Janice, "I believe you were the nurse who helped me last month. You and Dr. Reynolds."

"Oh yes, I remember you. How is the ankle?"

"Fine, and thanks for your help. Is the doctor still here?"

"No, he's gone. He encountered a legal problem and can't practice medicine here anymore."

The nurse looked past Janice and Shelley toward the men who had stepped onto a scraggly patch of grass in front of their house. Then she turned her attention back to Janice and looked closely at Shelley.

"How many weeks?"

"Nine," answered Shelley nervously.

"I wish I could help you, but for legal reasons I can't. Anybody can report me. Those people across the street got $15,000 for turning in Dr. Reynolds. They've made it a business, and they want more. They're parasites and dangerous. You can't stay here; you can't come in."

"Is there any place that. . ."

"Not that I know of. Now you best get in your car and leave here. Just driving this girl for the procedure is a felony. Those people will arrest and claim their reward if they catch you. Go, and don't stop."

The nurse hurried back inside and shut the door. From behind the door's glass window she again said, "Go! I never saw you."

Janice started the car and glanced out the window in time to see one of the men rushing back into the house. The two other men sprinted for an old pickup poking out of the garage.

"Where are we going?" asked Shelley as they sped past vacant lots, clapboard houses and bare trees. The windshield wipers swished back and forth as the headlights reflected on the wet road.

"Home. We've got to get back."

A few minutes later Janice looked in her rearview mirror. "I think it's those men," she said as she increased speed.

The road was narrow and winding. The car bounced over potholes, splashing brackish water onto the muddy pathway beside the road. Janice swerved to miss a fallen branch on a curve and was nearly hit by an oncoming truck.

The vehicle following was only six car lengths behind, its yellow lights on high beam glaring in Janice's side mirror. She gripped the steering wheel and, frightened by the near miss, peered into the gloom.

"We can't outrun them," she said. "They live here and know this road better than we do."

"Do you think they have guns?" asked Shelley, turning back in her seat.

"I'm sure they do. You heard the nurse. They capture people to get the money."

"Will we go to jail?" Shelley wailed. She was terrified.

"No, at least I don't think so. I can't talk now. I've got to find. . ."

There was a sudden jolt as the pickup slammed into the rear of the car. It backed off and rammed again. Janice tried desperately to retain control as the pickup remained only thirty feet behind.

Shelley began sobbing, and Janice tried to recall what Steven had taught her about evasive driving. It was shortly after he had bought her the gun that he had said, "You never know, someday you might have to do this."

"But it's raining," she had complained.

"All the better," he'd said. "Now hit the brake, turn, turn hard!"

But where to turn, she wondered, knowing that one more collision could disable the car.

Out of nowhere, her high beams illuminated a road sign. With little more than a tap on the brake, Janice pulled the steering wheel hard right and spun onto the dirt lane. A shower of mud and stones shot back, spattering the windshield of the truck. Unable to make the turn, it rushed past. From the corner of her eye, Janice saw its taillights glow as the driver hit his brakes.

The next sign Janice saw was a Dead End sign.

Janice came to a full stop, grabbed her purse, and after turning off the headlights, killed the engine. But for the patter of rain, all was silent.

Shelley said, "Janice, what are we going to do? I see headlights coming."

"Those trees, we go into the woods."

"Do you have a flashlight?"

"No. But maybe they don't either."

The truck came to a halt beside the car, headlights blazing.

"Grab the guns; they're in those woods," said one of the men.

"Don't shoot to kill," another cautioned as the doors of the truck slammed shut.

Streaks of light illuminated gaps between trees as Janice and Shelley picked their way from one to the next. Tripping over fallen branches they got up and scrambled onward. A flashlight was turned on and one man shouted, "You can't get away! Stop, we won't hurt you."

But another said, "They ain't gonna stop. You gotta do this."

The crack of a rifle shot sped high as the three men clambered over tree trunks, closing the range. Another shell clipped a tree ten feet from Janice. She stopped, reached in her purse, and pulled out the .38.

A figure appeared and she fired. The bullet went wide. She turned, grabbed Shelley's hand and said, "We have to split up."

"No, I'm not leaving you," blurted Shelley.

They struggled past a fallen log when Janice lost her footing and fell face first into a hole. The pistol flew from her hand as the men came into view. Bunched together, one shouted, "We got 'em!" as they were within five yards.

Janice's weapon lay beside the puddle. Illuminated by the flashlight's beam, Shelley grabbed it and with heart pounding, eyes blurred by rain, fired and fired until all the rounds were expended.

There was a whimper from one man, but seconds later it stopped. There were no sounds from the others. Shelley stood stock still, staring at the carnage. And then she began to shake.

"Oh God, oh no," she cried, dropping the gun.

Janice, soaked with clinging mud, picked up the gun, then pried the flashlight from one of the corpses.

"I killed them," Shelley moaned. "I just kept pulling the trigger. I couldn't stop, I couldn't. Janice, what . . ."

"If you didn't, I would have. It's over. They would have done whatever they wanted to with us. No one would have known."

"But what do we do now? Do we call the police? Will they arrest me?"

"We leave them. And we don't call anyone."

"But someone will find them."

"Hopefully, not for a while. There are hungry dogs and other animals around, and maybe by the time they are found they will only be bones."

Janice's car was wobbly but drivable. She drove slowly for six miles then, stopping beside the road, got out and walked toward a clump of trees illuminated by the headlights. She paced about until she found a deep hole surrounded by rocks. Taking the revolver from her purse, she wiped it down with a handkerchief and slid it into the hole. Once covered with rocks, she made her way back to the car.

"What did you do?" asked Shelley.

"Something I had to do. Say nothing about it, ever. And nothing about what happened tonight."

"So, where are we going?"

"I'm taking you home."

"My father will be there. What do I tell him?"

"That you had to get out of the house. You thought of running away, took a bus, then decided to come back but was too afraid to walk home alone at night."

"He won't believe me, Janice."

"Tell him you phoned me, and I picked you up."

"I'm really scared. He may hit me."

"Then call the police, or call me."

"Can I stay with you?"

"I would gladly have you stay with me, but I'll have to ask Goodwin. It's not my house. He's very touchy about people coming over."

"I don't think my dad should see you. He'll be very angry. Why don't you drop me off a few blocks away. I can walk from there."

"No, I'll take you home. I don't care if he's angry or not." She was silent for a minute then said, "Remember, no matter what he tries to get out of you, say nothing about what happened tonight."

"But what if the police come?"

"There's nothing to implicate you. The only person I spoke to was the nurse, and I doubt that she's going to tell the police that we were followed. In fact, she went back into the house before they left in their pickup."

"But she knows you."

"She won't say anything, of that I'm sure. It would implicate her."

A light was on as Janice pulled to a stop in front of Shelley's house. Her father was sitting in a straight back chair on the front porch smoking a cigarette.

A sudden thought came to Janice who said, "Was he ever in the military?"

"For a year or two. Marines, I think."

"Do you know what he did in the marines?"

"Not really. He doesn't speak about it. I think he got thrown out, but he once said he did dangerous stuff with things that get people killed."

Palmer got off his chair and stood by the driver's side door.

"Where the fuck did you take my girl?"

"I didn't take her anywhere. I offered her a ride when she called me." Janice was glad the darkened car interior hid the muddy state of her clothes.

Palmer snorted then looking at Shelley said, "You get out of the car and go inside. We'll have to talk."

"Touch her and you go to prison," said Janice, as Palmer turned to follow his daughter into the house.

"Fuck off," said Palmer. "I'll do what I want, anywhere, anytime."

Shelley glanced back, her shoulders slumped, her body drained.

"I'll call," said Janice, as Shelley opened the door of the house.

"Don't bother," answered Palmer, slamming the door.

CHAPTER 6

FLIGHT

Oh my God, what have we done? thought Janice as she drove around the block three times, not wanting to pull into the driveway of Goodwin's mansion. It had been self defense. Her hands were shaking.

Finally pulling into the drive, she sat and stared into the black night. She had told Shelley that there was no way of being traced to the murders, but now she wasn't so sure. Of course, it wasn't she who pulled the trigger but. . .

And there was the man who'd sighed, then became silent. Was he really dead? She had assumed he was, but what if he was able to crawl to the road and signal for help?

It was all so horrid, she thought. She knew that Shelley must be in shock. Tormented by the failed abortion attempt, the shootings, the threatening presence of Palmer, would the girl become paranoid? Might she even consider suicide?

Goodwin, as usual, was sitting in his recliner, drink in hand, when she entered. He put down his glass, rose and stared at her.

"What in God's name happened to you? You look like you've been run over by a truck?"

"I slipped and fell into the mud. It's nothing. I just want to clean up and go to sleep."

"I was getting worried. I can make you a drink. I think you need one."

"Thanks, but no. Come to bed when you wish, but I'm in no mood for anything tonight."

"Sure, I'll try to not wake you up. But tomorrow night. . ."

"Yeah, maybe."

"You look troubled, Janice. It's not like you. Is there something you'd like to talk about?"

"No, just tired. Got to get some sleep."

Sleep did not come easily. She thought about the gun and assured herself that no one would ever find it. Should she buy another one? she wondered. She had never had to use one before, but these were dangerous times. No, she thought, it would have to be registered and she didn't need unwanted attention.

The shaking came again. She got up and took two sleeping pills and told herself to call the rabbi in the morning. But what could he possibly say?

*****

"Of course, I'll be happy to speak with her," said Joshua Rabinowitz, "but it sounds like she already made up her mind. As you said, she's now an adult. The decision in other places would be hers, but unfortunately, not in Alabama. There is a provision allowing the procedure if the pregnancy endangers her life or if the fetus is deceased, but you say that neither is the case. And rape is not considered justification."

"Rabbi, she's physically okay, but I'm worried about her mental state," Janice responded.

"I don't doubt that."

"She's living with her father, who is abusive. Her mother died a year ago."

"May I ask who her father is?"

"Stanley Palmer, the former radio host."

"I know of him, a real anti-Semite. It is only a suspicion, but I think his rantings were responsible for the vandalizing of several Jewish businesses, along with death threats. Him being Shelley's father puts a different light on the subject. Perhaps it would be best if she can get away."

"She wants to, but she wouldn't know where to go. Palmer intends to keep her at home. And he has a following that will watch for her. He's very controlling."

"Is that because he loves her or for some other reason?"

"I honestly don't know. She considers herself a failure in his eyes but has always tried to please him. In that, she has failed miserably."

"Let me think of what I can do. It's good that you are her guardian angel, a *mitzvah*, as we say. And how are you? It's been a long time since we last spoke."

"I'm okay. Well, sort of. I'm going through a divorce."

"I see. Well, divorce is a difficult thing."

"It is. Look, Rabbi, Shelley and I would like to schedule an appointment. She thinks you might have some ideas that might help."

"Some in my congregation think I'm sometimes helpful, but this is especially difficult. Tell Shelley I'll do what I can. And Janice, I wish you the best. Shalom. Peace be upon you."

*****

Stanley Palmer sat in President Lee's office, virtually salivating over his exalted position as chief of internal security. Hands folded in his lap, he felt a sense of adulation as he gazed at the president of the NCRA, waiting patiently for Lee to finish scanning a report on climate change by the U.S. Department of Agriculture.

"Utter nonsense," Lee said, closing the folder before turning to Palmer. He gave Stanley his best politician's smile and said, "I'm glad that you have chosen to join my cabinet. I believe, yes, *believe*, that you will do a fine job. I have always been a listener of your broadcasts, indeed, a fan of yours. Appointing you security chief was a no brainer."

"Yes, sir, thank you, sir. And I sincerely thank you for the condolence card you sent me upon the death of my wife."

"The passing of Alice was tragic. The card was the least I could do."

"Most kind of you. You asked me to report to your office for a particular assignment. How can I be of assistance?"

Lee steepled his fingers as he usually did before making a pronouncement. A scion of the old south, Lee liked to think of himself as a professional and an avid student of history, a very astute one, and a staunch proponent of values. He looked directly at Palmer and said, "A number of people alien to our Christian values have succeeded in entering our sacred land, and have, with a certain guile, polluted, indeed poisoned, the minds and culture we hold so dear."

"Exactly, sir. And in my radio commentaries, I have often noted how terrible a scourge they are and how necessary it is to remove them."

"Skillfully put," said Lee as he leaned back into a copy of the ancient swivel chair designed by Thomas Jefferson. "I do not wish these people any particular harm, but I would like them to vacate our new nation and find solace in states less beholding to Christian ideals."

"Mr. President, in line with that determination, we do have a Jewish population, a congregation, in fact, that may have interest in relocating. I believe their Rabbi is Joshua Rabinowitz. Would it not be to our advantage to assist them in that quest?"

"You're reading my thoughts. Indeed, it would be considered a humanitarian gesture, good for them, good for us. We will start small fundraiser. I would gladly find funds for transport to, say, California, if the Rabbi Rabinowitz and his congregation approve. And, as a matter of fact," he paused, eyes lighting up. "I know of no one better to organize such a worthy endeavor than you, Mr. Palmer. Would that be of interest to you?"

Palmer was stunned and several seconds passed before he said, "Sir, I would be honored to take on that mission. Yes, yes!"

"Very well, we shall coordinate through my office. This project will delight all those who wish to see this land, the land of our forefathers, rid of an alien element."

*****

On page two of the *Montgomery Daily Sun* appeared the following article:

Yesterday, two teenage boys were hunting in a wooded area about a hundred miles west of Montgomery when they came across the bodies of three men, all shot at close range, according to the police. A vintage Ford pickup truck belonging to one of the men was found at the site. Beside them were footprints of what might have been several women.

As of yet there is no motive nor any information on who might have shot the victims, and no weapon or other identifying material has been found. Police are conducting a full-scale investigation. Records indicate that the men had been the recipient of monies relating to information provided to authorities of illegal abortions. Previously the men in question admitted to being members of a Montgomery neo-Nazi organization.

Janice put down the newspaper when the phone rang.

"I just got the strangest phone call," said Rabbi Rabinowitz. "It was, from all people, Shelley's father."

"Why would he phone you?" asked Janice, surprised to hear Palmer's name.

"He said that the president of NCRA, Jeff Calhoun Lee, is making it possible for Jews to leave Montgomery and relocate to California, or somewhere else if they wish. And Palmer's been put in charge of arranging this. The idea was apparently from Lee."

"Palmer? Completely out of character."

"Strange thing is, he sounded rational. He said that he knew through his contacts that a considerable number of my congregation have received death threats, which is true, and are seriously thinking of leaving the state."

"Are you?"

"If the majority of my congregation chooses to go, then I must. Jerry, my son, wishes to graduate with his class at Manassas High School, but he and many others are having difficulty with the new teaching guidelines and religious requirements."

Janice thought for a minute, then said, "Rabbi, do you know how many in your congregation might be leaving?"

"Not exactly, but I'm guessing around one hundred and sixty. My wife, Tania, and my oldest son Danny will be coming with me if we go. But one reason I called is about Shelley. It will require a bit of subterfuge, but if she still wants to leave Montgomery, we can bring her onto the plane. It will be a charter flight, and we can change her name for the manifest. In effect, she'll be traveling as a member of my congregation."

"I think she'll be delighted. A grey wig, old lady's makeup and a veiled hat, and she might be able to get on board. Of course, not a word can be said to her father. When's the flight leaving?"

"In about three weeks. There's a lot of preparations to be done. Houses to be put on the market, resumés to be sent out, furnishings to be sold, a million things. This is a very big deal. To most of my congregation, it feels like Germany and Austria in the late 1930s. I think we'll be greatly relieved when we're in a safe place."

Janice said nothing for several seconds until the rabbi said, "Should I be worried?"

"You should be cautious. Consider the man who is presumably helping you. I'll tell Shelley to say nothing to Palmer. And if Jerry needs anything, have him call me."

"I will, but he'll be staying with my cousin Levi until I get settled."

"Okay, and thanks. We'll keep in touch."

Janice ended the call and glanced back at the paper. There was nothing to implicate either her or Shelley, but still, a feeling of despondency fell upon her. And then there was Palmer and Lee and their bizarre offer.

Maybe they were trying to prove a point—that the Alabama Jews were not going to be welcomed. She recalled reading that Hitler sent a boatload of Jews to New York harbor, but FDR refused to let them disembark. Britain took a few hundred, but the rest went back to Germany, where they were incinerated before the war's end.

But that was Germany a long time ago. She sighed. *It will be okay,* she reassured herself. California for Rabinowitz and Shelley. A *mitzvah*, the Rabbi would say.

CHAPTER 7

SH'MA YISRAEL

All pre-flight passenger checks had been waived; one hundred and sixty-two passengers climbed the roll-out stairs, happy to get out of the pervasive drizzle. There had been a delay due to a mechanical problem, but the four-engine Boeing was finally approved for takeoff.

Stanley Palmer had appeared earlier that day. He did what he came to do. He'd entered the aircraft but said little to the crew. Not wishing to answer any questions, he departed before the passengers arrived.

The only media on the tarmac was Von Hoffmann of *Freedom America*. His camera panned the members of the rabbi's congregation, then focused on those choosing to remain who waved behind a wire fence.

"Rabbi Rabinowitz, would you care to make a comment?" asked Von Hoffmann.

"I will just say that we are appreciative of the administration's effort and particularly that of President Lee. That is all I wish to say at this time."

"Very well, we wish you a pleasant and safe flight," said Von Hoffmann as the camera panned back to one elderly woman who followed the rabbi and waved to someone behind the barrier.

Janice watched as the door closed and the stairs pulled away. The aircraft maneuvered onto the taxiway. Moments later, its wheels left the runway the plane rose into the cloud-covered sky.

As she walked to her car, she overheard a teenager say, "Uncle Levi, maybe I should have gone. I really don't care about a diploma from Manassas."

Janice turned and said, "Are you Jerry, the Rabbi's son?"

"Yes, I am.

"I'm Janice, and I am so thankful to your father for his counsel and assistance. Your dad's a very special person. You must be proud of him. Are you also thinking of becoming a rabbi?"

"Not really. My great uncle here was a sergeant major, and I'm thinking of ROTC at Stanford before joining up."

"So, you'll be leaving here soon."

"If I can. I am afraid that I might not be able to get there."

"I'll get him out," said a man standing next to Jerry. "I did plenty of special ops in my day."

"Yeah," said Jerry, "Sorry, I forgot to introduce you. This is Levi, my uncle."

"Well, I wish you the best. Say hi to the Rabbi for me when you talk to him. He's a really fine man."

*****

Danny sat in the rear of the aircraft while the Rabbi, his wife and Shelley found seats near the front. Amongst the passengers, there was a sense of anxiety mixed with relief, having left a region in which they were not welcome. Many phoned friends and relatives who would be meeting them in Los Angeles, the plane's destination.

The FAA was tracking the flight, but communications began to break down over. California, which was attributed to particularly foul weather as well as a problem with on-board computers. All attempts to contact the plane proved ineffectual, and sixty miles from LAX the aircraft began to pitch and shake violently.

A dozen overhead compartments swung open, spilling luggage into the aisle. Then, quite suddenly, the radio came to life and the pilot received a brief message telling him to proceed to the Palm Springs airport. A request by the pilot for more information went unanswered.

Rabbi Rabinowitz, holding onto one seat after another, walked unsteadily down the aisle comforting those who looked up at him with growing fear. The jet lumbered on, losing altitude as it began its descent to the runway, still twenty minutes away.

The pilot came on the intercom and said that despite the extreme turbulence there was nothing to worry about. But everybody should remain in their seats with safety belts secured. Following the announcement, he attempted to contact the tower, but there was no response. Puzzled and concerned, he grew anxious, not being at all familiar with the terrain.

Fleeting breaks in the dense clouds made it possible for the pilot to spy mountain peaks ominously close. Intense wind and blowing sand whipped the plane. Visibility was down to several hundred feet. As the plane dipped lower, the pilot glanced at his second officer and said, "Jeremy, do you see the runway, any lights?"

The co-pilot stared into the blackness. Out of nowhere, several explosions rocked the aircraft. One knocked out all lighting and instruments in the cockpit; the other destroyed the hydraulics that operated the flap on the port wing.

The plane immediately lurched, and there were terrified shouts amongst the passengers. Many turned on their cellphones, illuminating the cabin in a sepulchral light.

There were cries and prayers as the aircraft corkscrewed in the unstable air.

Once again, the pilot frantically attempted to call the tower, but there was still no answer. A third explosion ripped away the front landing gear and left a gaping hole beneath the craft.

"Fasten seatbelts! Stay in your seats!" said the pilot over the intercom.

Terrified, Shelley gripped the rabbi's hand. The plane began to shake and rattle as pieces of the undercarriage ripped away.

"Are we going to crash?" asked Shelley, staring at the rabbi, who was frantically speaking into his cell phone.

Across the aisle, an elderly man wearing a yarmulke held onto his wife and offered the prayer for those about to die: *"Guide me, Holy One, on the final journey, Your hand pointing the way, Your loving eye upon my face as I seek my new dwelling. Surround me with your kindness, Embrace me with tranquility. Soothe my fears with surety of Your care. . ."*

"No!" cried Shelley.

I'm sorry, I'm so sorry, Shelley," said Rabinowitz. "It is partly my fault that you are here."

Shaking, Shelley said, "It's not your fault the plane is going down. Oh, I don't want to die!" She wanted to curl up into a ball that nothing could hurt or harm. *The baby!* she thought. *Why didn't I just stay home and have the baby? Or is it better this way for both of us?* Without her mother, that house had become truly unbearable.

She gripped the arms of the seat and said, "Rabbi, who will be there for us?"

"Your mother, Alice, will be there for you with open arms. And God will be there, too."

Rabbi Rabinowitz felt a hand on his shoulder and looked up. His son stood in the aisle. He looked into his son's eyes and shook his head.

"Danny," he said, "I made a terrible mistake. It was too good to be true."

"Don't blame yourself. You tried to do the best for the congregation."

"I think we're going to crash. It must be God's will."

"No, it was someone else's. If I live, that man will pay."

The rabbi said nothing as the plane dropped another hundred feet.

Danny took his parents' hands and said, "I love you. We all do, and we will be together again." He sighed and said, "I must go back to my seat now."

"Yes," said his father, "We shall hope for the best."

The Rabbi kissed his wife and then began the prayer said for thousands of years, *"Sh'ma Yisrael, Adonai Eloheinu, Adonai Echad. Barruch Shem Kvod mal chu-to lo lam va'ed."*

Tania repeated it. *"Hear, O Israel, Adonai is our God, Adonai is one. Blessed is God's glorious kingdom forever and ever."*

"Yes," whispered Rabinowitz, sounding suddenly at peace as the plane shuddered once again. "Shelley, you are a wonderful person. Fear not, for the Lord promises the gift of peace. We shall all be at peace in His keeping."

Tania, Shelley, and the rabbi clutched each other's hands and laid their heads beside one another.

Yes, Shelley thought, *Mom will be there. I will be in the hands of the Lord, but..."*

A break in the clouds gave the pilot a chance to peer left and right. A faint moon illuminated the 11,000-foot Tahquitz peaks that suddenly appeared before them.

"Pull up! Pull up!" cried the co-pilotl "Oh God, no controls." The plane grazed the boulder-strewn mountain, shearing off the starboard wing. The plane cartwheeled, and the rear section ripped off. The main section hurtled toward the desert floor and exploded in a devastating ball of fire.

The aft section, including the last five rows of seats, skittered to a stop on a plateau seven hundred feet above the ground.

Stunned and shaken by the impact, Danny sat immobile in his seat, unable to grasp the fact that he was still alive. But for the burning fuel below, all was dark. And except for the moans of a woman and a wailing child, there was silence. Grief washed over him at the realization that his parents had been in the forward section.

A few boulders clattered down, bouncing menacingly toward the bottom of the steep decline. Finally, unfastening his seat belt, Danny inched his way back and knelt in the aisle. The woman stared at him, unable to say anything. The baby settled into a plaintive cry.

"We have to get out," said Danny. "We are unstable, it could roll."

There was another moan from two seats back. A man shakily came to his feet and held onto a seat where a passenger, dead from a jagged piece of metal, stared lifelessly.

"Do you see anyone else alive?" Danny asked the man.

The man shook his head and said, "No one."

Danny steadied the woman as she rose from her seat. Then she and the baby passed through the jagged hull and onto rocky ground. The other survivor followed. They were immediately drenched as rainclouds scudded past.

Hundreds of feet below, the carcass of the fuselage glowed as the last of the fuel burned away. A cacophony of sirens could be heard in the distance. Danny stepped toward the edge of the narrow plateau and looked down. He then made his way to the rear of the aft section and saw it wedged between two boulders. Returning to the man he said, "This part of the aircraft isn't going anywhere. I can't see any trail going down, and it's very steep. We'll have to wait for dawn when they can airlift us out. We could go back inside and get out of the rain. There's nothing else we can do."

The aft section held several coats belonging to the crew, as well as emergency supplies. There were flashlights, and Danny grabbed one, shining the beam toward the crash site below. Moments later, an answering beam flashed toward the aft section. And then it went out.

Shortly after dawn the storm cleared, and a rescue chopper arrived. Taken to the Eisenhower Health Center in town, Danny was peppered with questions from members of the FAA and FBI. Their findings were still inconclusive; the recovered "black box" was yet to be examined.

One FBI agent, upon observing the wreck, muttered, "No runway lights, no voice communication, three explosions. It only points to one thing. Someone wanted them all dead. And they nearly all were."

CHAPTER 8

THE REMAINS

Stanley Palmer sat in his chair on the front porch till very late in the night. He had already gone through a half pack of Marlboros, the butts littering the ground on the other side of the weathered railing. It would be the second time in a month that Shelley had stayed out late. He was peeved that he'd neglected to get Janice's number, for certainly she would be the guilty party. He pondered why she would have taken any interest in his daughter. Shelley, he reasoned, had nothing to offer. A mediocre student, a blob of a girl with no money or skills, why would anyone, especially an attractive and presumably secure woman, want to put herself in danger over an abortion?

He found Shelley's cell phone on the vanity in her room. Why hadn't she taken it? She always did. He checked her closet; the suitcase was there, as were her clothes, including the fancy ones. It made no sense.

He lit another cigarette, inhaled, then considered the fact that she hated him. Did she know the truth? Had Alice ever admitted to her the rape? Would he have shown Shelley real love and attention if she were his own child?

Well, that was water under the bridge, he decided. But maybe not. Maybe, if she really knew, it was the real reason she loathed the idea of giving birth to the offspring of a rapist.

No, he had little love for the girl, but here he was, sitting on the front porch waiting for her. *That had to mean something*, Palmer thought. Maybe he should make amends, do something that might show approval, but there was damn little approvable in the girl. And as for Janice, well, there would be an accounting.

A passage from the Bible came to mind, Exodus 34.7: "... *visiting the iniquity of the fathers upon the children, and upon the children's children, unto the third and to the fourth generation.*" Was that what had happened? The iniquity of one father had tainted his household for nearly 19 years, and the same thing was about to happen all over again. Well, if he had anything to say about it, the iniquity of this father was going to fly right back home to roost. He'd put up with Shelley
for Alice's sake; not again, never again.

He considered calling the sheriff, putting out a missing person report, but she would have had to have been gone for more than a few hours. He breathed heavily, stomped out the cigarette, and went to bed. He would think of what to do in the morning. He was a light sleeper and would hear her come in. Then he would find out what the hell was going on.

He hardly ever worked on Sunday and rarely went to church, though he made sure that people knew he was a God-fearing Christian who despised those who were not. He thought he would sleep in and deal with his daughter later in the day. So, he was miffed when his phone rang at nine thirty in the morning.

"You awake?" asked Jefferson Calhoun Lee.

It took a moment for Palmer to recognize the voice of the caller.

"Yes, sir. What can I do for you, Mr. President?"

"Turn on the TV. Call me in ten minutes."

Palmer, still groggy, turned it on and sank into his well-worn sofa. His phone rang again.

"Palmer, its Hoffmann. Are you watching this?"

"Just turned it on. President Lee called me a minute ago. What the fuck is so damn important?"

"Just watch. We'll talk later."

"This is Mohammed Shuri of BNN at the crash scene in Palm Springs, California. Only four individuals—two men, a woman and an infant—survived the horrific disaster that took place last night. It is estimated that approximately 150 passengers, along with pilots and crew members, died in the fiery crash.

"The flight from Montgomery, Alabama consisted of a Jewish congregation attempting to find a new life in California. The FAA and FBI are beginning a thorough investigation, since one survivor stated that there were three on-board explosions prior to the crash.

"A memorial for the deceased will be held two days from now. Numerous government officials and family members will be in attendance. The services will be conducted by Rabbi Bennet Sanders of Temple Beth Israel. Security for the event will be substantial, according to Steven Whitinghill, FBI director."

Palmer sat silent for several seconds as CNN replayed the scene of the crash the previous night and the charred remains of the main section of the fuselage. From above the peaks, a helicopter filmed the aft section wedged between rocks. Shards of metal glinted in the sun, and water-logged clothing from torn open suitcases, along with laptops, personal papers, and refreshment carts littered the slopes.

It would be a tense discussion, and Palmer tried to gather his thoughts. Nine minutes passed before he placed the call.

There was no preamble. "You were supposed to see that it all went smoothly. Do you have any idea how bad this looks? Who the fuck put bombs on that plane?"

"Mr. President, it could have been any one of thousands who heard about our proposal. Sure, I looked the plane over before they all boarded, but the airline was responsible for security. I hope you don't think I went to that aircraft with a box full of bombs and willy-nilly tossed them around."

There was a long, painful sigh on the other end. "Palmer, I'm not blaming you. But that investigation has legs, and I can't be implicated in anything. All I did was make a suggestion, nothing more. The FBI will surely come down here. Not that they have any right to, but I'm damn certain they will question both of us. No finger pointing, you hear? You tell them that it was a flight of compassion, one that the people strongly desired. We merely complied with the Rabbi's wishes. And for God's sake, no racist anti-Jew talk."

"Yeah. I'll try to sound compassionate, but that's not easy."

"Just do it. I think you should go to the memorial. Just for looks."

"No, sir, I'm not going to stand there bowing my head and listen to some goddamn Jew preacher giving a eulogy. Sorry, that's a bridge too far. But since it was your idea, maybe you should go."

"I might do that. It's about looking good."

Palmer stopped, thought for a second then said, "Mr. President, maybe you could help me with something, since you know just about everybody. My daughter has gone missing, or should I say, she didn't come home last night. And she was with that Janice, the bitch who hangs out with Goodwin. I detest her and it's not the first time she's interfered. I gotta put some sense into that woman, and I think Shelley's with her."

"I'd go easy there, Palmer. She is divorcing her husband, but you could find yourself in deep trouble. Not that he can do anything directly, but he *is* the director of the FBI."

"No shit? I suspected that Goodwin was fucking her, and here she is, as Goodwin's aide."

"And my spokesperson. I think you know that. She's a smart lady, so I would keep my distance if I were you. But Palmer, I do hope all is well with your daughter. And let me know what the FBI says when they call." Lee was about to hang up when he said, "By the way, were you in the army?"

"Marines, long time ago."

"What was your MOS? What did you do?"

"Same as everyone else. Basic, advanced infantry. But never in combat."

"You play with any ordnance?"

"You're talking about bombs? Shit, we threw lots of grenades and played with explosives. But that's another story and I don't care to go into it."

"Sure, we all have bones in the closet, don't we?"

"Life ain't Disneyland," responded Palmer.

"If I hear anything about your daughter, I'll call. But kids run away all the time. And some don't come back at all."

*****

The next day, Palmer decided to give James Goodwin a call. "Mr. Goodwin, this is Stanley Palmer. President Lee gave me your number. I'm trying to get in touch with Janice Whitinghill. It's very important. She might know about the whereabouts of my daughter, who failed to return home last night."

"Mr. Palmer. Janice is not here. But I know about Shelley and how you have treated her. Janice is her friend and would do nothing to harm her. As for your daughter's whereabouts, I have no idea. Good day, Mr. Palmer."

It wasn't until noon that Palmer rose from his front porch chair and drove his pickup to the newsroom at the strip mall.

"I thought you'd call me," said Von Hoffmann looking up from the morning's paper.

"I was on the phone with James Goodwin, the guy who's fucking Janice Whitinghill. I was hoping that she would know where Shelley was. I'm not in a very cordial state right now, Hoffmann."

"You rarely are. But since you were in charge of the flight to California, this article will make you even less cordial."

Von Hoffmann slid the paper across his desk, indicated a chair and said, "Have a seat and read it. There's going to be a lot of questions flying around."

Palmer made a dour face, lips compressed. With trepidation, he peered at the page one article. It was entitled "Murder, Intrigue and Mystery in Palm Springs."

Gregory Hamilton, the Palm Springs air traffic control officer, told FAA and FBI investigators that he entered the tower before the crash and was startled to find all runway lights off. He assumed that it was due to a power outage, a result of the storm. He rushed up the stairs but was knocked unconscious and didn't wake up until after the crash.

"Mr. Hamilton is unaware of who struck him but assumes that whoever did wanted the lights off and no communication with the approaching aircraft. That individual is still at large.

"According to explosive experts, the bombs could have been activated by air pressure as the plane descended or even set off by someone on the ground using an electronic signal. It may have been intentional to have the aircraft diverted from LAX to Palm Springs, where weather conditions were

further deteriorated. It is believed that there was an intent to destroy the aircraft regardless of its destination.

Palmer pushed the paper back across the desk and said, "I'm going home."

"Not leaving Montgomery, are you? The Feds will want to talk to you. You're definitely a person of interest, if not a suspect, in FBI speak."

"I ain't running away, Hoffmann. I'll be at the house if they come looking. By the way, have you seen Shelley?"

"Nope. Why would I? She doesn't particularly care for me. She's gone again?"

"Yeah. You see her, you tell her to get home, right quick."

*****

"How many times do I have to tell you, I was only responsible for securing the aircraft and having a look at it," said Stanley Palmer. Three days after the crash, he and Special Agents Eli Barett and Leandra Sutter sat stone-faced at his kitchen table.

"This is a criminal investigation; I wish to remind you that any false statement will be held against you. We are talking about murder on a huge scale and a life sentence for whoever is responsible. We have already talked with Mr. Jefferson Lee," said agent Sutter.

"If I was guilty, do you honestly think I would be here to answer questions? Hell, passport in hand I would have lit out for Ecuador, Paraguay or somewhere in the Philippines. But no, here I am. Tell me the charge if you're gonna arrest me. I'll see you in court."

The TV was on mute and Palmer glanced at the Palm Springs coverage, still at the top of the news cycle.

"What the hell!" he blurted, grabbing the remote and turning on the sound.

The agents turned their attention to the broadcast, the camera focusing on rows of people rising from their chairs as the *Kaddish*, the two-thousand-year-old prayer, was uttered by a Rabbi. President Lee, wearing a *yarmulka*, solemnly bowed his head and looked every bit a distinguished patrician. Standing beside him was an aged man who eyed the NCRA president with askance. A youth, no more than eighteen, dabbed his eyes and stood beside a stoic mourner who stared straight ahead.

Next in the line was a dark-haired, slender woman, her only adornment a pearl necklace.

"That's her. The bitch who kidnapped my daughter. You want to arrest someone. You arrest her!" said Palmer, turning to the agents.

Barett and Sutter studied the screen and Barett said, "That woman did not kidnap anyone. She's the wife of—"

"I know who she's the wife of!" shouted Palmer. "And I don't know why the fuck she is even there! What does she have to do with a bunch of Jews anyway?"

"It's not for us to make a judgement on the matter; we're not here to question her motive. But I am sure we will have more questions for you," said Agent Barett. He and Agent Sutter rose and returned to their vehicle.

*****

Two weeks later, an article appeared on page four of the Boulder, Colorado *Grand Union Press*.

Mr. Leland Galway, age twenty-three, died yesterday when his vehicle plunged off a mountain road. Son of multi-millionaire businessman Douglas Galway, it was reported that Leland had spent the previous hours at a fraternity party.

RON SINGERTON

Although an investigation of the crash is in its early stage, police indicated that the vehicle, a Mazda MX-6 Miata, was in poor condition and its braking system may have been in need of repair.

CHAPTER 9

THE ARRANGEMENT

Twenty years earlier, Los Angeles
Eli pulled the letter from the envelope and read it twice. He shouted and started jumping up and down, pumping his fist into the air. The letter gracefully settled to the floor.

> *Congratulations, Mr. Barett,*
> *Your request to enter the Federal Bureau of Investigation's Academy Training Program has been approved. Your class will begin on the date indicated at the bottom of this announcement, at which time you will report to Quantico, Virginia. Best wishes for a successful career with the Department of Justice.*

Eli was tempted to phone Julie and give her the great news, but upon reflection he decided that he wanted to see her expression and delight. Their date was for the following evening and, with this announcement, it would be dinner and champagne at the Los Angeles Hilton. Expensive but worth it.

Remembering that his best suit was at the cleaners, he picked up his car keys and headed out to his ancient VW, letter in hand. *Got to wash the car,* he thought, as he put the key into the ignition and started it up. The engine coughed and sputtered as a plume of smoke fouled the afternoon air. He jumped out and popped the rear engine compartment.

"Shit," he growled, as oil oozed over the engine. He grabbed a rag from the floor of the car and wiped off as much as he could. Getting back in, he tossed the envelope onto the passenger seat and drove the five blocks to the run-down garage where Tom, his twin brother, worked part time. It was a quarter to five, but Tom often stayed late, swilling beer with his buddy James Goodwin.

Tom knew all about cars and had two of his own: a new Mustang—his delight—and an old Ford pickup. The Volkswagen ground to a stop at the rear of the garage beside Tom's twenty-foot racing boat with its twin Evinrude outboard motors. "Fastest thing on the water," bragged his brother.

"Tom, my VW's burning oil. It's wasted. I got to borrow your Mustang for tomorrow night," Eli said as he entered the garage.

"I told you that bug was junk. Keys are on the rack; take them and go. And it's your hide if you put a scratch on it."

Goodwin handed Tom a rag to wipe up an oil spill near the front door.

"Sure, thanks," replied Eli, taking the keys.

A black sedan with a lowered chassis pulled up to the front of the garage. Two Hispanic men got out, one with an attaché case.

Turning to the man with the leather case, Goodwin said, "Hey, Antonio, just give it to me. I'll deal with it from here."

"Yeah, more coming tomorrow. Alberto has some cash for you."

As Antonio walked into the garage, Alberto spied Eli and said, "Who the fuck is he?"

"My brother," said Tom. "I have to fix his car. He's just leaving."

"He knows?"

"Knows what?" said Eli, turning toward Alberto.

"*Nada*, nothing," said Tom.

Antonio slipped in the oil and toppled backward. The attaché case spun out of his hand, struck the concrete floor and sprung open. A half dozen clear plastic bags spilled out, one splitting open.

Eli stared at the white powder that spewed across the floor. Tom knelt and tossed the bags back into the case as Eli said, "What the hell! Is that what I think it is?"

"Oh, shit!" said Goodwin, grabbing the mop.

"You deal with this son of a bitch! Any *problemo* and you're dead!" shouted Antonio.

"Yeah," said Goodwin as the two men sprinted back to the car. Seconds later, tires squealed as the sedan sped into the early evening traffic.

"You didn't hear anything, didn't see anything," said Tom, slamming the case and sliding it under a workbench.

"The hell! What's that? Cocaine, meth? You're dealing, aren't you, Tom? That's how you get money for the fancy car, the boat, the clothes."

"Eli, keep your mouth shut. I warn you," said Goodwin, his hand reaching for a heavy wrench.

"Bullshit!" said Eli, turning and walking to the rear of the garage.

The wrench slammed into the back of Eli's skull with a resounding crack. He let out a sudden cry, reached for the back of his head and slumped to the floor.

"Shit! Shit, shit!" blurted Tom kneeling over his brother. He heard Eli faintly moan before he lay inert. Tom tried to stem the blood streaming from Eli's cracked skull, to no avail.

"Eli, can you hear me? Can you. . ."

"He's dead," said Goodwin, standing over Tom and the corpse.

"You killed him. You killed my brother," said Tom, shocked and staring up at Goodwin.

"You think we had a choice? He was going straight to the cops. We would have been toast."

"We could have gotten rid of the stuff. He wouldn't have proof. Just his word against ours."

"He was a goddamn boy scout. There would have been an investigation, and maybe he saw the car's license plate. They could track that, and he might identify Antonio or Alberto. The cops know the gang, and they would finger us in a heartbeat."

In a daze, Tom said, "So, what do we do now? What do I tell my mom?"

"Not a damn thing. We get rid of him now, tonight. He becomes just another missing person. Waylaid by someone, robbed, beaten, gone. Not a trace."

"But how? Where?"

"The ocean. We put him in the boat. Let's move!"

It was dark by the time Eli's body was bundled into shop blankets and stowed in the cramped boat cabin. Then they pushed Eli's car into a weed-infested lot between two rusting trucks. Tom opened the glove compartment of the Volkswagen, found a flashlight, and shined it into the interior. The light shone on an official looking envelope and curious, he slipped a letter out and read it twice. He shoved it into his pocket as the envelope fell onto the floor of the car.

"FBI Academy," Tom said to himself. "Oh shit, oh shit," he repeated.

Goodwin was connecting the back-up lights of the boat trailer to the pickup when Tom joined him.

"Are we going now?" Tom asked.

"Yeah, while there's still traffic. We'll go slow, real safe like."

"You know of a specific place?"

"A mile beyond the cove where we used to go fishing. Nobody's ever there, especially on a week night."

It was a one-and-a-half-hour drive on a moonless night. The boat, unhitched, slid off the trailer and bobbed in the high tide. Ten minutes later they idled past the cove as shore lights dimmed behind them. They pulled Eli's body from the cabin, chained the anchor to his legs, and lowered him over the side. Tom watched as his brother sank into the inky black water.

He sat remorsefully as Goodwin piloted the boat back to the trailer.

"I found a letter in the VW from the FBI," he said quietly.

"A letter? No kidding?"

"Yeah, he was accepted into the academy. Passed the investigation and would have been a full-fledged agent: badge, gun, everything."

"And he would have put us in prison."

Tom brooded, then said, "Mom would have been overjoyed about him becoming an agent."

"But she's losing it, right? Senile and in that institution."

"She has her moments. Sometimes she comes out of it and is as clear as a bell."

"Yeah, maybe. But she can't tell the difference between you and Eli."

They drove for an hour in near silence when Goodwin slapped Tom on his knee and said, "I got it! Hot damn, and it's perfect!"

"What are you talking about? We just dumped my brother into the ocean. There's not a damn thing that's perfect."

"That beard you're growing; you shave it off tonight."

"Why?"

"Because you're taking his name, his identity. You're not Tom anymore; you're Eli and you're going to the Academy. You're going to be an FBI agent, and a damn good one, too."

"That's crazy! They'll know."

"Bullshit! You know how he talks, he behaves, treats people. You must become him in every way. It's the best cover we could ever have. Kind of like a double agent. We keep on dealing, making money, and you have a great career and get a government check every month."

Tom stared at Goodwin with incredulity. "You expect me to be an imposter, a completely different person for the rest of my life? That's one hell of an act, and there will still be questions about Eli's disappearance. I mean about no one ever seeing him again."

"*You* are Eli. Don't you get it?"

"And what about me—Tom?"

"I already told you. He disappeared. Never said a word to either of us about where he was going. He just. . .vanished. It happens every day."

"What about Julie?"

"Did you ever meet her? Does she know anything about you?"

"I never met her. Eli thought I might try to take her from him. Never introduced me and I never saw her."

"Good. What did Eli tell you about her?"

"Damn little except that she's smart and very pretty."

"Nothing about what they did, where they went, their sex life, friends?"

"Nope. Eli kept a lot to himself, especially about her. Do you think I should talk to her about. . ."

"Are you fuckin' stupid?"

"You said I should take his identity."

"Think, man! You don't know her. Looking like Eli won't cut it with her. You're thinking of dating her or something? What if she says, 'We agreed, no oral sex, or why are you taking me to McDonald's? You know I can't stand that place?' So, you apologize three or four times, and she gets suspicious. Then she says, 'Don't you remember anything we discussed? You're not the Eli I used to know.'"

"It was just a thought."

"One fucking bad one. Especially when she begins to doubt who you really are, begins to think there's foul play and demands to see your brother. When you can't produce him, she gets scared and goes to the cops. No, Tom, you can never see or speak to her. End of story."

"And Julie never knows the truth?"

"Not unless you'll enjoy prison food for the rest of your life."

Tom pondered the black hole he'd been sucked into then said, "We got to get out of the business. It's too damn risky, especially if I'm around agents every day."

"Bullshit! You get assigned to narcotics, learn what investigations are going on, cozy up to people in the know. You do intelligence gathering for us."

"That might be more difficult than you think. I bet a lot of that is departmentalized, secret unless, what do they call it? A need to know?"

"Then use your brains, angle for it. Make up a story, say it's heinous and you want to help end it. Make it your core reason for joining. Gotta be passionate about it."

Goodwin stopped at a traffic light then said, "We made a lot of money doing this and we can make a lot more. We have the contacts, the clients. I don't want to give it up. I just hope we're on the same page. If not, you let me know right now. And no, I'm not going to kill you, but you better keep your mouth shut. We're both guilty of disposing a body in case you forgot."

Tom thought for a very long moment then said, "Yeah, I'm still in. But if they're onto me then I'm bailing."

"You just give me a head's up so I can get out of dodge."

"Sure, unless I'm behind bars."

Another moment passed and Tom said, "So, what are you going to do? I mean as a cover?"

"Like you, I've got a degree. My pop made a name for himself in the Alabama State House. I might go into politics, run on his coat tails, go for Congress. Maybe even the Senate down the line. That's what I'm going to do. So you see: new lives for both of us."

"You've got it all planned out."

"We're going to make a great team."

"You sound real cheerful, considering what we did tonight."

Goodwin was pensive for a minute, then said, "A confrontation was going to happen sooner or later with him in the bureau. Then what? A shootout with the feds? We'd both be killed. Maybe him, too. I know he was your brother, but you two weren't really that close. He didn't even introduce you to his girl. That tells you something, doesn't it?"

"Yeah, I guess. But what if Julie or my mom plans a memorial for him?"

"You can't make it. You're on your way to the academy. As of tomorrow."

"That will seem odd."

"Do you like orange?"

"Why?"

"That's the color of jump suits. Need I say more?"

CHAPTER 10

THE PRONOUNCEMENT

Manassas High School, Montgomery, Alabama

Senior high school student Jerry Rabinowitz tapped on Dr. Bhavna Sanvi's door, then entered her classroom. Bhavna was forty-one years old, the biology and anthropology teacher at Manassas, Montgomery's most prestigious high school. She looked up, smiled and said, "Jerry, I'm surprised to see you here. I'm so sorry about your loss. I greatly admired your father. He was a fine man. Are you sure you want to stay in the class?"

"Thanks, but he would have wanted me to. He had a real appreciation of your devotion to learning, and I'm not a quitter. So here I am."

"You are a brave young man, Jerry. I know that you will do well despite the tragedy," she said, then accepted an envelope he handed to her.

"The principal saw me in the hallway and told me to give this to you."

"Thanks. Did Mr. Talbert say anything about it?"

Jerry shrugged and said, "It might be about the meeting. I think everyone's going to be there. It was even announced in the paper."

"So, I noticed," said Bhavna.

She glanced at the envelope, then handed Jerry his term paper. The grade was 'A' minus. "Very nice science, Jerry, but terribly convoluted sentences. Great for a composition in Victorian form but not for a biology composition."

"Yeah, it's a bit florid. I was reading nineteenth century lit and got caught up in the descriptive stuff."

"Well, just cut it down to straightforward facts." She grinned then said, "So, you graduate next week. What are your summer plans?"

"My Great Uncle Levi is taking me camping in the Smoky Mountains. He knows all about guns, tracking, and survival stuff. He was a sergeant major, Army. Then I'm signed up for a chemistry class at the university."

"Very nice. Except maybe the guns."

"Umm, well, I would like to learn how to shoot. Just for sport, you know."

"Uh-huh, well, you know I'm not a fan of firearms."

Jerry appeared momentarily downcast, but then in a spritely manner said, "I told Mr. Talbert that I would help him this afternoon. There's a shipment of new books coming in."

"Any for science class?"

"I don't know. But I'll check. Things have been a little weird for a while. At least since. . ."

"I know," said Bhavna, a concerned look on her face.

Jerry shrugged, and left the room.

Bhava opened the envelope and read the brief note, the same one given to each faculty member.

As announced earlier, this is to remind you of a mandatory meeting of all staff in the school auditorium at seven this evening. It will be addressed by Mr. Wendel Talbert, followed by some remarks by Pastor Everitt Martel, superintendent of schools.

Please be prompt. Be advised that the public is invited and discussion regarding the matters at hand must be kept to a minimum. All topics have been approved by the Board of Education and their decisions are irrevocable.

Bhavna sat back in her swivel chair and contemplated the ominous note. She had been aware of faculty room talk, but despite having the respect and admiration of most of her colleagues, after eleven years in the community she still felt like an outsider and often kept her own counsel.

She had several hours before the meeting and spent the time grading the remainder of the compositions. At six forty-five she joined the flood of teachers and the public into the large, ornate auditorium.

Once everyone was seated and the general conversation had abated, Mr. Talbert asked everyone to stand and follow him in the new pledge of allegiance. This was followed by an invocation led by Pastor Martel.

Bhavna stood but remained silent throughout both, earning some unpleasant glances from those around her.

Once everyone in the audience was again seated, the principal began by saying, "I wish to thank y'all for coming tonight. The announcements we will be making extend far beyond the confines of this academic institution. They are an integral part of the laws of our land. So, I wish to announce that in conformity to the ideals of our nation, all classes and assemblies will begin with the pledge of allegiance we just shared, followed by a Christian prayer. Each instructor will either offer the prayer or appoint a student to recite an appropriate passage or a prayer approved by the authorities."

Once Talbert had finished, he handed the mic to Pastor Martel, who said, "The purpose of the exercise is to bind together the common desires of our people. Speaking the word of God has a calming and thoughtful effect on the student body, which will most certainly result in improved temperament and academic progress. I'm absolutely certain that the vast, vast majority of righteous Christians throughout the world will approve and applaud this monumental endeavor."

His remarks were followed by applause, but Bhavna stood and raised her hand. Both Talbert and Martel gave her a disapproving look, but courtesy dictated that they recognize her.

"Sirs, as a faculty member, I wish to state that I have one hundred and fifty-three students enrolled in my classes. Of that number, twenty-six represent religions other than Christianity and they, along with their parents, will be put in a disagreeable position of having to partake in a prayer service of a faith not their own.

"However, if the board insists on daily prayers, the matter might be mitigated if prayers of various religions be allowed at intervals: Hebrew, Moslem, Hindu, Buddhist, Native American, Shinto and Druid. The latter includes the Gorsedd Prayer of the Gwyddoniaid from the Great Book of Margam. It's quite lovely and speaks of God, love, light, truth and goodness. Highly recommended."

Derisive laughter and calls to "Sit down!" rang out, matched by apoplectic looks from the two men on stage.

"That is absolutely ridiculous," blurted Talbert.

"So is the imposition of mandatory religion in a secular environment," said Bhavna, over the guffaws. "And what of the students who will not take part? Do they stand outside the classroom? Must I stand outside during the Christian prayer? Lack of classroom supervision is contrary to school procedure. I think the board is opening a real can of worms, and lawsuits are bound to follow. I strongly recommend a rethinking on this subject."

"As stated in the notification sent to all faculty," said Talbert, "there will be no further discussion of the matter. The decision of the state and the board is final. This assembly is now concluded."

Bhavna, still standing, would not be silenced. "Sirs," she said, "what you are advocating will be thrown out by the court."

"No, they will not. We control the courts!" shot back Talbert. "This is Alabama, and we will do exactly what we intend to do!"

Bhavna slept fitfully that night. She awoke early, made herself a cup of tea, and sat on her front porch awaiting dawn and the testy confrontation that would surely come later in the day. She felt walls closing in, just as she had when fleeing her Indian village. She had been promised by her father to a man she refused to marry and a mother-in-law who, according to tradition, would rule her life for years to come.

She remembered gathering a handful of coins, riding the train, then a bullock cart, and finally walking the five hundred miles to New Delhi, where she scrubbed floors and worked in a factory in order to pursue her dream: entry to the university. A decade of intense study had resulted in a doctorate in biology.

Returning home, she'd hoped to be congratulated, but nothing had changed. Instead of praise, she was condemned for violating the norms of society and was shunned. Once again, she fled a stultifying mindset and arrived in America. And now she felt wary. Though not incapable of compromise, she was determined to confront the trials coming her way.

To her relief, there was no retribution or condemnation for her views of the previous day. She had fully expected to be summoned to the principal's office for a stern admonishment, but that did not happen. As usual, she remained at her desk preparing lesson plans after school was dismissed. From outside her classroom, she could hear boys unloading boxes from a truck parked a few yards away.

From her open door she saw Jerry Rabinowitz and two other students carrying boxes to a room across the hall. A few minutes later he entered her class with a heavy box and placed it on a side table.

"Three more coming, Doctor," he said. "One box was open and I peeked in. It's a biology text with a real weird cover. You might want to take a look at it when you have a chance." He stopped and continued, "Mr. Talbert told me to put two large trash cans outside all classroom doors. I saw him with Pastor Martel coming this way."

"Toward my class?"

"I think so."

She rose and walked to the door just as Talbert and Martel entered. Talbert merely nodded to Bhavna then, along with the pastor, scanned the shelves of textbooks. He turned to Jerry and said, "I want all of these in those cans. We'll lend a hand."

"Why are you taking my textbooks?" asked Bhavna with alarm.

"They're not in conformity with the revised teaching. You have new ones coming in."

"Jerry, you and your friends bring in the rest of the books when you're done with this," said Talbert.

"Yes, sir," said Jerry, giving Bhavna a concerned glance.

She watched as armloads of texts were taken from the shelves and dumped into the cans outside. When finished, the two men left without a word. Moments later, Jerry returned with another box and a print in a gilt frame.

"The pastor said that this picture will be in all the classes."

"Jesus Christ? Am I to actually display this on the wall?"

"That's what he said. Have you seen the textbooks yet?"

Anger rising, Bhavna tore open the cover of the box, removed a biology book, and stared at the cover.

"Jerry, please put all of these boxes in the hallway. They will not be in my classroom."

"Okay, but. . ."

"Close the door when you're done. I'll be back soon."

"Where are you going?"

"To see Mr. Talbert."

*****

"He's in a meeting," said the principal's secretary.

"He's having one with me," Bhavna stated, bursting into Talbert's office.

"This is a private conference. I don't care for an interruption," said Talbert. Across from him was Pastor Martel. The room seemed close; she had only been in it once. Now in early June it was stifling. A cross, a diploma, and several framed articles hung on the walls.

"Exactly what is this?" she asked, abruptly laying the book on his desk.

"Your new textbook. Biology, right?"

"And this cover represents the material within?"

"As a matter of fact, it does. It falls in line with—"

"Creationism? This book has a very colorful cover, but it's a joke! Here you have four individuals in biblical clothing in a very pretty valley, surrounded by animals, all quite content in each other's company, even though half of them are apex predators and the other half are prey animals."

"Yes, indeed," said Talbert. "As it was some six thousand years ago."

"I see. So, here we have in total harmony, a brontosaurus, a saber tooth tiger, an imperial mammoth, sheep, a lion, horses, and oh, yes, a tetradactyl flying overhead and Jesus

90

below and staring up toward heaven. This is utter nonsense! Dinosaurs died off sixty-two million years ago. There's no way they were contemporaries of ice age animals."

"They were all there six thousand years ago," said Pastor Martel. "It's in the Bible."

"I have read the Bible and it is not," said Bhavna. "The earth is four and a half billion years old, and our bipedal ancestors were around over a million years ago. All serious scholars of the Bible agree that Yahweh's "day" was a metaphor for eons. Have you any idea how you got six thousand years?"

"It's not something I question. Everyone knows it's true."

"Have you heard of John Usher?"

"Should I have? Is he relevant to this?" asked Talbert, clearly out of patience.

"He was an archbishop of Armagh, Ireland, who in an attempt to determine the age of the world added up twenty-one generations, starting with Adam and Eve. This was in 1650, some seventy-five years before the Enlightenment, when not a single scientific subject was taught. Adding up the begats, the good archbishop concluded that four thousand and four years before 1650, on the twenty-third day of October, Julian calendar, the world began. Add some four-hundred years and you arrive at six-thousand. Is that what you really expect me to teach? I have a doctorate in science. I deal with facts, not dogma or mythology. I will not, cannot, teach this."

It was a full minute before another word was spoken. Then Talbert said, "I don't think there is a place for you here any longer."

"Mr. Talbert, I love this school and my students. But there is truth and there is falsehood. I cannot abide by the latter. I will tender my resignation in one hour's time."

"That is best," said Talbert. "Unfortunately for you, there will likely be no other academic institutions that will employ you in this nation. And you should not expect any monetary compensation. None at all. Good day."

Jerry helped Bhavna load boxes of teaching materials into her car and said, "I wish you weren't leaving. There are so many here who will miss you."

"And I will miss them. I really don't have a choice, do I? There is fact and there is fiction, and science can only exist where facts are recognized. President Lincoln said, 'You can fool some of the people all of the time and all the people some of the time, but you cannot fool all the people all the time.' I don't wish to fool anybody. So I have to say goodbye. Let's stay in touch."

She put her purse on the front seat, started the car, and drove out of Montgomery County.

Three days later, on page four of the *Montgomery Journal*, an article announced:

Miss Bhavna Sanvi, a former biology teacher at Manassas High, has been dismissed from her teaching position for noncompliance with academic instruction. Miss Sanvi has not announced her future plans.

CHAPTER 11

EDITH BARNES

It had been a hardscrabble life, growing up poor in the Cochella Valley near Indio, California. As a child, Edith Barnes was an ardent, bright champion of the underdog, always on the lookout for righteous crusades. And if none were in sight, she would create one. It didn't matter to her if it was worker's pay for the harvesters of date palms, the staple crop of the valley, or a head start program for Hispanic children, whether they were legal or not.

With a tangled forest of unruly blonde hair, an unremarkable face, and ever present blue-rimmed glasses, Edith Barnes was not one that men lined up for. Dates usually ended within twenty to thirty minutes, after she launched into an intense dissertation on women's rights or some sidelined portion of the citizenry.

As a teen-ager she eschewed make-up, designer clothes, and had absolutely no interest in popular fads, though her intensity resulted in being the star of the girl's high school soccer team. An admirer of determined people, the walls of her bedroom were plastered with photos of Winston Churchill, President Ulysses Grant, Sojourner Truth, Mahatma Gandhi, George Washington Carver, and aviatrix Amelia Earhart.

Often frustrating her teachers with pointed questions, probing for accuracy, but earning straight A's, she was on the road to graduation by the age of sixteen.

Her one true companion was Iris Leon, an immigrant from Haiti who enrolled in her high school as a junior. Edith befriended and coached her in English, earning the girl's everlasting gratitude.

Edith's wealthy uncle, Wilbert, who made his fortune shipping oranges to the east coast on refrigerated box cars, attended the girl's graduation where Edith, the valedictorian, gave a no-nonsense speech. Her topic, unlike the usual "How hard we worked to graduate," or "It's Party Time," centered on the fragility of democracy and how to best serve the nation. He was impressed by her sincerity.

Wilbert greeted Edith following the ceremony and said, "Well, is it Stanford, UCLA or Harvard?"

"None, unless Iris goes, too."

He stared at Edith then said, "You are serious, aren't you?"

"Absolutely."

Hands on hips in her usual stance, Iris gave him an ingratiating smile and said, "I think Harvard would be nice. Dat's what I think."

Wilbert shrugged, looked at Edith and Iris and said, "So, it's Harvard for both of you. Fine, I guess I'll come to that graduation, too."

Iris was sassy and irreverent. In honor of her Caribbean roots, she often wore a cloth head scarf and a floral dress. Under her graduation robe there was a flash of green and scarlet. She reached into her shoulder bag and pulled out a large, floppy hat banded with bright colors.

"I bought dis hat for dis very occasion. Do you like it, Edith?"

"It's very becoming on you, Iris."

"Do you think the Harvard men will like it?"

"Of course! It will attract them like bees to honey."

"Mmm, I do like honey. And maybe I will find a nice college boy. I feel so special."

"You are special, Iris," said Edith, as they walked to the reception. *So now we will start to make our mark,* she thought. *Someday we will change the world.*

After their graduation from Harvard, Iris was there for Edith at her marriage, subsequent divorce, and the adoption of a one-eyed indolent cat named Sam Grant.

For Edith, city council led to California Assembly, then the House, followed by ten years in the Senate, and her triumphant election as President of the United States, with Iris, her steadfast assistant, by her side.

On the day following the NCRA inauguration of Jefferson Calhoun Lee, President Edith Barnes entered the Situation Room of the White House accompanied by Iris. She glanced at the cabinet members, as well as FBI Director Steven Whitinghill. They were all standing silent as ghosts, somber but not defeatist.

"Please be seated," she said while taking a chair on one side of the polished table. At fifty-five, trim, with her hair in a bun and a touch of grey, she moved with characteristic energy. Today she wore an immaculate grey pant suit with a toned-down silk scarf. President Barnes removed her glasses and glanced at a folder.

Having already reviewed the President's Daily Brief, she said, "We know that the NCRA consists of the states of the old Confederacy and a few in the Midwest. There are still others that support the interests of the secessionists but have chosen to remain with the federal government. Though not the twenty-five states Mr. Lee hoped for, it's still a horrific rupture. So, the question is, how do we deal with it? How do we put the Union back together? As President Washington said: 'Advise and consent."

There was a long moment of reflection, after which General McRae, head of Joint Chiefs of Staff and the nation's highest-ranking military officer, said, "Madam President, I do have a recommendation, one that will end this farce in about two or three hours' time, depending on its implementation." He spoke in his cherished John Wayne accent

With studied patience, Barnes wondered if he was going to add, "Little Lady." He did not. "And what, pray tell, might that implementation involve?"

"An immediate assault and capture of their Capitol in Montgomery, Alabama. I, with your consent, can issue an order to seal off the county by deploying the Eighty-Second Airborne as well as troops from Fort Rucker. My second order would be to arrest every traitor in their government. If there is resistance, I would recommend an air strike on their Capitol. Cut off the head of the snake. Blow the thing into little pieces, put it in the shredder and it's over. End of story."

There was absolute silence as all eyes turned from him to Edith Barnes. She stared at him for what seemed eternity then in a very quiet voice said, "So, you are advocating the killing, no, the murder, of former citizens of the United States?"

"If you want to end it. Why pussy-foot about? Why pander to secession? Kill it, get it over with, then discuss the legal or ethical ramifications. Otherwise, this heresy can go on for a very long time. And if the NCRA gains foreign support, it can become very nasty indeed. Also, there are potential supporters in the U.S. military stationed in secessionist states. The longer you wait, the more subordinates they can enlist. It's called a chain of command."

"And what do you do with officers and men who want to defend the NCRA?"

"Simple. Disarm, arrest, charge them with treason and invoke extreme disciplinary action. That's what, Madam President."

"I see," said Barnes, her eyes unflinching. "The 'shredder' you speak of will be seen on TV screens and in social media around the world. The headlines will be 'U.S. military lays waste to historic site and annihilates hundreds of civilians.' No, sir, that will not happen. There are other ways of dealing with Mr. Lee, but declaring war is not one of them."

Her eyes fell on Alexander Petrovich, a one-time child refugee from the former Soviet Union. Rotund and extremely fond of Edith Barnes, he spoke with the an accented, gravely voice reminiscent of Henry Kissinger, who had been advisor to President Richard Nixon. "Speaking as Homeland Security chief," he said, "It is my sincere belief, Madam President, that the NCRA will begin to disintegrate when its citizens come face to face with stark reality."

"Go on."

"Deny social security, Medicare, and no imports from the United States. In effect, sever all relations with them. Blockade their ports and allow no aircraft from their states to cross borders. And then block roads and only allow the exit of refugees. In other words, strangle them."

Gerald Chu, Secretary of the Treasury, said, "The point Secretary Petrovich makes regarding business and monetary matters is very telling. If the military option is off the table, there are numerous ways of crippling the NCRA that do not require violence."

Forty-one, balding and academic, Doctor Chu was the financial guru. Before heading the department, he'd worked closely with the FBI in tracking down off-shore accounts that evaded taxation.

Chu continued. "Politics and defense aside, governments are primarily about finance: directing the flow of monies to projects of national importance, and seeing to the financial well-being of their citizens. Cripple the banks, suspend federal loans and assistance, spread uncertainty in whatever currency they devise, and their nation faces financial disaster."

"Can you elaborate?" asked Barnes with sudden interest.

"Well, since the FDR administration, bank accounts have been insured by the FDIC." He smiled and said, "Technically, it's not part of the Treasury Department, but I do have connections. Withdraw that insurance, and money in a bank is no safer than under the mattress. You've got, in a financial sense, a nuke going off in several thousand banks throughout the NCRA."

"That might have a terrifying effect," said Terence Chenault, Secretary of State. He ran his hand through a head of curly blond hair, then twisted an upward pointed moustache reminiscent of Wilhelm, German Kaiser during World War I.

"But won't the NCRA establish their own FDIC? It's not exactly a destitute region."

"They could attempt that," replied Chu, "But that can take weeks, if not months, and there would be an enormous disruption to their banking system. And, without the gold reserves of Fort Knox or that in New York, their currency would be virtually useless. The term used after the American Revolution, 'not worth a continental,' comes to mind."

"It would be like Black Thursday, October 1929," said Petrovich. "A run on the banks to retrieve uninsured funds. I hope there aren't too many suicides when banks shut their doors."

There were some chuckles before the room turned serious once again. The President turned to Steven Whitinghill, who set aside a legal-sized brown envelope he had forgotten to leave in his office.

"Director, besides the matter of secession, has your office discerned any NCRA threats against the U.S.?"

"Nothing on the radar, Madam President, though we monitor all of their communications. That includes cyber, internet, social media and phone. We have also been watching home-grown groups. There are quite a few, and they are disturbing. But we're not sure if they might be targeting U.S. or NCRA locations. I suspect that the secessionists are more worried about us than they are about a few terrorists."

"Damn right they should be," blurted General McRae.

The President glanced at him, then turned to Hamilton Sherwood, Postmaster General, who said, "I suggest that all mail from the U.S. into the region be terminated. Choke them off. No FedEx, no UPS, no trucks or rail. Have the Navy terminate ocean transport of supplies, and any ocean travel out of the NCRA. Right now, the leaders of the NCRA think they're a budding magnolia that will grow in Alabama sunshine. Make it shrivel, and there will be perilous discontent. Once that occurs, it's just a matter of time before they implode."

"I agree with the Secretary," said Barnes. "I will instruct the governors to employ the National Guard to seal the borders. And General McRae, you may employ regular troops if there is any violent assault upon the United States. However, I'm opposed to having Congress declare war. To do so implies that we are recognizing a sovereign nation, and I refuse to do that."

Despite her disdain for the General, she felt compelled to work with him. She was gratified when he puffed out his chest, one filled with hard-won medals, nodded, and said,

"The military will comply. As Lord Nelson said at Trafalgar, 'Every man will do his duty.'"

"And woman," the president added mildly.

"And woman," agreed the four-star.

"Very well," said Edith Barnes. "One more matter before we meet again tomorrow. The NCRA is not a monolith. There are entire regions of residents still loyal to the United States, areas that may come under pressure from vigilante groups and militias. These people, the ones who choose to remain in the seceding states, as well as those who attempt to reach U.S. borders, have to be protected. So, General, how do you recommend we do that?"

Surprised, but pleased that she was asking for his advice, McRae said, "I can order our military to airlift troops to the endangered sectors." He raised his hands and added, "No shooting, unless we receive incoming. To which we will reply with appropriate response."

"That works," replied the President. "I will be giving an address to the American people tomorrow. I think we have finished our business today."

As all the cabinet members headed for the door, Edith Barnes said, "Steven, have a moment?"

"Of course."

They paused as the others filed out of the room.

"Have you heard from Janice?"

"Not since she left with Goodwin for Alabama."

"I've known her for a long time, and she's a very smart lady. I'm worried about her. Is she aware of the trouble she could be in?"

Steven shook his head and said, "I don't think she's considered all the ramifications. She fell in love with James Goodwin and will follow him like a lap dog. There's not much I can do."

Steven showed Barnes the legal-sized envelope and said, "I suspect it's from her attorney."

"That's not good." Edith was silent for a while, then said, "Regarding terrorist groups in the U.S., we have to keep an eye on them. We don't want an incident that can precipitate violence in the NCRA or revenge by the secessionists. Please keep me informed."

"Yes, Ma'am."

Deep in thought, Steven returned to his office and opened the envelope. It was postmarked from two days before the secession. He scanned the divorce papers, sat back in his chair, and stared at the far wall.

Special Agent Eli Barett, who never knocked, entered Steven's office, glanced at the papers, and said, "Surely you're not surprised. You knew it was going to happen. What's she asking for besides everything you own?"

"Not quite everything," Steven replied. "I retain the vacation property and half the money in American funds."

"That's all? Well, hell, Stevie, it could be worse. She could have asked for Rambo."

"He's not negotiable," Steven replied, picking up a very cold cup of coffee and taking it to the micro. "The mutt's mine," he said, glancing at a framed photo of himself and the ever-slobbering, watery-eyed bulldog. Flopping into his well-worn sofa, he glanced again at the papers and said, "To be honest, I didn't think she'd go through with it. I knew they were having an affair, but I assumed that she would tire of him."

"Janice has always had a thing for danger. You've been married for what? Twenty-one years? That's a good run, better than most. There was a time when you two were damn tight, had lots of friends, spent time together. But face it, pal, not since you got this job. Goodwin is a blowhard, insufferable, but he's a whirlwind, attracts excitement and can seduce almost any woman he wants."

"Including my wife."

"Fraid so. She's still a fine-looking woman and is attracted to flamboyant men. And she hasn't been terribly secretive about her affair with Goodwin. So, you being a workaholic, what did you expect?"

"I don't know. I thought we could talk things out, maybe go somewhere together."

"Like Montgomery, Alabama? Well, if it makes you any happier, those divorce papers don't mean shit. They're an act of futility, and probably an expensive one, too."

Steven frowned and said, "Care to explain?"

"Mr. Director, are your brains on hold? You're living in the U.S. of A. She and her attorney are residing in a political entity not recognized by this country. The document has no legal standing as long as she remains in the NCRA. And, as long as she is married to you, she can't marry Goodwin. And that's a fact."

"Maybe you just earned beer and lunch."

Eli snorted and said, "You still love her, right?"

"Yeah, I do. This would be a lot easier if I could put all those years into a little box, never to open it again, But I can't. I've lost her and it hurts."

"It's going to hurt a lot more if she's charged with treason. You might speak to her about that if you ever get the chance. There's gonna be a real comeuppance when the NCRA implodes."

"She won't speak to me. She's in Goodwin's camp, or bed, and he's calling the shots," Steven said, sipping his coffee.

"Then have Evelyn call her."

"They're not speaking either."

"Well, I hope the lady sees the light before the power goes out. Damn shame, pal, a damn shame. I'm all ears if there's anything else you want to tell me," said Eli. He saluted with two fingers, then left the room.

What does he think I'm going to tell him, thought Steven, *what a great lay Janice is? Or was. . .*

He felt a dark, ominous cloud descend upon him. "Oh shit!" he shouted, his coffee sloshing onto his desk.

*****

"I've got you, babe," James Goodwin hummed, holding Janice tightly, their bodies entwined. Having reached a too quick orgasm, he slipped off the sheath and murmured the only words he recalled from Sonny and Cher's long-ago tune.

"Mmm," sighed Janice, content in his arms. "I love it here, the old South—laid back, refined, full of romance."

"It draws one in—the epitome of charm, vintage, elegance. It's like a flower, a perfumed essence, my dear. It's all about living. And dying, too, but dying in splendor. Magnificent splendor." Then he whistled a few bars from "Dixie."

"Are we going to be all right?" she asked wistfully as his hand reached for hers.

Drifting off after his carnal exertion, he said, "Of course. We'll be just fine. As they used to say, 'We're living in high cotton.' Those people up north will bluster and fume, but what can they really do? Make hollow threats against a hundred million? Lordy, no. They're just twisting in the wind."

She grinned at his slow southern drawl then said, "Do you really hate Steven?"

The question disturbed his reverie. "Honey, he's a sore subject with me. I wish you wouldn't bring it up. Hate him? He did me wrong, made me look like an ass during a congressional session, and I'm not the forgiving type. I think you know that. But I'm the victor."

He leaned over, kissed her, and whispered, "I have you. And Steven lost the most delicious thing in the world."

CHAPTER 12

THE HERO

President Edith Barnes sat at the Resolute desk in the Oval Office. She removed her glasses and said, "I wish to address our loyal citizens this morning, as well as the Americans who have defected from our great Union. It has been nearly three centuries since the first patriot shots were fired to establish a nation free from the constraints and unequal representation imposed by a distant power.

"This endeavor was engaged in by people in all thirteen colonies. Regretfully, many of their descendants, as well as more recent arrivals, have forsaken the cause for which our ancestors so nobly gave their lives and fortunes.

"In 1789, the Constitution was signed and our Republic was born. The concept of a democratic nation led by representatives of the people was, in foreign capitols, regarded as unworkable, democracy being regarded as rule by the mob. Our republic was, and still is, an experiment in democracy. How sad it will be if it fails, for is it not the shining beacon on the hill? If it flounders due to partisan short-sightedness, how dark will the shadow be that falls upon the world? And what chance will there ever be for that beacon to be relit? And by whom? Surely not by a dictator or autocrat who would deny life, liberty, and happiness to those different than he.

"When asked about the nature of our government, Benjamin Franklin said, 'It is a republic if we can keep it.' And until recently, we, the people, all the people, have done just that.

"We have, through wars, depressions and other calamities, striven to adhere to President Lincoln's words spoken at Gettysburg: that our fathers brought forth a new nation, conceived in liberty and dedicated to the proposition that all men are created equal. He went on to say that we are engaged in a great struggle which would determine if this nation may endure.

"This nation, now sundered, is engaged in a war of ideology, of principle, of concepts of right and wrong. So this I declare: this nation shall be reunited, not through the fire of cannon and blood, but by the voice of reason. We are all humans, we make mistakes, we can be cut adrift by raving sensationalism, by displays of passion contrary to reason, goodness, justice, and law. There are those who will turn away from the light and from brotherhood to further their own ambitions, their own inadequacies, and cast dispersion upon others to deny their own failures."

She paused and in a somber voice said, "We will welcome back to our union all those regions that have forsaken the liberties and responsibilities for which we stand. But we will hold accountable those who instigated insurrection and harm brought upon loyal citizens. This, I believe, is only just."

*****

In Montgomery, President Lee sat at his desk, arms crossed and scowled. "Turn off that damn TV," he said to James Goodwin. "I can't stand the sight of that woman. Never have."

"Are you going to make a counter-address?" asked Ralph Prescott, his Secretary of Agriculture.

"What good would that do? I already set out the guidelines of this country in my inauguration. There's no need to repeat it. Besides, am I to defile Lincoln's words with some ranting? My base wouldn't have tuned into Barnes anyway. No, we'll just let it go, ignore it. But there are other things we can do."

"Against the United States?" asked Stanley Palmer, hoping for new and exciting responsibilities.

"Perhaps. But I'm thinking of ways to deal with certain groups of people, undesired people, right here in the NCRA. And that, Palmer, might come under your jurisdiction."

"People in opposition, certain minorities," said Palmer.

"Something like that," said Lee. "Points we enumerated in the Constitution."

Prescott remained stoic but uncomfortable.

"And what might that be?" said Goodwin.

"Something that will be swift and thorough," said Lee.

"Fantastic," said Palmer. He offered a rare toothy grin and said, "Boom."

*****

Shortly afterwards, a news article in the *Los Angeles Sun Journal* one month later reported:

The U.S. Coast Guard in conjunction with the DEA intercepted a rare electric narco submarine with six tons of cocaine and Fentanyl. The sleek craft, built in Columbia near the Cucurrup River and costing one and a half million to construct, was being intentionally scuttled by its three-man crew in the

Gulf of Mexico as the littoral combat ship USS John Paul Jones *came alongside.*

While older cartel subs were only semi-submersible, the newer craft, propelled by twin electric motors, is capable of fully submerging for over thirty hours. Many of these are constructed with fiberglass hulls, making them harder to detect by naval vessels and circling patrol planes.

On board the Jones *was LEDET, a law enforcement detachment including members of an FBI dive team which located the narco vessel in one hundred feet of water. FBI Director Steven Whitinghill said the drugs recovered had a street value of one hundred and fifty million dollars.*

The illicit drugs, weighing nearly five thousand pounds. were packaged as kilogram bricks and wrapped in waterproof sacks on which the crew slept when not tucked into a claustrophobic stern control compartment. Battery powered, the sub was forty feet in length. The Columbian crew was apprehended and revealed that the vessel was heading to an inlet on the Louisiana coast where it was to be met by Americans trafficking in the distribution of drugs.

The government has expressed concern that a large quantity of the confiscated drugs were to be smuggled into the U.S. market. Although not confirmed, it is considered likely that profits from the sale of the drugs were going into the coffers of the NCRA and that their Internal Security Service may be involved.

The Coast Guard has stepped up its search for more subs and is currently patrolling the NCRA coastal regions.

*****

Eighteen years earlier, Washington, D.C.

"Hold one moment, I'm transferring you now," the FBI operator said.

"This is Whitinghill, senior special agent. Please state your name and the purpose of your call."

"Um, I'm Tony Eland, the son of Garand Eland, the man in the most wanted poster. That's what I'm calling about."

The youth spoke rapidly, his voice fearful.

"Are you in immediate danger?" asked Steven, frowning and glancing at Eli, the agent trainee, and Special Agent Crawford.

"No, but my mom and I ran away after he robbed that bank in Virginia and killed those people."

"Where are you calling from?"

"Maryland, just outside of D.C. I saw his picture on TV and the FBI number. That's why I'm calling. He knows I'll turn him in. My mom and I are really scared."

"Do you know where he is?" asked Steven, silently pointing Eli and Crawford's attention to the wanted poster on the bulletin board.

"Yeah, at least I think so. He's not at home. Pa's got a trailer back in the woods."

"Can you meet with us? Can you show us where he is? We'll make sure you are safe."

"Okay, I'll tell you where to meet us. Kinda hurry, will you?"

The location was approximately a fifty-minute drive away. Steven, Eli, Crawford, and Field Agent Williams raced to their gear-loaded SUV. "The bank teller just died of her injuries," said Steven. "The bank's security guard is in critical condition. I'm calling for backup, but we will be first on the scene."

Steven turned on the emergency lights and wove past cars pulling to the curb. It had snowed recently, and while the roads were mostly cleared there were piles of snow between the sidewalks and the streets.

"There were two shooters, right?" asked Eli.

"Yeah," said Crawford. "Baltimore PD put out an APB, found the car, but lost the trail. They'll be following us in."

"Good, but we're in charge," said Steven.

In Maryland, they spotted the boy and his mother standing in the alcove of a coffee shop. In a quick, tremulous voice, Tony described where his father was hiding, and the hazards on the trail. "My pa is real good with hidden trip wires. He never liked anyone coming around."

"I would like you to go to our Baltimore office with Agent Williams," Steven told Mrs. Eland, when a backup police car arrived. "I suspect there's a lot you can tell us. It's very important."

The woman, filled with anxiety, nodded and said, "Be really careful. Garand has an automatic pistol, the one he used at the bank, and his friend, Denny, has a rifle." She hugged her son and was escorted to the PD car.

"There's just a trail," said Tony, when Steven pulled the SUV off the road a half hour later. Thick patches of ice littered the ground as the four carefully picked their way through dense thickets of brush and bare trees. They found and deactivated three trip wires along the way.

Tony stopped and pointed. "You can barely see it, but the trailer is hidden in that clump of trees."

"Crawford, stay here with Tony," said Steven. He and Eli moved forward into the clearing. Suddenly, the trailer door opened and two men burst out, guns blazing. Drawing their guns, the agents sought cover, but Steven slipped and fell heavily onto the ice, his weapon sliding out of reach. One round ripped into his calf as Eli fired at Garand's accomplice, bringing him down with his second shot.

Eli ran to Steven, grabbed him by the collar and began pulling him to safety. In the chaos that followed he managed to fire three rounds, hitting Garand who fell onto the ice, blood pooling beneath him.

Eli holstered his gun and radioed in "Officer down, both suspects down, ambulance needed." He then began to tend to their wounds.

"How are you feeling?" Eli asked when he entered Steve's hospital room.

"Better than I would be if it weren't for you."

"Just doing the job, boss."

"Well, I owe you."

"Maybe a beer. Naw, make it two."

"Steven grinned and said, "I know just the place."

CHAPTER 13

ON THE TRAIL

Arizona, twenty one years earlier

It was already warm at nine in the morning. Steven sat on a decrepit mare watching the guide determine which horse would be suitable for each of the riders.

"I'm Glen," said the guide, a man in his early seventies, wearing a battered slouch hat. "You look like an experienced rider," he said, taking in Steven's relaxed demeanor.

"Fair to midlin,'" said Steven with a lopsided grin.

"Good enough. I should have put you on a better horse. Anyway, I'd like you to remain in the rear in case there's a problem. Not that there's been any for years, but nature's a wild card—rocks, sudden storms and such."

He glanced at Steven's camera and said, "Just taking a vacation?"

"Got to get away from the office. It gets claustrophobic, and I like Arizona's open air and big sky."

The old man nodded and said, "I've been doing this for forty-three years. Kinda gets into your blood, you know?"

Steven grinned and said, "Yep, lots of things do."

Of the nine riders, three were children, one not more than five years old. It took twenty minutes for the old man to adjust all the stirrups, get people mounted, and strap children into the saddles. With that finally accomplished, the he mounted his gelding and signaled that they would begin the eight-mile ride along the canyon's rim. The ride would conclude at a staging area from which the riders would be transported back by air-conditioned van.

Steven wondered how many times his nag had been on the trail, which snaked above a sandstone canyon three hundred feet below. It could probably navigate it with its eyes closed. The slope was forbiddingly steep, studded with cacti, boulders, and mesquite. He was perplexed why anybody would take young children on such a ride.

A young woman seated on a bay mare rode just behind the guide, who had just finalized the order of their procession. She turned for a brief moment, glanced at him, then turned back as the horses began a slow walk. *Nice looking lady,* Steven mused. Perhaps he might get to speak with her on the way back. *Never know what might come of it.*

Two miles into the journey, the five-year-old boy's horse dallied and lagged behind the horses ridden by the child's parents. Then, suddenly alert, it trotted to catch up. Joggled up and down, desperately clutching the saddle horn, the child began to scream. Glen halted the riders, dismounted, and approached the child's mother. "Ma'am, the boy's terrified, and I can't allow him to go on riding solo. You can hold him in your lap instead. I'll have to take this horse's reins."

Comforting her son, the woman readily agreed. The ride re-commenced, with Glen back in front. Steven, relaxed in the saddle, watched billowing clouds gather on the horizon.

The woman riding behind the guide glanced back once or twice. She saw that everybody, save the rider at the rear, was holding a death grip on the saddle horn. "Can't control a horse if you don't have the reins," her daddy had told her. Except for that man, there was not a rider in the bunch.

What she did not see was the diamondback slumbering beside the trail. Disturbed by the clomping of hooves, it decided to assert some territorial dominance and launched itself with blinding speed to sink its fangs into the leg of the third horse in line. The mare reared, half spun, then toppled over the side of the precipice, plummeting toward the bottom of the chasm.

Janice screamed as she tumbled down, dislodged from the saddle. Instinctively she protected her head and face with her forearms. He body struck against a boulder before rolling into thick mesquite.

There were gasps and cries amongst riders as horses skittered nervously. Glen strove to calm the horses down to prevent any other disaster. Steven swung off his mount and began to descend into the gorge.

When he reached the woman's side, she lay in a fetal position beside a narrow deer trail partially hidden by brush and granite boulders. It was obvious that she had a broken leg, along with numerous bruises and bleeding scratches. "Can't get up. Can't walk," she murmured. "The horse, is it. . ."

"Gone," said Steven, looking into her worried eyes.

There was little to no cell phone coverage in this desolate area, so any air rescue would be long in coming. He assessed the path that snaked up towards the trail.

"This will hurt, but I will get you out of here," he said. He gently lifted her and draped her over his shoulder in a fireman's carry. The path was steep and he had to stop numerous times to rest, sharing his canteen water with her.

"Maybe you should leave me here and go for help," she said, gritting her teeth to speak through the pain.

"That's what the other riders should be doing. I'm not leaving you here alone. In addition to snakes, there are gila monsters in these parts. Besides," he said grinning, "this is a great way to get to know each other."

"I can think of better ways, but you're very courageous for helping me."

"Yep, 'fidelity, bravery, integrity.'"

"Is that a motto?"

"FBI. That's why I'm required to plow through cacti, bound over rattlers, plunge down chasms, and rescue fair damsels. Now if you were ninety years old and wrinkly, I'd have just shouted down, 'Are you okay?' and waited for the cavalry."

She managed a laugh and said, "So, my hero, what's your name?"

"Steven Whitinghill, special agent, at your service, my lady."

"Wow, impressive. My name's Janice. Now how about getting me out of here?"

She looked forward to his hospital visits during her recovery. Attentive, considerate, and academic, with a dollop of dark humor, he made her the focus of his romantic attentions. When she finally succumbed to his persistent efforts, they married and found a modest home nine miles from Washington D.C. Their daughter, Evelyn, their only child, was born two years later.

In time, Janice found work at the Treasury Department, and she and Steven began to hobnob with colleagues and politicians at numerous social functions. At one such event, she met James Goodwin, who mentioned that he was seeking a highly capable aide. He was delighted when she agreed to work with him. Very delighted indeed.

RUPTURED

*****

Late spring, Present Time, Baltimore

"Professor Rathmore, I wish to disagree," said Devin Winfeld, sitting at the rear of the class. Tall, authoritative, older than the undergrads, he exuded an air of superiority and commanded everyone's attention when he spoke.

"Yes, social changes often come incrementally, but real revolutions with dynamic structural change comes, as Chairman Mao said, 'from the barrel of the gun.' Just look at the overthrow of emperors of China, Tsar Nicholas, the French and American revolutions. They were all violent. That's the way to change the course of history. And it needs to be changed again," said Winfeld.

Evelyn Whitinghill raised her hand and said, "Doctor Rathmore, didn't Thomas Jefferson say that there should be a revolution every twenty years? Perhaps Mr. Winfeld is correct. I mean, wouldn't the situation with the black population of this be very different if a great revolt had happened in the eighteenth century?"

The professor smiled indulgently then said, "Jefferson said that as a very young man, but he certainly changed his mind after becoming president. And in regard to your second point, there was the Nat Turner slave revolt in the early 1830s that ended disastrously. In fact, it resulted in a much stricter laws, fear, and retaliatory violence. One must be very careful in picking a revolution to join or starting one. Besides, sometimes regimes implode without violence. I'm thinking of the Soviet Union, a society so corrupt and hollow that it collapsed under its own weight."

"But that," said Devin, "took seventy-nine years."

"True, it was a slow death, and you advocate revolution. But it is often the case that the revolutionaries are the first to be eliminated after the fall of a government. Their continual insistence on violence becomes an impediment to establishing order. They become expendable. Robespierre comes to mind."

Other students, already riveted by the testy exchange, sat upright when Professor Rathmore gave Devin a long, hard look and said, "So, allow me to ask, are you planning a revolution, Mr. Winfeld? And if so, against whom?"

"That, sir, is still pending, but there are enemies that must be dealt with."

"Through the barrel of a gun?"

"Yes, through the barrel of a gun."

*****

"Thanks for supporting me," said Winfeld as he and Evelyn walked across the quad.

"I think you presented a cogent argument," she said admiringly. "I also believe in justice for the oppressed, especially in places with systemic racism."

"Is that so? And exactly how have you demonstrated that?" he asked, brushing lank black hair from his brow.

She looked into his eyes, mesmerized. "I've been on Black Lives Matter marches and lots of other demonstrations. Perhaps even more than you."

"I doubt it. Look, to be effective, marches must have impact. They cannot just be angry chants ignored by the opposition. They have to result in violent upheaval that causes fear amongst the ruling class. It must lead to their demise, their extinction. Do you agree?"

"Well, that does seem extreme. Is that what you intend to accomplish? Extinction?"

Winfeld stopped and gazed at the young woman who stared back.

"I like your spirit, Evelyn, but I'm hardly going to reveal anything specific. I once read that if you don't write your own epitaph, somebody else will, and it may not be complimentary. I don't want to be remembered as a footnote on the bottom of a page. I want to be the first sentence in the next chapter, if not its heading."

"And what if I want to be the next line?"

He said nothing for several heartbeats. She stared at him, enraptured.

"Then you will have to commit to a course from which you cannot deviate. Nothing can interfere. What I am considering won't be child's play, and it demands very serious thought. As Jefferson said, revolutions are not made for light and transient reasons."

"It sounds dangerous but terribly exciting," said Evelyn, feeling emboldened and excited in his presence.

"Dangerous, exciting, yes, but excitement is not the goal. The results can be cataclysmic and, even if successful, will end in the deaths of many, including, perhaps, our own. So, think about it, Evelyn. Think really hard."

CHAPTER 14

THE KLAN

Alabama, twenty five years earlier

Eighteen-year-old Antoine and his mother, Melli Winfeld, left their pew and walked onto the steps of the AME church, where they were met by Reverend Amos Brown. He shook Melli's hand with an ingratiating smile, then addressed Antoine. "Well, young man, are you staying out of trouble, or is Mrs. Winfeld taking an ugly stick to you?"

Antoine, at six foot two, laughed and said, "Oh, no, Rev, I ain't misbehavin'. No, Mama won't tolerate that."

"He got that right," said Melli, as she adjusted her fancy Sunday hat and folded her fan. "I keep close watch on Antoine. Indeed, I do."

Antoine grinned and said, "Please excuse me, but I have to get to work, Rev."

"Not coming to the social? Kisha will be there. You know how she has her eye on you," said Amos Brown.

Antoine sighed and said, "She nice, but. . ."

"Uh-huh. So, you're working on the Lord's Day?"

"Just a few hours. Plantin' a few trees for Mrs. Jessup. Won't take long, then I'll be back."

He fairly skipped down the steps, walked along the tree-lined streets and modest homes, and got into his old Chevy pickup. His tools were in the truck bed. He drove three miles outside town until he came to an ornate iron gate of the Jessup home. He got out, pushed the button on the call box, and waited for the gate to open. He was happy, but not necessarily about the money he would be making.

"Celine, it's me, Antoine."

"One sec, I'll be right down," answered a voice as the gate slid open.

He got back in the truck and moved along the broken asphalt drive between the one-hundred-and-sixty-year-old willows until he stopped before the former plantation house. Once a splendid Italianate mansion, it was now in need of considerable repair. Five chipped marble pillars supported a portico and Grecian frieze.

Stepping out of his truck, he cast his eyes over the expanse of an untended field, previously a source of cotton, many decades before. And at its edge, he knew that there were remains of huts once occupied by people who looked like him. Their skeletal remains were buried not far beyond.

The thought of that quickly dissipated as Celine bounded down the driveway, her smile dazzling, her blue eyes sparkling.

If Gordon Jessup were not in his study by the second-floor window that looked down upon them she would surely have thrown her arms about him.

"Good morning, Miss Celine," said Antoine with a grin and a deferential bow, knowing that she would roll her eyes and say, "Oh please! You are so silly." She did.

"He's here?" asked Antoine looking up at the window reflecting in the sunlight.

She nodded and said, "Yeah, I'm afraid so." Then she said, "My mama wants the trees planted by the old carriage house. They were delivered four days ago and I fear they are starting to wither."

Antoine removed a shovel from the truck and walked with Celine across a field to the aging building. The chestnut trees were only five feet high, and Celine showed him where they should be planted.

"A two-foot-deep hole should do," she said. "There's a spigot and hose around back."

He removed his shirt and tossed it over a post then said, "Lord, you are one beautiful girl."

She shrugged, smiled, and said, "I want to go away after I graduate. Maybe we can go together."

"I'd like that but I have to finish my senior year. And won't your pa go looking for us? You know what he's like. Is he still in the Klan?"

She nodded. "I think so. He doesn't talk about it, but he does go to the meetings."

"He's dangerous," said Antoine, thrusting the shovel into the ground.

"You're not afraid of him, are you?"

"Him personally? No, but his kind . . ."

"Mama told him not to use the strap on me anymore. Or do anything else."

Antoine stopped. "Use the strap and do anything else?"

"You know. Touch me and stuff."

"And has he stopped?"

"For now."

"You should have a way of protecting yourself. Have you called the police?"

She gave a mirthless laugh. "They're his buddies and in the Klan. They would do it too if he let them."

Her eyes downcast, voice barely audible, she said, "I'll be eighteen next month, right after graduation. I saved some money from babysitting. I'll go, if Mama doesn't get any worse."

"She goes for treatment, right?" asked Antoine, moving a tree toward the hole he dug.

"Yeah, but it makes her sick, the radiation and all." Antoine worked in silence, planting the seedlings.

Mr. Jessup came walking across the field. He looked at the newly planted trees, then at his daughter with a turned down mouth. "Celine, go into the house, you got work to do. Your mama needs you."

She glanced at Antoine and hesitated until Gordon said, "I'm not paying him to stand here and ogle you. Get along now."

Antoine dug the shovel back into the dirt and attempted to ignore her stepfather. Gordon, with his bulging stomach and skinny legs, watched for several minutes, his eyes hard. Finally, Antoine turned to him and said, "Mr. Jessup, sir, you have something to say?"

"Sure do. No niggah sweet talks my daughter. Hear? That's how bad things happen. You been comin' round a bit too often."

"You hired me."

"No, actually, my wife did. She wants this plot fixed up and made purty. But I won't have you do that. Now you finish this and get gone. And best stay away from Celine. Or, as I said, bad things can happen."

Furious, Antoine planted the last tree, watered them, then strode to his truck. He glanced up at Celine's bedroom window. It was open, the day being hot and the old house devoid of air conditioning. She looked down, gave a small wave, then quickly turned away.

It wasn't until nine o'clock that night when he realized that he had not been paid. He considered forgetting about the money, but a bitterness welled up and he jumped into his truck, rammed his foot down on the accelerator, and tore down the road, ignoring one stop sign after another.

Parking outside the gate, he skirted the wooden fence until he came to a row of broken planks. Moments later, he pounded on the door. It was opened by Mrs. Jessup, who looked at him with apprehension.

There was a shout then a scream in an upstairs room. With a resigned, weary look, she pointed to the second floor.

"He's . . . busy right now. If it's about the money I'm sure he'll pay you later."

There was another shout, and the snap of leather followed by a long wail.

"Shit!" said Antoine, taking the stairs two at a time. When he slammed the door open, he saw that Gordon had already thrown Celine onto the bed. Her blouse had been ripped open and Gordon had unbuttoned his pants. He suddenly stopped, staring at Antoine, his eyes bulging. With spittle oozing onto his long salt and pepper beard, he screamed, "Get out!" and raised the leather belt.

The blow from Antoine slammed him against the wall. The second one broke his nose. A loud "Ahh!" sound escaped his throat as he slid to the floor.

Clutching Celine's hand, Antoine pulled her off the bed and they rushed downstairs.

"What happened?" asked Mrs. Jessup as they bolted for the door. That was followed by, "Dear Lord, where are you going?"

"Away!" shouted Celine as they sprinted for the fence. She tied her blouse as they scrambled into the truck. She glanced back at the house, a light now on in her bedroom. A face stared out of the window.

"It's him," said Celine. "Go, just go!"

Once they were six miles away, Antoine slowed the truck and turned into a dense thicket of trees and brush. He stared into the darkness, his heart pounding.

"We're in trouble," he said, slumping into the seat.

"He was going to rape me again. I knew it when he told me to go back into the house this morning. I could see it in his eyes. I wanted to kill him. I really did."

"So did I," said Antoine, his breathing short.

"I can't go back. Not tonight, maybe never," said Celine, holding his hand.

"So, what do we do? We can't stay here all night," said Antoine.

Celine was silent for a long moment then said, "There's an old house I know. A girlfriend of mine used to live there, but the family is long gone. No one will find us."

"Then what? What do I tell Mama tomorrow or the next day or the one after that? And what do you tell your ma?"

"I don't know. We'll think of something. Now let's drive. It's about ten miles from here."

It was a month later, and with morning sickness, Celine could no longer hide the fact that she was pregnant. And despite Mrs. Jessup's pleads, Gordon beat the truth out of his stepdaughter.

Gordon did not rant or shout as he left her balled up in a fetal position, welts rising on her face and arms. Instead, he made a phone call then walked to his car. Minutes later, he drove toward town.

The first one to see the body hanging from the tree two miles from town was a middle-aged white woman. The police arrived a quarter hour later. Within minutes, phone conversations flit on the wires as a stream of motorists arrived, both black and white. Melli Washington, accompanied by her older son Clarence, arrived as the body was being taken down, laid on the side of the road and covered with a tarp. Part of the rope still hung from a limb of the tree.

Word of the lynching spread like fire through tinder. Over five hundred people converged on the spot by eleven that morning, many in caravans from black neighborhoods dozens of miles around.

Reverend Brown arrived along with a coterie of church deacons and their security personnel. Police were dispatched from surrounding townships to redirect traffic, and numerous roads were closed off. The coroner drove up, and Antoine's body was about to be placed in the vehicle when the reverend reached down and unzipped the body bag.

"Y'all can come and view the body," he said.

The coroner glanced at the police lieutenant who shrugged and stood aside.

"He shouldn't be on the ground like that," said a black woman. "I have a big table, and I live just over there. Somebody help me bring it. He be dead but he's still our son."

One by one for the next half hour, a line of mourners, mostly black, passed the corpse, some making the sign of the cross, while Melli and Clarence solemnly greeted them. The murmurs amongst the mourners quieted, and people parted as a pregnant white girl approached the body. Tears ran down her cheeks as she placed a rose on the young man's chest.

"I loved him," Celine said to Mrs. Winfeld. "I really did. And he loved me. I'm carrying his child."

"I knows that," said Melli, giving her a motherly hug.

"Let us pray," said Reverend Brown and people bowed their head. The police and the coroner glanced at one another then removed their caps.

Gordon had hastily departed town after the lynching, and his wife had died days later. Some of Gordon's associates came minus their robes and hoods. Everybody knew who they were, but not a word was uttered. They simply looked on, satisfied with their work.

Minutes after the prayer, Antoine's body was zipped into the bag and placed in the van.

Celine said goodbye to Mrs. Winfeld and began her walk home. It was now an empty house, and she knew that her stepfather would never return and would never be apprehended.

As people began to leave the scene, Clarence, joined by his mother, asked Amos Brown to stay.

"Rev, you saw his clothes, all torn up, flesh ripped off his arms and the contusions. They beat then dragged him behind a car until they got to this here tree. They tortured him, just like during Jim Crow."

The clergyman nodded then turned his eyes toward the sky. "The good book says to turn the other cheek, to forgive, but evil is evil."

"A lot of people are not going to turn the cheek, not going to wait for God's wrath. There will be vengeance, Rev. Someday, somehow, and it may not be God's doing. There will be pain, of that I am sure."

Melli held her son's hand, her head bowed. When she looked up, she said, "I don't want to see killings, Clarence. Killings don't do any good. Maybe the Reverend can talk to the police or the governor. They may find the ones who did this to my boy. They be the ones who do the punishing."

"The ones needing the punishing were right here a few minutes ago, Mama. No police or governor is going to do anything. It's just another day in the old South. And if they be caught, what will be done to them anyway? Fine them, put them in jail for six months? No, someone else gonna have to make things right."

"But the innocents must be spared," said Amos Brown.

Clarence slowly shook his head and said, "Was not my brother an innocent man?"

"In the eyes of God, he was. But not here in Alabama."

"Then Alabama shall pay."

CHAPTER 15

THE ROUNDUP

Present Time, Montgomery

Just after dawn, Antonio Peralta watched warily from his twenty-two-foot trailer as trucks, cars and buses kicked up dust, approaching the small Mexican settlement in Montgomery County where the Peraltas lived. When he'd counted over twenty vehicles, he turned to his wife and said, "Teresa, wake Jesus and Olivia. Grab some food, bottles of water, and warm clothes. Do it now."

"*Porque?* The children are tired. We worked until late last night."

"Please don't argue. Just wake them."

Antonio was forty-one, stocky, with a ruddy complexion. He had heard the rumors spreading among the camps. Although he had lived in the United States for fifteen years, he spoke just enough English to understand the orders of the landowners on whose farms he toiled. His wife spoke even less English; they often depended on the children to interpret for them. Jesus and Olivia had both been born in Alabama and had attended school through sixth grade.

There were sleepy protestations as the children got dressed while their mother gathered belongings.

"Take the children across the creek and hide in the woods. Don't come back until I tell you," Antonio told her.

"What about you?"

"I don't know. Maybe they will just tell us to leave. If so, we can hook the trailer to the pickup and go."

"Where?" she asked, a tremor in her voice.

"North, away from here."

"Please don't argue with them. Don't get angry. I know how you are, Antonio."

"I'll try to stay calm. Now go, and make no noise."

"What if they take you? What if you don't come back?"

"I will. No matter what, I'll be back."

As the vehicles drew closer, a dozen families began to gather in worried groups. Mothers drew their children to them and stood close to their men.

As Teresa and the children crossed the creek, she looked back at the sight of armed men piling out of the vehicles. She heard shouting, threats and the protestations of dozens of migrants. She spied a tall, slender man with a dour expression directing the roundup. He gave orders that were quickly obeyed and seemed very pleased with himself. Within fifteen minutes, the convoy moved back down the road.

Hunkering in the brush, she listened for the wailing of police cars, but there were none. She told the children to remain hidden then, moving from tree to tree, she ventured into a clearing beside the trailers. Their doors had been left open. She called people's names but no one replied.

"Antonio, Antonio!" she cried, running toward deep brush beyond the trailers, hoping her husband would reappear. She put a hand to her mouth then wiped away a tear. She heard the voices of her children and turned.

"We didn't want to be alone anymore, and we were worried for you and Papa," said Jesus. At fourteen, he was three years older than his sister.

"Mama, will Papa come back?" asked Olivia.

"He said he will." She crossed herself and stood silently.

"Where did they take him?" asked Jesus.

"I don't know." She stared helplessly down the empty road.

From beneath the only double-wide mobile emerged an older woman, who put her slender arm around Teresa and murmured, "They think they have won, but they are wrong."

Teresa looked at the tiny woman, who straightened and wiped dust from her face and bandana.

"And who, besides God, will listen to you, Carlotta? Who will listen to any of us?"

"There is one. I knew her as a child in Ciudad Juarez. Her name is Maria and we used to swim in the Rio Bravo del Norte, the Rio Grande. She was younger than me but we were best friends. Then she came here and married a very rich man, a black gringo."

"Can she help us? Can you find her? I want my Antonio back."

"I will find her," said Carlotta, touching the medallion of San Judas, the patron saint of the poor.

*****

Devin Winfeld had driven on back roads most of the night. On several occasions, spotting lights in his rear-view mirror, he had pulled off the road and killed the engine. Even though the Ford sported NCRA stickers on its windows, there was no sense in attracting unwanted attention.

"How much farther?" Evelyn asked, from the passenger seat.

"Not much," answered Lawrence, a tall, lanky youth, one of two young men who sat in the back seat.

The sun had been up for only an hour. Now it illuminated a rural landscape of old frame houses, fields, and woodland.

"So, where are we?" asked Evelyn, still half asleep.

"Just beyond Coosada, about seven miles from Montgomery," replied Devin. "Our destination is two miles from here, off the road."

"We have the barn for the full year?" queried Thomas, a sophomore who attended the same class as Devin, Lawrence and Evelyn. Even though he was infatuated with Evelyn, he would do nothing to rile Winfeld. He knew the danger in that. She had become Devin's girl, and Devin was one you didn't cross.

"Yes, the lease is for the entire year," said Lawrence.

"We'll only stay at the barn for a short time today," said Devin. "I just want us to see the place again, and figure out where we'll put everything."

"But we don't need to get the stuff right away, do we?" asked Thomas. Evelyn detected nervousness in his voice. Except for Devin, they were all on edge.

"No, we'll get everything later," replied Devin.

They came to an unmarked dirt side road and turned onto it. Out of sight of the main road, the way was blocked by a rusty gate, which Lawrence opened. He got back in the car and they continued on to the barn. Devin removed the padlock to the barn and they all entered. Sunlight streaked in through windows high above bales of cotton and hay. Tack for horses, tools, and old coats hung from hooks. Dust mites spun crazily in the light, and the odor of horse dung permeated the stale air.

"We'll hide everything here," Devin said, pointing to a far corner.

They were back on the road ten minutes later. Rounding a bend, Devin slammed on the brakes and the car skidded to a halt. Four men stood in the road, ARs held menacingly in their hands.

"Let me do the talking," Devin said, as one approached. He circled the car, then stopped in front of the driver's door. Devin lowered his window and said in a self-assured voice, "Movin' them out, huh?"

"Got that right," said the man, looking them over, his eyes stayed on Evelyn for several seconds. "Whatcha doin' on this heah road?" he asked.

"Shortcut to the Capitol. That's what the GPS said."

The man snorted, shook his head and said, "Not really. Where y'all from? Got any I.D.?"

"Sure, we're from up north. NCRA fits our politics, our philosophy you might say. We're sort of refugees."

"Philosophy. Uh-huh. Well, as you can see we got some business heah. And it ain't nothin' y'all gonna be talkin' about, right?"

"Lips zipped," said Devin. He watched as dozens of Hispanics were off-loaded from trucks and moved to a distant field. They were herded into an enclosure topped by concertina wire that contained a number of dilapidated buildings.

"Lots of people," Devin remarked. "Who's going to feed them all?"

"Don't take much. Just a few tortillas. There'll be more. We're rounding them all up. No place for them heah."

Two vans with dish antennas drove slowly toward the vehicles still disgorging their human cargo. There was a shout, and the man standing beside the Ford turned and hollered, "Get them the fuck out of heah! Turn them around. We ain't givin' no interviews."

"Who's that?" asked Devin.

"The man in charge. NCRA chief of security, that's who."

"He's here, watching this?"

"You're asking a lot of questions, and that makes me a little suspicious. Should I be suspicious?"

"No, but if you want security, you might do this at night. Then nobody will see."

The man considered that then said, "Ain't my call." He gave Evelyn another long stare and said, "Mighty purty girl. She yours or. . ."

"She's mine."

"I see. Mighty purty."

"You're needed, Mr. Honniker. We got a problem communicatin'," called a thick-necked man.

The man turned to Devin and said, "You just move along. And you don't talk to no one, heah?"

"I heah."

"Don't you dare mock me. No damn Yankee does that. Unless. . ."

He waggled his AR, then strode away. Devin started the car and slowly passed an expensive vehicle parked a few hundred yards farther on. Beside it stood three suited men watching the proceedings. One held a pair of binoculars, another a cell phone. The third watched Devin drive by.

Evelyn glanced out the window and saw a middle-aged woman in the car's backseat. She appeared to be reading a magazine and looked up. Seeing Evelyn, she stared open mouthed. Their eyes locked as Devin drove past.

CHAPTER 16

I SAW YOU THERE

Maxwell Air Force Base, Montgomery, Alabama

Two military police with bloused boots and white helmets ushered Stanley Palmer into Major General Leslie Roth's immaculate office. The commander sat at his polished desk, bare except for several files, a laptop, phone, cup of steaming coffee and an embellished cigar box.

On the wall behind him was a photo of his grandfather in the cockpit of his P-47, taken in early 1945. The fuselage sported black iron crosses of the four Nazi Messerschmitt ME 109s he'd shot down over Germany, the same place his relative's lives ended in Hitler's crematoriums.

The general was talking into his phone. He did not stand or offer his hand when Palmer was escorted in; he had already heard about Palmer.

The NCRA official stood arrogantly before the desk. He glanced about the room with its framed decorations and photos, including one of the general standing beside his F-18 fighter at Bagram Air Force Base in Afghanistan.

Palmer heard the general say, "We have two fixed-wings up now and three helos. Nothing moves without us knowing about it. We're on standby. Got it covered, sir. And thank you for the birthday gift. I'll light one up with a brandy tonight. ...

My wife? She'll consign me to the garage. But I've got two stars so.... Yes, sir, as Sherman said of Mary Ann Bickerdyke, 'She ranks me.'"

There was laughter coming through the phone. With a grin, the general ended the call. Then, stone-faced, he stared at Palmer, who stared back. Mouth turned down, Palmer said, "It's only polite and customary for military personnel to stand in the presence of cabinet secretaries."

The general took a sip of his coffee, opened the lid of the cigar box, selected a fine Havana, bit off the end, then lit it with his grandfather's ancient Zippo lighter. He remarked, "I wasn't going to light this up until this evening, but now is a good a time as any."

Clicking the lighter shut, he drew in a puff, exhaled a cloud of smoke, and added, "I don't stand for traitors. You have thirty seconds. Speak."

Palmer made a show of disdain as the cigar smoke wafted towards him. He waved it aside, then said, "This installation is the property of and under the jurisdiction of the Nationalist Christian Republic of America. You will surrender it to President Jefferson Calhoun Lee at four o'clock this afternoon. At that time, the flag of the new nation will be hoisted and you will be relieved of your command."

"You don't say? That's very interesting, Mr. Palmer." The general regarded his watch and said, "You still have seven seconds left. Anything else?"

"I think I have made myself clear."

"Very well. Now I will take about ten seconds. You are a sycophant of Mr. Lee and a member of the Klan, a probable murderer and a low life piece of shit. You will be escorted off my base by military police. If ever again you attempt to enter this installation, you will be put under arrest. These proceedings are closed."

He nodded to the MPs and tersely said, "Get him out of my sight. If any of his people attempt to breech this base, you will arrest them. Put a few 50 cals on the perimeter. That is an order."

*****

It was early when James Goodwin received a call from Ralph Prescott, Secretary of Agriculture. Usually conversational, Prescott sounded troubled. In his baritone voice he said, "I just got off the phone with President Lee. He wants to see you this afternoon. There will be several from the cabinet, including Stanley Palmer."

"Palmer, eh? Sneaky bastard. Slicker than pig's snot," said Goodwin, winking at Janice.

"No argument there. I heard he went to Maxwell and nearly got shot," said Prescott, his crinkly white hair a contrast to his dark complexion.

"Doesn't surprise me. Somebody should shoot him. He hasn't the sense God gave to a goose. Now about Lee, he's not having a hissy fit, is he?"

"Not sure. But I am."

"What's all the fuss?"

"The fuss is that the FDIC has terminated its relations with every bank in Montgomery County. It's gone viral and people are panicking. If you haven't noticed, there's mayhem out there. The money is no longer insured. That includes mine and yours!"

"Just the county?"

"A lot bigger chunk than that. The FDIC can hit every bank in the NCRA. I suggest you get your ass over to the Capitol posthaste."

"That sort of a day, huh?"

"And it's just starting."

*****

"The last thing I heard when that damn Jew threw me out was him telling a soldier to set up a perimeter with machine guns. Can you believe that?" screamed Palmer in Lee's office.

"I think I can," said Lee. "And I strongly suspect that every commander will say much the same, Jew or not."

"So, what the fuck are we going to do? Just let the U.S. keep all its bases? We've got to have some sort of plan, some sort of defense," insisted Palmer.

"Against what?" asked Goodwin. "Hells bells, if Barnes was going to launch an attack it would have already happened. You're sweating like a sinner in church, Palmer."

"Okay, maybe their regular army isn't going to invade, but they have vigilantes, just like we do. What if they decide to burn a town or destroy industry? We just can't call up the local SWAT team against thousands of them. Sooner or later, we've got to take over the forts and bases. We've got to plan for that, maybe work with someone from the inside."

"We're not going to poke the bear, Palmer," said Goodwin, sitting on President Lee's office sofa. "As for their vigilantes, the FBI keeps a very close watch on them, and we have our eyes and ears in the FBI."

Undeterred, Palmer said, "We should deputize some of our boys: the militias and the neo-Nazis."

"A fair number of those are in federal prisons," pointed out President Lee.

"For every one of those there are ten more armed, free, and just waiting to pull the trigger," retorted Palmer.

"That dog don't hunt," said Lee. "It's going to be damn hard to control a bunch of wannabe special ops running around with ARs once they are recognized as an official NCRA fighting force. I see retribution if some go off half-cocked and kill people across the border. In fact, I would counsel tamping them down, getting them away from the boundary lines. The last thing we need is to give the feds an excuse to take every capitol in the NCRA with an airborne assault or ground attack."

We'd fight back," snorted Palmer. "On both sides of the border. Thousands out in the streets, fighting with everything they got."

"And it would be a bloodbath," replied Lee. "War is a goddamn bloody thing, and an AR or a shotgun isn't worth a damn against a main line battle tank. And we don't have those laying around. We don't want a war, Palmer, we want to live our way, not die their way. For now, the military bases are like little cysts: as long as they're encased, they don't bother us, and we don't bother them."

"Well, Jeff, you made me Secretary of Security," said Palmer. "I don't know what I'm allowed to prepare. If I can't put a real military force together then I might as well resign."

"No," said Lee. "Hang in there, we'll come up with something. Maybe beef up the SWAT teams, get them some real weapons from somewhere."

"Let me work on it," said Palmer. "I can do a lot better than that. I know people in the U.S. military who have our back."

He flashed a grin, his first in weeks, as he headed out the door.

"And I have another plan, one about some undesirables taking up valuable space they're not entitled to. And it's all legal. Yep, got that one planned out, too."

They heard him fairly skip down the hall. Goodwin turned to Lee and said, "He's as useless as a screen door on a submarine."

"Do tell," said Lee. "But if things go north, better to blame him than us."

*****

Washington D.C.

"On line six," Iris said, poking her head into the Oval Office.

Edith Barnes picked up the phone and heard a familiar and friendly voice.

"Madam President, this is Denise Eastman, representative of the Tenth District of South Carolina. I know that I'm certainly interrupting you, but I feel that it's imperative that I call."

"I'm glad you did. I always have time for you, Denise. It's been a while since we've chatted."

"Yes, we sat together at the Fourth of July luncheon last year. It was a wonderful time."

"Indeed, it was. A lot has changed since then, hasn't it?"

"Sadly, very much so."

The President waited, listening as Denise took a deep breath. "Madam President, I would like you to know that this monstrous thing, the NCRA, is not a monolith. My district is composed of a good mix of Republicans and Democrats, most of them loyal Americans. That has been borne out by a recent poll, and we want nothing to do with Jeff Lee and his demagogues."

"That's a breath of fresh air."

"Well, I'm sure there are large pockets of people in the NCRA who feel the same way. There have been demonstrations against the secession in my district, but we're beginning to feel like an oppressed people. And I'm afraid that things are going to get worse. A number of my constituents have been subjected to threats and harassment. And there have been acts of violence, several that have resulted in injury and death."

"I am aware of that, as well as of a particular individual encouraging it."

"Yes, so I'm wondering if your administration can do something regarding these crimes? To avoid bloodshed, I've had to discourage a number of citizens from marching to the Capitol of our commonwealth, taking it back and raising the stars and stripes."

"Painful as it is to discourage them, we don't want to see a bloodier version of the January Sixth insurrection against a state capitol. You did the right thing, Denise. I know that this is small compensation, but we would welcome any of your constituents who wish to enter the United States. And of course, we would assist them in every way we can."

"Thank you. I think a number of people here are considering that, but the vast majority cannot up and leave. So I'm open to suggestions."

"If your district is faced with the threat of mass violence, I will authorize the U.S. military to provide protection. But, if at all possible, I want to avoid a conflict that would result in major casualties across the NCRA. I can, however, ask Congress to make safe haven provisions for those who wish to relocate."

"I completely understand. But tempers here are frayed and I fear that things might spiral out of control."

"I am watching the situation very closely. I feel that the NCRA has sewn the seeds of its own destruction."

"I'd rather that destruction be sooner than later, Madam President."

*****

It had not been one of Janice's better weeks. She had learned of the relocation of Hispanic workers and had a run-in with Palmer. She had tried, to no avail, to beg off Goodwin's insistence that she accompany him and Palmer when they traveled to the remote location where the Hispanic workers were being taken. "I don't understand why you want me to go," she told Goodwin. They were on their way to oversee another internment.

"You are my aide and the mouthpiece of the NCRA. You are on TV and you should be aware of the nation's commitments. This is a necessary action, and a humane one, and you will be asked about it."

"It sounds like ethnic cleansing, and I don't see how it could possibly be humane."

"Well, it is. They're being put in shelters for their own safety. And that of the anglo population, I might add."

"Has there been any violence?" asked Janice.

"Palmer says there have been some incidents. No sense taking chances."

"It sounds like Manzanar," replied Janice, a reference to the internment of Japanese during World War II.

"And that was for their protection, too," said Goodwin.

"It was a land grab," said Janice.

Goodwin said nothing, merely turned up the back seat volume on the radio. They rode in silence until they arrived at the camp.

Janice observed the involuntary movement of Hispanic workers into the enclosed area. After several minutes, she pulled a magazine from an oversized purse and attempted to read, ignoring the shouts and protests. Janet looked up and saw a car go past with her daughter Evelyn in it.

What on God's green earth was Evelyn doing in Alabama? She was supposed to be in Baltimore! Janice wanted desperately to call Steven and ask what the hell was going on, but she couldn't. The phone calls to numbers outside the NCRA had a way of not going through.

A few days later, following an argument with Goodwin, she sat in a lounge chair behind the mansion. It was not the first exchange that had gone badly. She wanted desperately to avoid discussions about politics, but that subject seemed impossible to avoid. And there was something else, but exactly what she could not put her finger on. Downcast, she was watching heavy clouds blot out the sun. Her cell phone rang.

She looked at the caller's name, then sat bolt upright and took the call quickly. "Well, you surprised me, Evelyn. I didn't expect to hear from you. It's been months. I was worried about you. Why are you phoning me now?"

"Because of what's going on."

"What do you mean?"

"I saw you in that limo when all those defenseless people were herded into the concentration camp! And I know that you saw me. Were you trying to ignore it all, those goons and their machine guns, while staring at a magazine? Did you see the barbed wire, the ugly shacks and tents off the road out of view from TV coverage? Not that NCRA newscasters would disapprove. I imagine the asshole you sleep with isn't upset by it either."

"How dare you! Is this why you called? To insult me and James?"

The conversation came to a sudden halt. Evelyn could hear her mother breathing heavily and expected her to hang up. The air seemed dead.

"I had nothing to do with that. And for your information, I do not entirely approve. But we must enact certain measures, and—."

"Certain measures? I can't believe you said that. You once had a conscience, once cared about people. What happened? Beside being seduced mentally and physically by Goodwin? At one time you would have gotten out of that car and screamed at the indecency, the heartbreak those people were going through. But you just sat there pretending it did not exist, did not concern you. So, you are complicit in a crime against humanity.”

“I think you've gone far enough. You are too young, too naïve, and I'm hardly complicit. I'm not in lockstep with everything that goes on here, but those people”— Janice heard herself repeating what Goodwin had said on many occasions— “these illegal immigrants, are becoming the numerical majority in many districts, consuming community resources and changing how things are done. I's all about power.”

“And that's why you're with Goodwin? For power?”

“I have deep feelings for him, but I'm not after power. Here in the NCRA, people want order, a sense of one's place. Serenity, a restoration of what used to be.”

“Well, that's gone with the wind, and you and your boyfriend are on a runaway train headed for a cliff. The man's a rat, and you should be looking for an exit. I'd tell you to keep Dad's number handy, but you might already be on his target list. Actually, I suspect you are.”

“That's nonsense. I haven't done anything.”

“That's not how it looked to me. I'm so ashamed of you!”

“I don't want you to call me again if this is all you have to say.”

“Get out of there before it's too late. Please, Mom.”

Furious, Janice ended the call and fumed at her daughter's insolence. How little she knew about life. She sighed and wondered if the schism could ever be mended. *Maybe someday,* she thought, *but it would be a long time coming.*

CHAPTER 17

RESCUE

Each night, Antonio Peralta watched the changing of the guards. Rows of barbed wire coiled over the chain-link fence around the ten-acre perimeter. Towers with lights illuminated the barracks and shadeless grounds between the fence and the buildings. Considering it suicide, none of the Hispanic men or women attempted to climb over the wire in either direction.

Men had been separated from the women and children by a sturdy wooden fence. Antonio was glad that his wife and children were not here.

He noticed two different types of guards. One consisted of middle-aged men whose shirts could not cover their bulging stomachs. The other were cadaverous, dour and joyless individuals with cold, steely eyes. Few of them spoke to one another and none spoke to the prisoners except to shout when not being obeyed quickly enough.

All the guards toted weapons. On numerous occasions they took women to their barracks, which resulted in screams and cries throughout the night. Married male prisoners cringed, praying that the women being raped were not their wives or daughters.

But time, repetitive chores and boredom led to laziness and incompetence. Discipline broke down since, unlike the military, rank amongst the vigilantes was not established by law or tradition. Men assigned chores chaffed at being ordered about by self-appointed officers, and an undercurrent of grumbling and disobedience began to plague the encampment. Guards grew careless about checking the men's barracks at night. In inclement weather, guard towers would be abandoned for the comfort of the barracks. By two in the morning, those who patrolled the fence usually fell asleep.

One evening, Antonio merged into the darkness during a pouring rain as the prisoners were being herded into their barracks. He had noticed earlier in the day that a shed, which contained farming implements, had been left unlocked. Under cover of the rain and darkness, he slipped inside. He located a machete, a tool with which he was more than familiar, as well as a bolt cutter. At three in the morning, he slipped out of the shed and saw that the fence was unguarded. Only two sentries huddled beneath the portico of their barracks.

Kneeling, Antonio snipped one link after another until he had cut enough to squeeze through to the other side. He did so carefully, to avoid tearing his clothes or skin on the jagged edges of metal, and began walking.

The first pale light of sunrise was turning the eastern clouds grey when, in the distance, he saw a house illuminated by a single dim porch lamp. He approached cautiously, clutching the machete, not knowing if the home belonged to a vigilante, perhaps one who worked at the camp. He was just thinking the safest plan was probably to keep walking when he heard a distinctive click.

"Move and you're dead," said a voice behind him, speaking in a distinctively Creole accent. "And drop the weapons, all of them."

The machete fell to the ground. With his back turned, he raised his hands.

A Hispanic man approached and searched him for more weapons. "He's clean," said the man.

"Turn, real slow," said the first voice.

"*Como se llama*?" asked the man who had searched him.

"Antonio. Antonio Peralta. I escaped from the prison camp."

The Creole picked up the machete, eyed Antonio closely, then to his friend said, "I think he's okay. We'll bring him in."

A fire glowed on a hearth inside the small house, and Antonio moved toward it. The Creole called toward the kitchen, "Yolanda! Bring some dry clothes and coffee. This guy's soaked."

"*Si*, I just made a new pot," answered a female voice.

Antonio began to shake involuntarily as heat from the fire warmed him, then he yawned. "I was up all night, waiting for my chance to escape," he explained.

The Creole said, "From a prison camp, you say?"

"I know of it," said an elderly woman, coming into the small room. She came forward, looked closely and said, "Antonio, is that you? I thought I recognized your voice."

"Carlotta!" blurted Antonio. "How did you get here? Where are Teresa and the children?"

"At the camp. You didn't see them? They were taken the day after you were. The bad men came back."

"I didn't see them! I didn't know that they were there!"

Turning to the other men, Carlotta said, "Antonio is from the workers' village. I know his wife and *ninos*. I was hiding under my trailer the day they were taken, so the vigilantes didn't see me."

"But you got here," said Antonio.

"Yes, it was too dangerous to stay in the village."

"How many guards?" asked George, addressing Antonio.

"About forty, sometimes more. There take the women to their barracks, and sometimes outside *hombres* come for them too. Now I'm scared for Teresa and Olivia!"

A young woman brought Antonio a cup of coffee and dry clothes.

He thanked her, then glanced at an M-14 with a scope over the mantle of the fireplace. Against the wall lay a shotgun, and on a shelf was a photo of a man in dress blues. Below it a plaque read *Semper Fi.*

"Six years, platoon sergeant," said George, following Antonio's eyes. Then, pointing to Pablo, he said, "Army. Can't do much about that."

Pablo just shook his head at the jibe. "And we're not alone. We have friends, ex-military."

Carlotta sat on a frayed sofa and said, "Antonio, I promised Teresa that I would call someone important. Her name is Maria Estavo. She's married to a man who is powerful in the NCRA. I told her what was happening to the Mexican workers."

"But she's with the NCRA," objected Antonio. "What good can she do?"

"She's a relative of Enrique Sepulveda, the President of Mexico. I asked her to call him, tell him about the bad *hombres* who are taking our people away, and how all of us are being treated. He can do something, I know it."

"But that will take time," said Pablo. "And we don't have a lot of that."

"He's right," said George. "When they realize a prisoner has escaped, all hell will break loose. If we are very, very lucky, no one will have noticed the break in the fence, or a missing prisoner. Do they do a nightly head count?"

"They did at first. Not anymore. And sometimes a man, or several men, go missing. We do not dare ask why when it happens."

"Hmm. Do they have tractors there? Heavy equipment?"

Antonio nodded. "They have us do farm work. They used back hoes, tractors and plows. Prisoners aren't allowed to touch the heavy equipment. We had shovels and rakes, that sort of stuff."

"People use back hoes and tractors when they want to get rid of evidence. Cover everything up nice and tidy," remarked Pablo.

"Won't be the first time," said George. He rubbed his face and said, "Maybe it's time I made some phone calls. And Pablo, see if Walker is still playing around with that RPG. It might come in handy."

*****

Following George's instructions, twenty-two men blackened their faces with charcoal, cleaned and inspected a variety of weapons, and drank coffee made by Yolanda. The small house took on the scent of gun oil and the odor of men, some who had walked quickly, stealthily, for several miles through the woods. Nine large trucks were parked and camouflaged. Beside them waited their drivers.

"Remember, no talking, follow your leader. The object is to get people out, not to engage in a firefight unless absolutely necessary. We move on my command," said George. "Pablo is my second."

"Guard towers and lights go first," added Pablo. "You have knives. Use them, hand over the mouth, blade in the kidneys or across the throat. And take their ARs. In and out quick. George and I have flash bangs."

"And I have the RPG," said another man, introduced as Charles Walker. "Once we fire that, they're going to panic and shoot at anything, including each other."

At three in the morning, the cars and trucks left the house five minutes apart. The drivers parked a quarter mile from the enclosure; in squads of five the men made their way to the far corners of the camp. They had studied the layout drawn by Antonio and memorized the location of each building, ditch and guard tower.

In the darkness, George phoned each of his squad leaders and said, "Go!"

Bolt cutters went to work, and within five minutes the chain link fence was in pieces. With silence and swiftness, the men carried out the missions assigned to them.

Electrical wires were cut, and lights went out. The few guards not asleep or with women began calling to one another. Several flashlights came on, but those who had left them behind stumbled about the littered yard. One by one, their throats were cut or a cold blade was shoved into their kidneys.

Other teams scrambled up makeshift ladders to three of the towers and eliminated their occupants.

Now aware of the incursion, several guards began to fire at shadowy shapes in the darkness. From the fourth tower, a frantic guard sprayed the camp with bullets from a machine gun. Two guards on the ground were struck, and screams filled the night.

Charles Walker aimed his RPG and pulled the trigger. The shell, with its bulbous head, shot out, and there was a blinding flash as the tower exploded.

Antonio and George found the Quonset huts housing the women and children. Now fully awake, a half dozen guards came charging out, several hitching up their pants, shouting and raising their weapons.

Antonio's machete decapitated one, while several quick bursts from George's AR cut down three others.

Pablo strode to the guards' sleeping quarters and threw in a flash bang. The blast deafened and blinded those inside, but one managed to fire an AR toward the door. Pablo responded by emptying his magazine into the metal building. There was no more return fire.

When the rescuers went inside, they found about 20 men dead or dying on the beds or the ground. George put his pistol to the skull of each and pulled the trigger.

"Bring them out," ordered Pablo into his phone. Antonio rushed into the women's quonset, found Teresa and the children among the terrified prisoners, and hurried them to the waiting trucks. Once everyone was loaded on board, drivers started the engines and, with headlights shadowed, edged down the road. At the first crossing, they split up and headed for pre-arranged safe houses dozens or even hundreds of miles away.

*****

"They did what?" shouted Palmer, storming into President Lee's office.

"Killed the whole lot of them," said Goodwin, lighting a cheroot. "Some with a bullet hole right in the skull."

"According to the police, it was a precision military operation," said Ralph Prescott.

Palmer, lips welded together, turned his face to the Secretary of Agriculture and said, "You look pretty damn smug. Some of those men were my friends. I bet that makes you as giddy as a possum eating a sweet tater."

"Most of your friends are not very nice men," replied Prescott. "And some probably deserved to die."

"So, what do you want to do about it?" asked Goodwin.

"Retaliation. Hunt down every one of those sons of bitches and slit their throats. Make an example of them right on TV. That's what," sputtered Palmer.

"Not good for our image," said Lee. "Some people are getting squeamish, and we don't really know who carried out the raid. Who do we round up? Should the government do anything at all? We could write off the camp as an unauthorized exercise by citizens outraged by the invasions of illegal immigrants. Puts the blame squarely on the Mexican's shoulders for breaking the laws of due process. "

"Got to be careful about the Mexicans in particular," said Prescott. "My wife says that she's been contacted by an old friend of hers, a woman she grew up with in Mexico. And Maria has some pretty serious contacts."

"Like who?" asked Lee.

"President Sepulveda of Mexico, for one. He's made some alarming statements against the NCRA."

"What the fuck can he do?" said Palmer, hands on hips. "Mexicans thinking of going to war, starting a rebellion or something? Hell, we can damn well deal with that! It'll be a pleasure. Let's send some lead over the border in return for all the drugs they smuggle into this country!"

"You stir up that hornet's nest any more and you got a problem beyond all control," replied Prescott.

"Your wife tell you that?"

Prescott stood, walked to the door, and in a quiet but menacing voice said, "You don't want to fuck with Maria. Or me either, Palmer. But take my word on this; things are going to get bad. Real bad indeed."

Palmer stormed out of the office and passed Janice as he descended the spiral staircase to the ground floor. She was carrying an armload of papers and a steel three-hole puncher. He turned at the bottom of the stairs and snarled, "I haven't seen my daughter in weeks. You were with her, I know it. And I saw you on TV in Palm Springs after the plane crash. What the hell were you doing there?"

Janice stopped and said, "I was there for the memorial. The Rabbi and his wife were friends of mine."

"I don't care about the goddamn Rabbi. What the fuck happened to Shelley? You know, don't you? Don't you!"

She glared at him. "Maybe you should check the hospitals or reports of runaways. Maybe she committed suicide. Have you thought of that?"

"Bitch!"

The heavy puncher struck his forehead. He screamed in surprise and pain. Janice abruptly turned and entered President Lee's office.

"Mr. Palmer seems to have hurt himself, James," she said with seeming indifference.

"Where is he?"

"Last I saw, he was at the bottom of the stairs."

Goodwin slowly rose and went to find Palmer. He was leaning against the wall, a massive purple welt on his forehead. The hole puncher lay at his feet. Goodwin picked it up, gave Palmer a close look, and said, "Oh my, that must really hurt."

CHAPTER 18

LEVI GROSSMAN

It was not often that Levi Grossman was puzzled. He frowned as he watched Danny Von Hoffmann interview Janice Whitinghill on *Freedom America*.

"Of course, we mourn every loss of life in the NCRA. After all, it is the *Christian* Republic. I should point out it's possible that some of the men who were slain were innocent. It's also possible that a number of the Hispanics incarcerated in the compound were real criminals, and now they are free to carry out acts of violence."

"That's entirely possible," agreed Hoffmann. "As an aide to Mr. Goodwin and privy to sensitive information, can you verify that the movement of Hispanics into the compound was a government approved operation?"

"I have no specific information on that, but you might ask the head of Internal security, Mr. Palmer. I'm sure he'd be happy to answer whatever questions you might have."

"I have attempted to contact him and others in the government, but have received no replies at this time."

"I am not at liberty to say any more about the tragic incident, except that the whole thing might have been a terrible mistake."

"There were a few more polite exchanges before the interview conculuded.

How strange, thought Levi. She'd sounded so consoling when he met her in Palm Springs all those months ago. And here she was, the spokesman for the NCRA, making such an ambiguous statement. The only indication of distancing was the comment about Palmer. The entire scenario left him unsettled. *Where is her true allegiance?* He thought he detected a nuance of dissatisfaction with the NCRA but certainly no obvious break.

He clicked "mute" and considered Palmer, an outspoken anti-Semite and perpetrator of violent acts against Jews since the plane crash. Though not particularly religious, Levi decided something had to be done, but exactly what he wasn't sure. His mind wandered for a moment until he saw Hoffmann engaged in another interview. Grossman clicked the remote and listened to Rufus Clarendon, in full Nazi regalia, declaring that the crash in Palm Springs was an act of God.

Given free rein to speak on *Freedom America,* he touted the superiority of the Caucasian race. He became apoplectic when a guest anthropologist stated that all *homo sapiens* are descended from several hundred dark skinned women who lived in Ethiopia hundreds of thousands of years ago. So incensed and hateful was Clarendon that the female scientist walked out of the discussion.

In the NCRA's supportive environment there was nothing Clarendon had to fear. He was often seen in the company of Stanley Palmer, who attended neo-Nazi rallies. Palmer denied having membership but was quick to condemn anybody who criticized the organization.

Levi Grossman still carried himself like the soldier he had been decades earlier. He spoke little about his days in the field. But every month he would venture to the range with a few of his old buddies—all former Marines—fire a few rounds, then retire to their favorite pub and discuss fishing, politics, and the state of the world.

His old push-button, land line phone rang, and Grossman lifted the receiver. "Levi, it's Danny Rabinowitz, are you awake?"

"Of course I'm awake. I don't sleep past Reveille."

Danny laughed and said, "Yeah, 0600. Did you see on local TV about Clarendon's rally?"

"I must have missed it. Where's it going to be?"

"In the park outside the Capitol in Montgomery. They're expecting several hundred of his ilk a week from today. The Klan will be there in force."

"Not good."

"Not good at all. I'm thinking of a counter rally."

"That can turn bloody, and we can't count on the police."

"What else can we do?"

"Not sure, but I'll think about it. I'm sure your dad would have had some good ideas."

"Maybe. I miss him."

"So do I. But Clarendon may have some tough days ahead. He and his bottom feeders should be made very scared."

"Do I sense gears turning, Sergeant Major?"

"Just ruminating, that's all."

"Like Hitler's Gestapo, they would kill all of us if they could. They should be incarcerated in Bergen Belson or Auschwitz for a couple of weeks. Maybe have them sleep in a crematorium," said Danny.

"Fat chance of that, but sometimes strange things happen to very bad people."

*****

Levi Grossman had grown a long white beard since the crash in Palm Springs in the hopes it made him harder to

155

recognize. Now he stood at the checkout of a sporting goods shop and laid a bow and arrow set on the counter. "For my grandson," he said, smiling, his baseball cap pulled low, sunglasses hiding his eyes.

"Nice," said the kid behind the counter. "Lucky you found it; we're out of just about everything, including guns and ammo. People buying them up as if we're expecting an invasion."

"Maybe we are," replied Grossman.

"Nah, feds won't invade. They'll lose too many. Everybody has a gun now. Yep, we're all ready to defend the NCRA! Only crazies would attack us."

"Lots of crazies. But you're right. Not too much to worry about. And now my grandson can do his part."

"Damn straight," said the kid. "Hope your grandson likes the kit. Bows and arrows are sometimes better than guns."

Grossman merely smiled, picked up the bow and arrows and said, "Have a nice day."

Levi Grossman gave considerable thought to the degree of fear Clarendon and his allies should be made to feel. He thought of the Third Reich's "Final Solution" that had led to the deaths of countless relatives; he thought of the hundreds of thousands of American soldiers who died fighting the Nazis, and his anger for men like Clarendon grew by the hour.

Upon learning of Clarendon's address, Grossman climbed into his pickup, removed the license plate, and cruised by Clarendon's wood frame house on a weed infested lot. To his satisfaction, he'd learned that Clarendon was divorced and no woman lived with him, his commitment to the neo-Nazis being his only true interest.

At eleven pm, Grossman edged the pickup into a cluster of trees a hundred yards from Clarendon's house and empty driveway and waited. Thirty minutes later, the "colonel" parked his ancient Ford in the driveway, entered his home, and turned on the kitchen light. He poured himself a drink, sat in his recliner, and watched TV until he turned out the light and went to bed.

Dictated by the late-night meetings of the Montgomery Reich committee, Clarendon's schedule remained the same for the next three nights. It appeared to Grossman that the routine would continue, which pleased him immensely.

By driving to a rural area outside Montgomery, he found four dried bales of hay, which he placed in his pickup and offloaded into a storage unit. That same day, he stopped at a service station and filled two five-gallon containers with gasoline, which he also deposited in the storage locker.

Then he spent considerable time thumbing through the New and Old Testament to find the most appropriate passages before printing them out.

The night was exceptionally dark when he coasted into the cluster of trees. Clarendon's truck was in the driveway, and all the house lights had been turned off. With practiced silence, Grossman stacked two bales, one on top of the other, by the front and rear doors. He poured several gallons of gas over the bales and around the base of the house. In a dirt patch twenty yards away, he drove a nail through the printed paper, nailed it to a tree, and then wrapped a gasoline-soaked strip of cloth onto an arrow, fitted the notch into the bowstring and lit the cloth. Pulling back the string, he let the arrow fly. It struck the bale beside the front door, igniting the gasoline-soaked hay, and flames sped around the house.

Grossman started the truck and drove away. In the rearview mirror he saw a massive conflagration as fire engulfed the wooden structure. He was miles away before he heard sirens.

*****

Stanley Palmer and James Goodwin sat in the President's office the following morning, watching the TV. Danny Von Hoffmann was at the scene of the fire as investigators carefully sifted for evidence for arson.

"This was an act cowardice against a fine, upstanding citizen of the NCRA," said Hoffmann. "Firefighters have established that the doors had been targeted to prevent egress. This is now a murder scene, and the charred body of Mr. Clarendon has been recovered. He apparently struggled to get out, but the flames must have been too intense. The perpetrator has not been apprehended, and anybody with information is required to contact authorities."

Von Hoffmann held up a sheet of paper and said, "This is a copy of the note found staked to a tree that was discovered by the police. It contains words from Psalm 11:6, '*Upon the wicked, He shall rain snares, fire and brimstone will be the portion of their cup.*' What that has to do with Mr. Clarendon has yet to be determined. But rest assured, the perpetrator will be found and will face justice."

James Goodwin turned off the TV, took a sip of coffee, and said, "I'm surprised that Von Hoffmann didn't mention the Palm Springs incident. I mean, this passage about fire and brimstone is pretty obvious."

"Why should he?" asked Palmer, standing with arms crossed, his countenance dark. "This attack may be a mystery, but somebody was out to get Clarendon. Somebody around here who knew his comings and goings."

Jefferson Lee shrugged and said, "Sounds like a professional job, possibly a hit man. Maybe it's meant to be retaliatory for the Palm Springs accident. Perhaps someone with family on the plane targeted a home-grown Nazi. An eye for an eye."

"Possible," said Goodwin, "But I wonder if the demise of Clarendon is a one-off thing, or will there be more?"

"What do you mean?" asked Palmer.

"A vendetta against neo-Nazis."

"Maybe they need police protection," Lee chuckled.

"Screw that," replied Palmer. "They can fucking well take care of themselves."

*****

Despite the efforts of police detailed to protection duty, three days later, the corpse of Mr. Griffen, another neo-Nazis, was found in a ditch by the side of the interstate. His throat had been slashed, and a bayonet had been plunged through a piece of paper and into his chest. Once again, Von Hoffmann stood before the camera and read the notation.

"This one, possibly by the same assailant, is from Thessalonians 1:9. *'These will pay the penalty of eternal destruction away from the presence of the Lord.'*

"A Star of David was drawn on the paper. The coroner states that the murder was committed very early in the morning, certainly before first light. Mr. Griffen was reported to have left a meeting of his organization around two A.M."

A week later, the corpse of another neo-Nazi was found, an arrow through his skull. The late-night meetings of the leadership ceased, and an element of fear began to pervade the members of the Montgomery Reich committee.

CHAPTER 19

THE FORTRESS

"I thank you all for coming this morning," said Jefferson Calhoun Lee to his cabinet, gathered around the oval table in the NCRA Capitol. A copy of the Constitution had been placed in front of each of the members, as well as several attending governors. "I wanted to convene this meeting to discuss one of the most important provisions in our Constitution, one that, if implemented, might avoid serious disturbances in the years to come."

Members of the cabinet opened the slender document as Lee said, "I refer to the law stating that only citizens of European descent should be allowed to own high-powered rifles and semi-automatic or automatic weapons. This excludes revolvers and rifles that only fire a .22 bullet. Those can be used for personal defense or hunting rabbits and such."

Ralph Prescott, all too conscious that he was the only black member of the cabinet, glanced at the other cabinet officials, all of whom were nodding in agreement.

"This may be a major undertaking," said Randolph Demming, governor of Mississippi.

"It may very well be," replied Lee. "But if one of the provisions cannot be implemented, can any? I intend to enforce each and every article of our Constitution. I invited you here, Governor, because I think your state is a good candidate for enforcement of this law. And I am appointing Stanley Palmer to coordinate and implement it with one of your mayors."

"Very well, Mr. President. I personally think it may be problematic, but perhaps a good test would be in a relatively small community," said the governor.

"I know a mayor in Hattybend, grew up with him in Louisiana," said Stanley Palmer. "I think that would be a good place to start."

"Small town," said Demming. "I don't anticipate too much trouble there. More white than black," he added, giving Ralph Prescott a quick, troubled glance.

Prescott, who had been sitting back in his leather chair, sat up straight and turned to Lee saying, "Small town or not, Mr. President, this is not going to go down easily. I strongly suggest, for the sake of innocent lives, you delete that part of the Constitution. Nothing need be said about it. Just let it die."

"Nope, not about to do that, Ralph. I don't want a race war somewhere down the line, and disarming a portion of the population is one way to prevent it. I am the president and I order it done."

Prescott folded his arms, stared at Lee and said nothing more.

Stanley Palmer liked the idea, as well as the responsibility placed upon him in front of the cabinet and the governor of Mississippi. As a child, he had been severely beaten by his father for the least offense; later, having turned into a bully, he had been shunned by fellow students. He'd read voraciously about the Third Reich and wished to emulate Joseph Goebbels, the propagandist of the Hitlerian regime.

*****

Hattybend, Mississippi

Dilbert Walker, Mayor of Hattybend, stood authoritatively before the city council and a multitude of white citizens, with Stanley Palmer by his side. Walker felt particularly empowered with the presence of the Secretary of Internal Security.

"So, having addressed the measure before us, and having received my instructions from Mr. Palmer, the President's emissary, I intend to implement the order starting tomorrow morning."

Two members of the town's AME Baptist church, Pastor Elijah Thurgood and his friend, Benjamin Gaston, unobtrusively slipped in and remained at the rear of the assembly. They received some questioning looks but were not escorted out.

A woman stood and said, "Mr. Mayor, do you anticipate resistance when confiscating the guns?"

"I trust that our colored citizens will comply with the law, especially since my deputies will be with me."

"So, you will be leading this?" asked a heavy-set man, pistol tucked into his belt.

"Of course. It's my town. But I invite any of y'all to accompany me."

"Should we bring weapons? I mean, in case of resistance?" asked another.

"I think that would be wise, but I don't want intimidation unless necessary. This will be an orderly and peaceful action. We will have the honorable distinction of being the first community in the NCRA to implement this law. And, in fact, I have invited the famous reporter, Danny Von Hoffmann of *Freedom America,* to report our endeavor to the world."

"I've heard enough," said Pastor Thurgood to Benjamin. As quietly as they'd arrived, they departed City Hall. Soon after, their messages for the congregation to gather were spreading throughout the community.

There were only five hundred black citizens in the town, most of whom were now packed the AME church, located at the end of a row of modest homes. Pastor Elijah motioned for the congregation's silence.

After Elijah informed the assembly of the mayor's intent, a former Marine rose and said, "I don't care what the new Constitution says, I'm not handing over any guns. And Rev, after four years in the Corps, I know how to use them."

"I think a demonstration of our resolve is what's called for," said an elderly man. "They should know of our displeasure. A march to City Hall with every gun we have might put some sense into them."

"I think such a demonstration will more likely provoke them. They have every intention of disarming us," said Benjamin, standing beside the reverend. "What might be best, considering the probability of violence, is to find a defensive place where we can all be together. I was in the army and am aware of the need for concentrated fire, an escape route, and the possibility of a counter attack."

"This is nonsense!" said a thin grey-haired woman, rising from her pew. "Just give them a few guns, make a show of compliance, and they will think they won. Otherwise, we may be facing a massacre. And just where, Benjamin, is this fortification? We got no fort around here, and except for maybe eight or nine veterans, we ain't soldiers. Half of us are women and children. I never fired a gun and don't expect to either."

"They are not gonna be satisfied with us handing over a few guns," said a young man named Jesse. "They know we have lots of guns. They will be in the houses searching, and what happens when they find them? We just gonna say, 'Oh, sorry, I forgot about the shotgun and the AR.' And they say, 'Sure, no problem. Y'all just go about your business.' No, sir, they are not gonna be civil."

A tall, slender man stood and walked to the front of the nave. At seventy-four, Nathaniel Wilson was widely respected. His face was gaunt and the color of midnight black. The conversations ceased as the pastor motioned for him to come forward. Wilson remained silent for a long moment, then said, "As most of you know, I was a captain in the Corps and served two tours in Iraq. Benjamin is right. With the slightest resistance, they will come like a swarm of hornets, guns at the ready and itching for a fight. Now, we can demonstrate and appeal to their sense of reason, but in the end, it will be to no avail. We must think of defense, a place we can fortify and hold them off. It must be a bastion that will result in them taking casualties if they try to take it."

A sense of dread rather than excitement or anticipation fell over the congregation. They remained silent and fearful as Wilson continued. "The only possible location around here is the old cement factory on Ninth and Main. It has concrete walls and a second story with small windows. Only artillery can take it down, and the only piece in town is an old brass muzzle loader that hasn't been fired since the Civil War. That doesn't mean we won't come under heavy fire, but it does mean it won't happen quickly, or easily. During that time, we try to contact any outside help we can. I strongly recommend that we gather food, water, blankets and our weapons and get to the building as soon as possible. We must do it quietly, in small groups. Once there, we make it ready. They will come, of that I am certain."

*****

Danny Von Hoffman arrived just before six in the morning, with his communications van and two assistants. He was approached by Mayor Dilbert, who said, "I would like you to speak of this as an action being carried out by law-abiding citizens upholding the Constitution. I don't want to see pools of blood in the street perpetrated by us. You get my point?"

"Got it," said Von Hoffmann, shivering in the cold morning. This would be his scoop, but of course he would share it with the other networks once the matter was concluded. He could imagine BNN, FOX and NBC saying, "We are grateful for the special coverage provided by Von Hoffmann's *Freedom America*."

"Listen up," said Dilbert to the men who had assembled with their weapons. "I want only my deputies to approach a residence with me. The rest will wait here and be ready if trouble occurs. If it does, then I will indicate how much back up I need. And, by the way, I'll be telling folks that the city council will offer thirty-five dollars, NCRA, for every weapon we confiscate."

"That's taxpayers' money," protested one of the men.

"All we have to do is offer it. Payments will be spread out over a number of years, and budget cuts may delay it. That is, if funds are available at all. But for show, I do have some money with me," said Dilbert with a pleasant smile.

*****

The *Freedom America* van pulled up to the first house the mayor and his deputies approached. They were all surprised to see Reverend Elijah Thurgood sitting in his rocker on the front porch.

"Morning, Mr. Mayor," Thurgood said, with a gracious nod. "You're up mighty early. Care for some coffee? Got a new pot on the stove."

Dilbert grinned and said, "Actually, Rev, we're just paying a visit for a very specific reason, one which we hope that, as a man of peace, you will comply with. And, of course, instruct your congregation to do so as well," the mayor added.

Peace is a blessed thing," replied Thurgood. "So, how might I be of assistance?"

He rose from his chair and gazed calmly at the armed men at the foot of the steps.

Dilbert produced a copy of the NCRA Constitution and read the passage denying non-whites the right to carry firearms other than pistols and .22 caliber rifles. He read the passage, then, with a nervous smile, said, "So, you see, I am compelled to carry out the law of the land and I have been authorized to offer you money for any such weapons you might have."

The mayor pulled thirty-five dollars from his pocket and displayed it to Thurgood.

"Uh-huh," replied the reverend evenly, his eyes not leaving the mayor. "That's most gracious of you, but I really have no need of your money. And, I'm not in the mind to go surrendering my rifle, since I'm going deer hunting today. And I don't do that with a .22. In fact, you may join me if you wish. See, it's all loaded," he said, pointing to the weapon with scope leaning against the porch railing.

Dilbert took a deep breath, glanced at his deputies, and with affected exasperation said, "Rev, this is not a request. It is a command by the authorities of this state and the government."

Thurgood shrugged and said, "I think that's a matter for the court. And you're not a member of the court, Mayor. I intend to contest the law, and I suggest that you and your folks leave in peace. I think that would be best for all."

"Can't do that," said Dilbert, reaching for his holstered revolver. Thurgood picked up his rifle.

"My deputy will take that," said the mayor.

Thurgood shook his head and raised his rifle. A shot from Dilbert's revolver splintered the morning silence. Thrown back, Thurgood pulled the trigger. As the blast tore upward a second pistol round hit him between the eyes.

"Get his gun," instructed Dilbert, already walking toward the next residence. He turned back to a deputy and said, "Search the house. This is war."

The second home seemed vacant, but they smashed open the door. A man holding a .45 backed toward the wall and fired four rounds before being brought down. One of Dilbert's deputies lay dying outside the door.

"Get an ambulance," said the mayor. Turning to Von Hoffmann, he asked, "Did you get that?" Then he took the mic. "We have just suffered our first casualty in carrying out the law of the land. This deputy has been shot, and there will be hell to pay!"

Kneeling over the deputy, Dilbert glanced at another officer, pointed to the house, and said, "Burn it. Burn it down!"

When the next four houses were found abandoned, the mayor began to look anxious. How newsworthy could the operation be if only two people resisted?

A car pulled up, window lowered, and the driver said, "They're all at the cement factory. You should take your men there, Mayor. You can bag them all at once."

"Call up the reserves!" shouted the mayor, committing his people to savage battle.

With energized alacrity, men piled into cars and trucks as tires screeched. Once outside the factory, they sprang from their vehicles, some spraying the building with dozens of rounds.

Most cities and towns in the NCRA were divided into white and black communities, and so was Hattybend, where the railroad tracks were the dividing line. Built behind the tracks was a four-foot wall, a sound restraint for the more affluent section of town that rose up a low hill behind it. Twenty-five yards behind the wall stood the three story *Hattybend Gazette* newspaper building, long abandoned. Attempting to consolidate and organize the attack, the mayor ordered a half-dozen men to occupy the building since it towered over the cement factory.

"I want snipers on the roof," he shouted, as his cohorts rushed around the cement factory building, looking for unlocked doors.

Two blocks from the newspaper building stood a museum, in front of which was the community's brass cannon and a stacked pile of Civil War cannon balls. A block further down was the town's gun store. With the inauguration of President Lee, gun sales had increased, and the proprietor had decided to purchase thousands of rounds of ammunition. He'd also ordered barrels of black powder for muzzle-loading muskets used by black powder enthusiasts.

As rounds splattered off the cement factory, Nathaniel Wilson went to his veterans and said, "Remember your training. Short bursts when you have a definite target. Conserve ammunition. This is going to be a long siege."

He tapped the shoulder of a man with a sniper rifle. "Up there on that building. Take them out."

"What about the mayor?"

"Not yet. He's going to make a big mistake. I want to let him do it."

The mood amongst Dilbert's comrades was that of a Sunday picnic, southern comfort and all. The men on the roof of the newspaper building knelt to fire while others, seeing no danger, aimed bursts from a standing position. Those were the first to be blown off the roof.

"Sniper! Sniper!" shouted one of the remaining men, as they scrambled down from the roof.

Throughout the morning hours the firing continued. On several occasions, men would rush the front of the building in an attempt to break through the door. But old bags of hardened concrete had been stacked behind it, and their attempts met with failure. When another group brought ladders to gain access to the roof, Molotov cocktails lobbed from the windows ended that effort, with dead and dying men laying on the ground.

Seeing the futility of storming the building, the mayor approached, waving a white towel. "I urge you to lay down your arms and come out," he said, using a bull horn. "I promise that none will be harmed if you exit now peaceably. But we have reinforcements on the way, and I may not be able to control their actions. We shall breech your walls and a massacre will follow. The blame will be upon you. I pray that you believe me."

"Tell your men to go home and we might talk," said Wilson.

"Nope, can't do that," said Dilbert. "Surrender, or your community will suffer greatly."

When there was no response, he walked back to his men and said, "Burn every one of their houses. Don't spare a single one."

Fifteen minutes later, smoke and flames rose from the black section of town. No fire engines appeared and the conflagration roared unimpeded.

With no progress made against the defenders, one group purchased a barrel of black powder from the gun shop, while another removed the wooden plug from the muzzle of the brass cannon. They pilfered a ramrod, black powder scoop, and sponge attached to a pole from the museum's Civil War display.

"I wouldn't fire more than one round," said the gun shop proprietor. "I won't wager on the strength of the barrel. And be sure to stand way back when you pull the lanyard. Remember, the cannon is an antique."

Excited by the prospect of firing the historic piece, men waved off the cautionary note and chained the weapon to the rear of a utility truck, hauling it to within thirty yards of the factory.

Frowning, Captain Wilson stared at the dozen men milling about the cannon. He shook his head and said, "Everybody in the basement. Get away from the walls."

Black powder was ladled into the barrel, followed by a cannon ball. A measure of powder was placed into the touch hole that pierced the rear of the cannon while a man prepared to pull the lanyard. Another man, designating himself as captain of the gun, shouted, "Fire!"

The ancient cannon recoiled as smoke belched and a twelve-pound ball shot out, tearing away a three-foot section of concrete. A burst of applause rose from the gunners and others who had chosen to crowd around it. Enthused by the sight of the hole, the crew wormed out the barrel's debris from the first round. But in their haste, they failed to bring a pail of water to sponge out the tube.

"Load it again, load it again!" shouted the crowd from across the street. As ball and powder were again spooned into the barrel, a spark flared. The resulting explosion shredded the barrel, and shrapnel ripped through everyone standing within twenty yards.

Screams filled the air as survivors were carried away. Lacerated bodies littered the area. A six-foot-tall wheel had flown upward, only to plummet down on an occupied car.

Except for the moans of the wounded, silence descended on the smoke-engulfed scene. Wilson and the other defenders resumed their original places and stared as twenty-four acolytes from Saint Benedict's monastery approached, walking down the street. A priest in a black cassock held a six-foot cross as they silently passed the dead and wounded attackers.

Upon approaching the factory door, the priest called out, "In the name of the Lord, we have come to offer our assistance. We have food, water, and medical supplies. And though we will not fight, we will share all we have."

"Open the door," said Wilson. "Allow the priest and his young men into the building."

Desultory fire continued from a dozen of the mayor's people, but seeing the futility of the attack, and the carnage, the remainder left in disgust.

Danny Von Hoffmann had recorded it all. He had filmed smoke and flame rising from the burning homes, and he had witnessed the exploding cannon and its aftermath.

"This has been a horrific day," he said, his demeanor solemn as he and his cameraman walked to within a hundred yards of the factory. He held a white piece of cloth in one hand and the mic in the other. Speaking softly, he said, "We do not know how many casualties there are within the building. To the men who have followed the mayor, it seems impregnable.

"It is now getting dark, and nobody has yet ventured out of the building. It is probable that we are being watched by snipers. At least none of the ambulances were fired upon, nor were the brave men who removed the dead and wounded. I would imagine it was an act of mercy and discipline. Hopefully, nightfall will end this unfortunate bloodletting. We shall continue to report any further developments."

RUPTURED

As darkness descended, a few car lights pierced the night. Palls of smoke from businesses and houses still rose, as did flames from a gas line. At around six-thirty, a twenty-knot wind began to fan the flames and brush, and an untended lot caught fire. Ignited weeds were whipped along and embers descended on the community beyond the tracks.

One roof caught, then another. The flames began to consume houses along the prosperous avenues. People frantically phoned the fire department, which consisted of three engines, but only one could be manned since many of the volunteer firefighters had been killed or wounded during the siege. Only one engine responded, but as the conflagration expanded, its crew pulled away for reasons of personal safety.

Within a few hours there was nothing left of either community. Cautious and fully armed, Captain Wilson emerged from the cement factory. Smoke and ash covered everything. There was no one to oppose them; most of the townsfolk had fled.

Danny Von Hoffmann, however, had remained to record the demise of the town. He was about to load his equipment when he saw a tall black man surveying the remains.

"Sir, were you in the cement factory?" he deferentially asked Nathaniel Wilson.

"I was."

"Have you anything to say about this disaster?"

"Only that it did not have to happen. But if the NCRA continues its racist policies, this is only a microcosm of what is in store. Pray that it is not."

*****

President Lee convened his cabinet at ten the next morning. They viewed the footage taken by Von Hoffmann. Lee said, "I want to speak with the mayor."

"He was caught in the fire and was seriously burned," said Ralph Prescott. "The man is heavily sedated and not expected to live. Several of his deputies died in the fire as well."

Lee took off his wire-rimmed spectacles and said, "Okay, we can't let this happen again. I'm going to remove the prohibition from the Constitution."

"Congress will object," said Palmer. "It's a slippery slope. We delete one thing and that leads to another. We'll look weak and that will lead to an insurrection. I advise against it."

"I don't give a rat's ass what you think. The Constitution says I can overrule any decision, even one made by me. As Louis XIV said, *'L'etat, c'est moi'.'* I am the state and I make the law."

No one saw the smirk on Prescott's face as he left the cabinet meeting.

CHAPTER 20

THE GAMBLE

Montgomery, Alabama

President Lee scanned the report sent to him by the CEO of the petroleum conglomerate, put down the folder, and faced four members of his cabinet.

"They're telling me that reserves are down and they can't get parts for worn out equipment. A number of wells are going dry and fracking is getting too expensive. Some on the board are suggesting drastic action but aren't committing to anything specific.

"That's putting us in a real bind," said Palmer. "No oil coming in from Venezuela or any place else, and gas prices are going out of sight. I think it's time for that drastic action. Nothing says we have to maintain the territorial limit set by the U.S. We can move the limit twenty-five miles if we want."

"The U.S. won't recognize it," said Goodwin. "And their navy patrols those waters."

"Yeah, well what I'm thinking about won't be traced back to any of us here. It will be done by our citizens. A sort of popular uprising, spontaneous, beyond our control. Millions are fed up with the blockade, food and fuel shortages, everything. Lots of people are about to explode, and we can't have them explode against us. We have to do something, and folks don't give a damn how dangerous it is."

"I don't like it," said Goodwin. "Taking on the U.S. Navy or the coast guard is dangerous business. And you're talking about civilians without any command structure."

"So, what should we do? Just run out of oil?" asked Palmer. "What I'm thinking will be fast, over and done with."

"I know you're talking about oil platforms, and that, along with probable casualties, is a big problem," said Lee. "What you're contemplating is tantamount to piracy. The U.S. is going to respond and they won't ask for permission."

"Neither should we," sputtered Palmer. "They're strangling us. We're a sovereign nation, are we not? We should act like one, not some cowering banana republic. Once this is done, we own it and we keep it."

"Sounds like the last roll of the dice," said Goodwin.

"And it's gonna come up sixes," said Palmer. "You just wait and see."

"You don't do anything, organize anything, without my permission," said President Lee.

"Yeah, sure," said Palmer walking to the door. "Well, I'm taking a little trip down to my old haunt in Louisiana to talk to a few fishermen. And I've got some personal business down there, too. Swamp country."

"You be careful, Palmer. I don't need another damn crisis. And you call me before you do anything rash," said Lee.

*****

Sitting at his terminal on board an oil rig, Charlie Weston watched the signal sent by a drone two hundred feet above the Gulf of Mexico. It was just after daylight and the sun was peeking over the horizon.

"Daniels, come here, take a look," Weston said to his co-worker.

175

"Gotta be kidding," said Trevor Daniels. "How many do you think there are?"

"Two hundred and fifty, maybe three. Some probably tour boats, the rest fishing craft. And there are five helos."

"What the hell are they thinking?" asked Weston.

"Don't know, maybe some sort of demonstration in front of the rigs? Is that a naval vessel with them?" said Trevor, enlarging the picture.

"Looks like an obsolete escort vessel, decades old. Somebody might have liberated it and done a lot of fixing up. It has two three-inch guns and a few fifty calibers," said Weston.

"If they intend to fight with it, they need ammunition. Where do they get that? Unless the guns are for show and it's only being used to ferry men," said Trevor.

"Naw, I think it's meant for an attack. I wonder if the FBI and Homeland Security have heard about it. There's had to be a lot of loose talk in coastal bars. I'm hoping the navy's tracking them. There's supposed to be a couple of destroyers just over the horizon. I'll ring up our boss," said Weston.

Albert Stone answered the phone and said, "The navy is heading our way and sending helos, but they want us to get ready for a possible attack. I want a water cannon, anti-piracy hoses, slippery foam and nets to foul propellers."

"Never had to use that stuff before," said Weston.

"Brand new world," answered Stone. "And that sound device, the LRAD, we'll use that if we have to. They won't be able to hear anything for a week. And yeah, we got some compressed air projectiles and a few lasers, just like the ships. We'll give them a nice reception."

"Sure thing," said the former roustabout, listening in to communications as alarms went off.

"Navy's alerted all the rigs," said Daniels. "The helos will warn those boats to head back and not attempt to board any of us."

"A few rounds in the water might be influential," said his partner.

"Maybe. I just wish we had put the barbed wire around the platform legs. That would keep them off," added Weston.

"They won't get that close," said Daniels. "But the NCRA guys have choppers, too. What if they try to drop people onto the rigs? Guys with ARs?"

"I'm sure navy helos can take care of them. I wouldn't want to tangle with a Viper. But an explosion on any rig may cause a fire," said Weston.

"That would be bad, but think of what's worse," said Daniels.

"Oh no, not that," said Weston.

Binoculars in hand, Charlie Weston said, "Trevor, I can see them now. That big boat must be the old naval vessel. It's in the lead and the deck gun is manned. A lot of boats behind it."

"There goes a Viper," said Weston. "I can hear the warning on their loudspeaker. Boat people are ignoring it." He glanced out of his window and saw that a U.S. flag had been hoisted to the top of the rig's flagpole.

The Viper suddenly made a sharp turn as rounds from the vessel sprayed upward. Several dozen small boats suddenly broke away from the fleet and charged toward a rig a quarter of a mile away.

The Viper turned back and a burst of machine gun fire erupted in the water within twenty yards of the antique naval vessel. Again, rounds from the ship flew upward toward the circling helo.

Daniels saw the craft turn away again and said, "I can't understand why it just doesn't riddle the damn thing."

"That's why," said Weston, turning his binoculars toward a navy destroyer closing fast. A missile launched by the destroyer struck the bridge of the ancient vessel. An enormous explosion engulfed the entire forward section, setting the craft on fire. A number of survivors spun into the sea, waving frantically to passing craft but none stopped.

Two more navy helos flew over the rigs. One bore down on a civilian chopper carrying an assault team as it approached a drilling platform. The Viper fired a burst and the rounds struck the turbine engine and main rotor. Smoke and fire shot out of the craft before it cartwheeled into the sea.

The destruction of the helicopter and the long-retired naval craft did not deter a flotilla of fishing boats heading for Daniel's rig. As they came within one hundred and fifty yards, Stone shouted, "Weston, turn on the hoses and acoustics!"

The pain-inducing sound caused men on the boats to drop everything and cover their ears. So intense was it that those who could immediately burst into the boats' wheelhouses. Then roustabouts on the platform directed streams of high-pressure seawater at the boat's crews and onto the decks. Fishermen grasping their weapons fired wildly before being knocked off their crafts by jetting water.

Three boats that eluded the hoses closed with the platform. Men on their bows slung grappling hooks, several of which snagged machinery on the rig. With weapons slung over their shoulders, they began to climb knotted ropes. When they reached thirty feet above the water, Daniels had crewmen reach for axes and sever the ropes, dropping the climbers into the sea.

Far from entirely repulsed, other men slung hooks onto the deck. Weston directed the crew to use the "Pain Ray," an electromagnetic narrow beam wave. Suddenly the assaulting party screamed, as an unbearable heat scorching their skin. Only by throwing themselves into the water was there any relief from second degree burns.

Deterred, the remaining would-be pirates turned their boats toward the closest platform, one lacking the defensive gear on Daniel's. Relieved that his crew was out of immediate danger, Stone watched in horror as men on one of the boats aimed an RPG and fired. The projectile struck piping containing crude oil, which spurted onto the deck and shot up the tower, catching fire as it spread. Within minutes, the entire structure was ablaze. Men coated in flaming oil flung themselves overboard. Pipes ruptured and oil flowed into the sea, igniting and spreading across the surface of the Gulf.

A strong wind whipped the sea, and seven boats coated in the viscous black liquid became torches. Screams and cries could be heard as captains tried in vain to escape the inferno.

"The slick is coming our way," Stone said to Weston. "Get the men off the platform; do it now!"

The remaining fishing vessels turned about and headed to port, but most were corralled by arriving Coast Guard cutters. From their decks launched fast rigid hull inflatable craft with an array of machine guns. Eleven meters long and speeding at forty knots, they encircled the remaining fishing and luxury craft. Bullhorn warning demanded that all engines be immediately stopped and weapons be tossed into the sea.

One by one, the engines were silenced. Each boat was boarded, confiscated, and all on board arrested. Lines were tossed from the naval vessels and the civilian craft were towed to the cutters, where sailors armed with M4 carbines attended to prisoners.

One of the cutters assisted oil rig crews as they abandoned their platforms. Looking back at the fires and smoke rising into the sky, Daniels turned to Weston and said, "I wonder who's going to pick up the tab on this one?"

"It's the NCRA's terrorist action," said Weston. "One way or another they're going to foot the bill."

*****

"Palmer, I told you this would be a fucking disaster!" shouted President Lee. "You went off half-cocked and disobeyed my orders!"

"I merely talked to a few fishermen. The subject of the rigs came up, and before I knew it the whole thing got out of hand. It spread like wildfire, and everybody was running for their boats."

Seething, Lee stared at the TV as a CBN chopper flew over the burning sea, the navy destroyers, and prisoners on the coast guard cutters. There were closeups of the flaming rig and charred corpses being pulled from the water.

The female anchor of CBN looked aghast at the images and said, "This is not only an act of terrorism perpetrated by the NCRA, but it is also an ecological disaster. It rivals the 2010 Deepwater Horizon spill that did horrific ecological damage to the Gulf Coast. Surely the owners of the rigs and the families of those killed on the platforms will be suing the NCRA. We have just learned that those arrested will be tried in U.S. courts on terrorist charges."

The anchor turned to the screen and said, "My colleague Matt Graftin is still at the scene. Matt, what is the condition of that rig?"

"It has suffered major damage. Much of the flooring has collapsed and heavy equipment has toppled into the sea. Oil is still flowing. This is a disaster on a monumental scale."

President Lee's fury turned once again on Stanley Palmer. Glaring, face crimson, he hissed, "'Roll of the dice. They'll come up sixes,' you said. It's your head that should roll!"

"But it was you who extended our territorial waters," wheezed Palmer, his arms crossed in defiance. "And you did not exactly object to the operation."

Lee sat back in his swivel chair, deflated, the venom slipping away. "This one is my fault," he said, his words barely audible as he stared at the high, ancient ceiling. "There were economic incentives we could have offered the companies. We might have had them divert oil to us based on humanitarian grounds. Of course, Barnes might have stopped it cold but. . . Anyway, this is going to cost us. Not just in lawsuits but to our fishing industry as well."

"The immediate question," said Goodwin, "is do we have the equipment and the trained personnel to deal with the spill? The Deepwater Horizon disaster was cleaned up by the National Response Team led by the U.S. Coast Guard, the EPA and British Petroleum. Except for BP, those are all U.S. agencies. We might be able to deal with a small spill, a few thousand gallons, but nothing like this. If we want to save the fishing industry, not to mention the environment, we're going to have to talk to them."

"Ain't gonna get us anywhere," chided Palmer. "They're not going to do a damn thing to help us. They'll say we created the mess and we can clean it up."

"I've already gotten calls from fishermen's organizations who were not involved," said Lee. "They're pissed and are demanding we save the industry and save it fast. The only way is to mobilize thousands, get them the equipment and then pay them. They're not going to do it *pro bono*."

"None of the governors were advised beforehand, and now they're going ballistic," said Goodwin. "The governor of Mississippi is calling for the resignation of all of us and new elections."

"Well, that ain't gonna happen," said Palmer. "He's just whistling Dixie."

"Last I heard, Dixie didn't do too well," said Goodwin. "This is what the army calls a real cluster fuck. Are you going to call Barnes on this one?"

"I sure as hell don't want to. Maybe she'll call me, offer some help," said Lee.

"Well, let's try to extinguish the fires and begin clean up," said Goodwin. "Maybe in two or three weeks this will be old news. People's memories are short."

"But not short enough," said Lee.

CHAPTER 21

A PERSON OF INTEREST

Montgomery, Alabama

James Goodwin was in his office beside the bedroom and neither saw or heard Janice walk into the mansion. Entering the bedroom, she heard his agitated voice on the phone. She frowned, rarely hearing him so unsettled.

"You were supposed to monitor the patrols and alert us if there were federal ships in the area! Were you just negligent?"

Goodwin listened for a moment then said, "Goddamn it, Tom, that sub was scuttled with millions worth of product. You know what that means? We lose big time, and so do the cartels. And they expect their take."

After another moment of silence, he said, "You told me you were on top of it, had assurances from the *jefe* . . . What do you mean they can't trace it? TV reports said that some of the crew gave information about the construction of the boat, where it was built and who was in charge. They also said where it was to rendezvous with our people, including Palmer. If the feds ever get their hands on him, we're. . ." There was silence while the person on the other end of the line responded.

"So you say. No more fuck-ups, Tom, got it? Your cut is on the chopping block. What? Don't you dare threaten me. I'm in a foreign nation in case you forgot. You are in the U.S. of A. I know somebody there who would love to interrogate you. Goodbye, pal. Just watch your back."

Janice had quietly retreated to the front room by the time Goodwin emerged from his office. Upon seeing her, his demeanor instantly changed.

"Hey, how was your day?" he said brightly.

"A bit stressful. Not much on the supermarket shelves."

"Yeah, the embargo is not helping. Hey, babe, can you pour me a drink? My day's been a bit ragged, too."

"I'm sorry to hear that. Lee's giving you a hard time? He does follow your advice, doesn't he? You're his best advisor."

"Pretty much. But I only tell him what I think he should know."

"I bet you know more than he ever will. I'll get you that drink."

The overheard phone conversation bothered her. Like everyone else, she had heard the news cast regarding the interception of a sub by the U.S. Coast Guard. And she had seen her husband announce the capture of the Columbians by the FBI. Solid, serious, and totally responsible — she recognized the character of the man to whom she was still married. The fact that he might be prosecuting her if or when the NCRA collapsed, gave her a sense of dread. And although he was entirely capable of a good laugh and playful moments, she knew that he was no one to cross, especially when it involved the law.

For the briefest of moments, she compared Goodwin to Steven and wondered if she had made a terrible mistake.

The name "Tom" came to her mind. *Who was he, and how did he connect with Goodwin, she wondered. They must know each other very well, and this Tom must be in a precarious position. Apparently, he had contacts with a criminal element as well as some very dangerous people—cartel people. And more chilling was the talk of drugs and money. And again, the name Palmer.*

A sudden thought assailed her mind. *In addition to aiding an insurrection against the United States, was she associated with a gang of drug-running criminals?* She shivered despite the warmth of the room.

Cocooned within the highest ranks of the NCRA, did she dare reveal what she'd learned to U.S. authorities? And what proof was there in just overhearing a conversation? Even more frightening, what would happen to her if Goodwin learned of her betrayal?

Say nothing, she told herself. *Pretend that I overheard nothing, show no suspicion, ride the train as long as it remained on the tracks.*

She wondered if she could share carnal moments with Goodwin and still be responsive in their love-making? And if not, what suspicions might come to his mind? *Pretend, pretend, pretend. Let the chips fall where they will. Maybe it was time to consider a Plan B,* she told herself.

*****

"I can sure use a beer right now," said Eli, as he took a slice of pizza from the box on Steven's living room table. It was after hours, and they were trying to unwind after an 80-hour week.

"When do you not need a beer? Lord knows, you drank all of mine."

"Aw, shucks," said Eli. He leaned back in Steven's recliner and pushed the button that lowered the back. "I was going to ask you, after all these years, how you wound up in the FBI?"

"I thought the idea of tonight was to forget about work for a while."

"Just curious. I imagine it's an exciting story, becoming director."

"Not that exciting. My pop was a cop and so was my grandad. I was a scrawny, academic kid—shy, too. When I was seventeen, my grandad, then retired, took me to his ranch in Montana. Taught me how to ride and shoot, and we rounded up cattle all summer. I confessed that I had no idea of what to do in life, so he suggested the Marines or law enforcement. Said he knew people on the D.C. force. After graduating from Colorado State, I became a cop, worked the streets for ten years, applied for the FBI, and the rest is history."

"That's it?"

"That's it. There's a six pack of cokes in the fridge. Help yourself." He looked at his watch and sighed. "Recess is over. I've got work to do."

***

After receiving an incoming call at the D.C. Bureau, the receptionist responded, "Sir, I won't be able to connect you to the Director. Yes, I understand that it's important."

She listened for a moment longer and said, "I will forward a message to the area agent. His name is Agent Barett. What is your phone number Professor? And, yes, he will contact you, but it may take awhile.

Professor Benjamin Rathmore's phone rang twenty minutes later. "Thank you for calling me Agent Barett. I am a political science instructor here at the University of Maryland and as I mentioned to the operator, I have a graduate student in my class whose views greatly disturb me. They are quite radical and rather threatening. Were he an eighteen-year-old freshman or sophomore, I would write off his pronouncements. But, he has military experience, perhaps even special forces, and a commanding presence. He speaks of revolution and I think he means what he says."

"So, we're talking about domestic terrorism, are we?" said Eli.

"I'm afraid so."

"Can you give me his name.?"

"Devin Winfeld, age twenty-six. And, by the way, I have a young lady, a freshman in the same class by the name of Evelyn Whitinghill. Could she be related to the FBI Director?"

"Possibly. He has a daughter enrolled in a political science class at the University. Does she have a connection or a relationship with Winfeld?"

"I'm not sure. I'm rarely aware of student relationships, but I think she does support some of his views."

"And you say that Winfeld is a graduate student. Is this an undergrad class?"

"There are some graduate students enrolled who are interested in the subject; 'Revolutions Throughout Modern History.' You should know that he will receive his Masters at the end of the semester and then will likely leave the campus to parts unknown."

"That might be worrisome. Can you tell me if he is involved with any group or individuals that might be associated with domestic terrorism?" asked Eli becoming more concerned.

"I'm not sure but I think he's entirely capable of it. If Evelyn is the daughter of the Director, he might be concerned about Evelyn's relationship with Devin. I can't see any way of removing him from my class since he hasn't done anything against school regulations yet."

"Professor, we greatly appreciate the information you have given us. The Director will be very interested in it too. And, because of the possible connection of his daughter with Winfeld, you may be receiving a call from him. Thank you."

Eli ended his call and went to Steven's office. The Director listened to Eli and then immediately made the call.

Steven introduced himself to the professor and said, "I'm very pleased that you phoned us. I do believe my daughter is in your class. And from what you told Special Agent Barett, we might keep our eye on Mr. Winfeld."

"I think that would be advisable. What might you suggest about your daughter? Should she be placed in another class?"

"No, that would raise Mr. Winfeld's suspicions."

"Director, I am also a councilor to students. They talk and I listen. Perhaps I may learn of something dangerous or imminent."

"Evelyn has always been a bit of a firebrand and a romantic. I'm afraid she can easily be manipulated, especially by a very imposing man."

"If it is permissible, Director, I will call you if further information comes to my attention."

"I would appreciate that professor. Let's keep in touch"

*****

Several days later, Steven Whitinghill received a phone call from Professor Rathmore.

"Director, I hope I'm not interrupting you."

"Not at all. I was hoping to hear from you."

"Good. I'll be brief, something my students always pray for. I just wanted to tell you that both Devin Winfeld and your daughter have dropped my class without prior notice. It's important to inform me, since failure to take the final exam will greatly influence a grade. I might be able to grant

188

an incomplete, but that requires some consultation and a very valid reason."

"Of course, but I wonder why they would have both dropped?"

"Good question. Since I hadn't seen either of them for five class sessions, I decided to do some sleuthing, something I have never done before. I went to the university enrollment office and found Mr. Winfeld's records, including his cell phone, an old one, and address—material he offered a year ago. My curiosity was up and I stopped by his apartment. He wasn't there and the place had been vacated. I also noticed a realtor sign on the grass."

"Did you speak to the realtor?"

"Yes. She said that Winfeld had left with no notice, no forwarding address. She tried to phone him but there's no new number."

"And what about Evelyn? Do you think she was with him?"

"Well, the realtor found a woman's sweater in the closet when she went to investigate."

"Did she tell you what the sweater looked like?"

"Blue with silver buttons on the sleeves. I've seen your daughter wear it, and I asked if I might have it in case she showed up for class."

"So we must assume that Evelyn was visiting his apartment. Do you think they've dropped other classes?"

"I believe so. They were in a chemistry class together and they dropped that. I find it rather worrying, Director."

"I do too, and I have no idea where she might be. I just hope she calls me before there's trouble. Thanks for the information, and please phone me if you see either of them. Based on your observations, I think this is worrisome."

The professor signed off, and Steven thought that there were only two people his daughter might contact.

"Eli," Steven said, as his friend slid back into the recliner, "has Evelyn phoned you during the last few weeks? She does confide in you."

"Haven't heard from her. Isn't she still at the university?"

"No." Steven summarized the professor's observations and deductions.

"I suggest you call your wife. Evelyn may have gotten in touch with her."

"They are not exactly fond of each other right now. I can't imagine Evelyn phoning Janice. What could she possibly say? 'I'm dating a possible terrorist'?"

"Not exactly. Maybe she needs someone to confide in besides the director of the FBI. Call Janice. Hell, she might know something we don't. Maybe even about the NCRA and Mr. James Goodwin."

"Goodwin, huh? I'm sure there's a lot she knows that we don't," said Steven. "I'll consider it."

"I'm worried for Evelyn. I think she's playing with fire."

"I think you're right."

*****

One week later, Jackson, Tennessee

Marjorie Phillips knew that she was doing what God expected of her. Having spent the entire morning with the volunteers of the Ohio Methodist Congregation, the five trucks were finally loaded. It was her responsibility to organize the food drive, determine the best route into Tennessee, and make the border crossing with the blessing of the U.S. government.

Marjorie was pleased the NGO faith-based organizations were permitted to bring food to the draught-stricken secessionist states. But her sense of Christian righteousness

190

would have compelled her to do it anyway, even if it was contrary to administration policy.

She had friends and family in Jackson who appealed to her for relief. Many of them attended the Grace United Methodist Church, and she reasoned it would be the most logical place for the distribution of the supplies.

It was five-hundred miles from Columbus to Jackson, and it was agreed that the seven-hour trip would require two days. And although Marjorie was the official leader, she was not the driver of any of the trucks. The lead driver was Grady Wills, a twenty-five-year-old parishioner with eyes much keener than Marjorie, who was sixty-seven.

The first night was spent in southern Kentucky, but there was a break-down of one of the older vehicles, and the convoy was not able to continue until the third day. The congregation at Grace United would be anxiously awaiting their arrival. Marjorie called ahead to advise them that they would not arrive before dark.

It was already dusk when she glanced at her cell and noticed that the map showed a long red line for the main roadway ahead. An alternate route was suggested, and the convoy trundled onto a narrow two-way lane that meandered through farmland interspersed with thickets of trees and high shrub. The road was rarely traveled and was in poor repairs, which explained why so few of the local drivers had resorted to it. Clearly, they knew better.

Marjorie sighed, knowing that it would be several more hours before they would reach the church. Not wanting to keep the congregation waiting, she phoned and told the pastor that they would be staying at a motel for the night and would meet the volunteers in the morning. The pastor replied that he would send everyone home and signed off for the night.

"They're all on the twenty now," said Cresper Foy to his brother Erik while watching with his rag-tag accomplices.

"That's good," replied Erik, watching eight vans pull over at a curve in the road. He swiped his finger over his phone, touched a name, and waited.

"Troopers are clearing the wreck now," said a voice. "We should be joining you pretty soon. Is everybody in place?"

"Yeah, and we got a tree down across the road. They'll have to stop."

"We're ready," replied Erik. "Everything should be delivered before morning. I see lights ahead; it's got to be them. The guys are in position."

"Do it fast. You know what to do. Don't be squeamish about it," said the voice.

"Something in the road ahead," said Grady Wills, slowing the truck to fifteen miles per hour. The five trucks behind him slowed to a crawl as Grady approached the fallen tree.

"It's pretty big, Marjorie. Tell all the men that I'll need their help."

She placed the calls and soon six men of the convoy were on the road, flashlights illuminating the thirty-foot oak. As Chantelle, a young volunteer, watched from the last truck in line, eight men dashed out from the trees, aimed ARs, and sprayed the men who were attempting to remove the tree.

Screams erupted as they fell. One after the other, they were silenced with a shot to the head. Appalled and terrified, Marjorie opened the door and started for the massacre but was shot before she could take a dozen steps.

Just as the shooting ended, Chantelle slipped out of the vehicle and ran as fast as she could into the deep brush.

"Cresper, get two guys and put those signs around the curves. Yeah, the ones saying 'road closed.' I don't want any cars coming either way," said Erik. Then he turned to his crew and commanded, "Grab all you can from the trucks, shoot anybody still in them, and get the hell away!"

It took twenty minutes to transfer the boxes and slip down the road until they came to the highway. As planned, when they first learned of the shipment from a homeless informant, each van headed to a different location. The foodstuffs would be sold to retailers or find their way to swap meets where the hungry would pay top dollar for cans and boxes of preserves.

Chantelle, still in possession of her cell phone, called 911 then sobbed as she silently prayed for Marjorie and each of the men.

A lieutenant approached her and listened to her account of the killings. In a state of disbelief and trauma, her words were barely coherent. They cautioned her not to speak to the press until she regained her composure and gave a full accounting
at precinct headquarters.

The local news vans arrived minutes later and Wendy Crossman, a reporter from WBBJ Eyewitness News, began a sketchy account of the murders and the theft of the food supplies as their camera scanned the nearly empty trucks and tarp-covered bodies.

"This is a horrendous outrage," said Wendy, as sirens of ambulances were heard in the distance.

"These people were good samaritans from a faith-based organization that traveled from the United States to bring food to our citizens. Now all but one is dead. We are anxiously awaiting the account from the only survivor, a young woman whose identity we have not yet learned."

Her camera man focused on Chantelle who entered a police cruiser and was driven away, the car's flashing lights having been turned off.

At ten the next morning, Marvin Gordon, governor of Tennessee, phoned President Lee and said, "The FBI just called me, and they weren't particularly courteous."

"What did they say?"

"There will be a full-blown investigation. I told them that they have no jurisdiction down here and they read me the Riot Act."

"On what grounds do they claim jurisdiction?" asked Lee.

"That the murdered people are citizens of the United States. And since the crimes were committed across state lines, as if we were still part of the U.S., they will do whatever is required to apprehend the perps. They also demand that we turn over all information we acquire. And they want the immediate return of the sole survivor."

"News of the theft will enrage our entire nation, but it's really a state matter," said Lee. "However, I suggest that as governor, you phone Edith Barnes and say what has to be said."

Gordon went to his office and put the call through to the White House. He was passed on to the Oval Office line in an alarmingly short time.

"I'm listening," Barnes said.

"Madam President, as governor I wish to express my condolences and that of my nation, as well as those of my president."

"I appreciate your call and your sentiments, but I was expecting to hear from Lee."

There was an awkward pause before Gordon said, "I spoke with your FBI, and I told them that I have directed every law enforcement agency in Tennessee to hunt down the perpetrators and solve this heinous crime. I wish to assure you that an APB has been put out and every Tennessean is committed to assisting the police. Once apprehended, the criminals will be handed over to your government. So, there is no need to expend the resources of the FBI in the search."

"Time is of the essence, Governor. But I realize that state enforcement may be more familiar with local neighborhoods than our agents. I will grant you three days, Mr. Gordon. If the criminals are not found by that time, I will order the FBI to take over the case."

"I understand, and I want to say that my office will pay for all funeral expenses."

"That would be appreciated. Now Governor, I am not sure when or if I will allow NGOs and faith-based entities to re-commence deliveries. But any future ones will be accompanied by armed security. And I mean security provided by my government."

"That would be a transgression, Madam President. I'm quite sure that any state within the NCRA can provide escort."

"I think I have made myself clear, Mr. Gordon."

"That sounds like an ultimatum."

"Yes, I believe it is."

Appalled by the murders and the theft, the citizens of Tennessee hunted down each of the actors responsible for the crime. Within three days, they were handed over to the FBI. A week later, a convoy of trucks resumed delivery escorted by a dozen federal marshals as well as a contingent of local police.

CHAPTER 22

REACHING OUT

It wasn't often that James Goodwin took Janice to a high-class restaurant, but he was feeling good that evening. In every respect, he had become the president's right-hand man, the one Lee went to when things appeared to be spinning out of control. He hoped that the intimate atmosphere in the swanky Hilton, along with a few drinks and a fine dinner, would do wonders for the strain that had seeped into their relationship.

Dazzling in her black silk dress and diamond necklace, Janice looked incredible. And Goodwin felt smugly pleased that eyes followed her to their reserved table overlooking the city.

He ordered a fine bottle of Pinot Grigio, kissed her hand, and said, "You look absolutely magnificent. I don't think you realize how good I feel in your company."

She smiled demurely and said, "And I enjoy yours, James. I like us being together, but I think we should get away every once and a while. Things around here are getting really tense. And it's so terribly hot. Everything is scorched, especially the crops."

"Yeah, climate change, I guess. I would love it if we could find a nice, cool place beside a lake, just you and me. But unfortunately, I can't get away, not now."

"I want to understand, but I am getting worried," she said, picking at her food.

Goodwin gave her a long look and said, "I know that things are not exactly going the way we expected. This heat wave, the embargo, and the financial situation are all problems. But I think there was a time when you were interested in what I was doing. Nowadays you seem distracted, if not disinterested. Is there a particular reason?"

She considered the question and was tempted to ask him about the late-night phone conversation, but thought better of it.

"I think we're twisting in the wind, James. Us and the country. I suspect people are getting tired of the restrictions, the continuous vilification of the U.S., the rules."

He laid down his fork and said, "Okay, I agree that Lee, Palmer and a few others are pretty dogmatic, but they're true believers in the supremacy of the white race and Evangelical's righteousness. Every society has rules. This is the Nationalist Christian Republic of America, and it's what our people want. The beliefs are rooted in our DNA, always have been, always will be. It's said that politics is the art of compromise, but on religion and racial superiority, there is no room for compromise."

"And you agree with that?"

He shrugged. "I'm a southern boy, Janice, born in the Bible Belt." He grinned, and, leaning back in his chair, said, "And who knows, I might even be in this for other reasons, too."

"Good reasons?"

"Good reasons? Well, let me put it this way, darling. I've always been a business man, always wanted nice things, including those diamonds adorning your pretty neck. So, let's stay with the program. You and I might not agree with everything going on here, but we're far away from people like

Edith Barnes and Steven Whitinghill. And I really prefer that."

He grinned again and said, "Look, it's a beautiful night. Let's put aside politics and enjoy the time we have together."

He laid a hand on hers and said, "The steak and wine are great, right?"

She nodded agreeably and said, "Dessert would be nice. Something sweet."

He leaned over and kissed her. "I also would like something sweet, and you're the sweetest thing I know."

Yes, she thought, *as long as you don't know what I know.*

*****

Washington, D.C.

Steven pondered the matter for most of the morning. Perhaps Eli was right and he should call Janice. If the discussion only concerned their daughter, it might not turn into accusations and bitterness. The tone would have to be business-like, professional, devoid of anything relating to their estrangement.

Janice picked up on the second ring; at first she seemed wary. But his salutation was neither hostile not recriminatory, and in reply she said, "Steven, I was considering calling you."

"Good, perhaps we're thinking about the same thing. I believe there's something going on with Evelyn that's potentially serious. Has she phoned you lately?"

"A while back. The last conversation we had wasn't pleasant. I had hoped to reconcile with her and tried calling, but the message said that there was no such number."

"That makes sense. I'm sure she's with a young man named Winfeld. They both dropped out of the university, and I think Winfeld's very dangerous."

"That's scary. I don't like that at all. Is this Winfeld a terrorist?"

"I did some checking and found that he was in the Army and trained with explosives. I'm worried that Evelyn might become an accomplice if he does something criminal. We have to get her away from him."

"You think she'll get arrested?"

"I think she'll get killed."

"Oh my God. Has he committed any acts of terrorism before?"

"Not that we've found. And to be honest, we don't know if he'd target the U.S. or the NCRA."

"But you think he has one in mind?"

"Just a theory right now. I'm hoping Evelyn either calls you or Eli. I expect she thinks of Winfield as a knight in shining armor who will never let any problem befall her, but terrorists are users, and it's all to easy to manipulate hero worship and blind faith."

"You and I know that Evelyn has always sought excitement and talked about revolution. So Winfeld became her hole in one."

Steven paused for several seconds before saying, "How are you doing?"

There was a moment of silence before she said, "We're having problems here. I guess you know that."

"With Goodwin?"

She hesitated. "Yes, some. And the government is unstable. It seems like we have a noose around our necks and it's just getting tighter. And, well, James has changed, too. Maybe I shouldn't say this, but he gets late night phone calls and goes into his office thinking I can't hear. I suspect there's something going on besides government business. But exactly what, I don't know."

"He's always been a shady character. Very slick, very manipulating. You know what I mean."

"In some ways. I should say that one of those late-night calls was with someone named Tom, probably an associate. Do you know anyone named that?"

"Not without a last name."

"James talked to him about drugs and the loss of that sub. He was really upset and said that they lost a lot of money. To a cartel."

"That's interesting, a cartel. I always suspected that he was into illicit stuff and only went with the NCRA to escape prosecution."

"That scares me," said Janice, her words barely audible.

For a moment he thought the line had gone dead, then she said, "Am I in trouble, Steven? From the FBI, the government?"

"That depends on what happens when the NCRA implodes. There may be amnesty for some. I don't know what category you fall in, being so close to the top. If you're asking if I can help, at this point I can't say. It's not entirely up to me."

"I'm afraid. We have this drought—food's scarce and people are so edgy. There's been riots in markets, and there's this thing with apartheid, censorship and arrests. And then there's Palmer."

She stopped for a moment, and when Steven didn't reply she haltingly said, "I'm impulsive, you know that. I was smitten with James and thought it would be a great adventure."

"You were bored with me. I wish things could have been different. Look, I didn't want to get into this thing about Goodwin. You know what I think of him. I called because of Evelyn. It's imperative that you phone me if you hear anything. The FBI has a long reach once we know where to go."

"I will. Can I ask you this? What if I need to come back? I mean, for safety's sake?"

"You might be taken into custody. For now, stay safe and don't engage in anything detrimental to the U.S."

"I won't."

"And if you learn anything more about this fellow Tom, let me know."

*****

Janice, Goodwin, and Palmer were in President Lee's office when Dr. Prescott, a former professor of agronomics at Brown University, and the NCRA Secretary of Agriculture entered. Despite Lee's general disdain for people of color, he had a grudging respect for Prescott.

After some light chatter, Lee said, "Professor, I'm aware of climate change, though I disagree with the claim that there is a human factor. All that EPA stuff about fossil fuels bores the hell out of me. But yeah, it's getting damn hot, and my wife's petunias have died a serious death. So, Mr. Secretary, what elixir have you? Can we muddle our way through without more food riots and crop failures?"

Prescott shook his head, his countenance dark. "Muddle through? No, sir. Not in my estimation."

"So, what do you suggest?"

"I recommend a government program to purchase millions of tons of grain and foodstuffs and distribute them for free when required."

"It's going to be that bad?" asked Goodwin.

"Maybe worse. We now have the most serious drought in a century, and the predicted weather patterns suggest that winter will bring horrific floods that will likely destroy any remaining crops. And on top of that, we have another problem for agriculture."

"And that is?" asked Lee.

"Workers. Your neo-Nazis, the Klan and vigilantes have expelled, intimidated, or incarcerated or outright killed most of the people who would have harvested the remaining crops. And I don't see any of your friends showing up to pick apples. I've received dozens of calls from growers pleading for farm workers."

"We must have plenty of people willing to work," said Palmer.

Prescott snorted and said, "Most white people aren't willing to do stoop labor, and the few who are willing — and there are not enough of them — aren't skilled."

"Hell," said Lee, "We were the bread basket of the nation a year ago."

"That's history. I think, in addition to rationing and government hoarding, you should start looking for other sources of relief. As in the North."

"No!" shouted Palmer. "Maybe some NGOs, church groups, but not the U.S. We won't kneel down before Edith Barnes."

Prescott shrugged. "Sure, Palmer. Just save all your grits and greens. Maybe raise some chickens, too."

Turning to President Lee, he said, "Perhaps, sir, you might think of making that phone call. She might help on humanitarian grounds."

"I don't think we're there yet, Prescott. But I'll keep it in mind."

CHAPTER 23

DECEPTION

Fort Benning, Georgia

Stanley Palmer was seething mad. The NCRA, that shining beacon of hope for mankind's future, seemed to be wallowing in ineffective measures, ricocheting from one catastrophic failure to the next. It was time for decisive action that would bring worldwide acclaim to the nation, and perhaps to himself as well.

For weeks, he had evaluated one plan after another, discarding those that would only make a ripple in a sea of despair. It would have to appear spontaneous, a true rising of the people against the insidious bastions of the government of the United States. And the most obvious were the military installations that remained a malignant growth within the NCRA.

It was imperative, thought Palmer, *that the operation be undisclosed to President Lee, Goodwin, and everybody else in leadership.* The plan he conjured was so audacious that it would be instantly rejected by the cowards in office. But it was so daring, so in tune with the fervor of the citizenry, it could not possibly fail.

He knew insiders within the U.S. military who, given the slightest chance, would rally to the NCRA, even if it cost them their lives.

So, at nine in the morning, Palmer met with Major Randy Benson in a park twenty miles outside Fort Benning, Georgia, where he was a member of the 163rd Infantry Brigade.

"I heard from several sources that you are an ardent supporter of the NCRA and may be willing to contribute to its strength and success. If not, let me know now."

The major was wearing "civvies" instead of a military uniform. He gave Palmer a long, hard look. "I am in complete agreement with the philosophy and efforts of President Lee's government. I am a staff officer in the United States Army and the commander of battle-ready troops. But I'm not going to put my career and my life on the line for some half-baked idea that results in a debacle like that mess in the gulf. I suspect you have a military action in mind."

"I do but it will also involve thousands, perhaps hundreds of thousands, of civilians."

"Who will lead all those people? What's their mission?" asked Major Benson, wary of a man he would not trust with a practice grenade.

"The mission, to start with, is the takeover of Fort Benning and its annexation by the NCRA. I envision a massive march on the fort led by a civilian, a pastor who is loved and respected in Montgomery County. I have known him since childhood, and he is a true believer. When Fort Benning is ours, other forts and bases will follow! We must rid the South of U.S. military installations if the NCRA is ever going to be a sovereign nation. It's as simple as that."

It was also widely believed that the military bases contained enormous stockpiles of food. If these stockpiles became available to the NCRA, Palmer would be a hero, and that miserable excuse for a Secretary of Agriculture, Palmer, could go pick his own apples.

The major smirked then said, "A march on Fort Benning by civilians, armed or not, is hardly going to result in its capitulation. They will simply be turned away at the gate."

"Very true. That's where you and your men come in. We need people on the inside loyal to our cause. And a leader. Meaning you."

The major looked about and noted that, it being a workday, there were few people in the park.

"Let's take a walk," said Benson, lighting a cigarette.

A stiff wind blew his smoke away as they headed towards a clump of trees. The major said nothing for several minutes.

"Yes, there are hundreds of troops in my brigade who would support the NCRA. However, scuttlebutt is one thing; an actual revolt is something else. I will not do anything unless I have the total support of at least three hundred men and an assurance that your persuasive friend will show up with a substantial show of civilian support."

"Of course," said Palmer. "I know that you would be taking a chance, but this can be done. Surely you're aware of how many millions would champion your leadership in this matter."

"Perhaps."

Benson stopped, looked hard at Palmer, then said, "I heard that you approached the commander of Maxwell Air Force Base with a demand that he surrender it to the NCRA. It didn't go too well."

"I didn't have any backup, and nobody on the inside. I won't make the same mistake twice. Are you with us or against us?" Palmer said abruptly.

"I won't know until I meet with my junior officers. You have to understand that to take over the fort we would have to neutralize the MPs, take out the communications center, arrest all senior officers, and deal with all the troops loyal to the United States. That's a damn tall order, Mr. Palmer. And will President Lee be issuing a call to arms? A nationwide uprising against the dozens of military facilities in the South?"

"He will, once Fort Benning is secured. He will have no choice. But I don't want to speak with him about the takeover until it's a reality. His other cabinet members are pussy-footers, not like you or me, and Lee sometimes get persuaded by them."

"He had enough backbone to secede from the United States. As I said, I have to talk to my people. And, by the way, have you discussed this with the pastor?"

"Yes, but not in detail. I don't want him to organize until I have a commitment from you."

"This may be an act of suicide on his part, Mr. Secretary. If the demonstrators get out of hand at the gates, if the guards start shooting before I or my men can arrive on the scene, your friend or some of his followers could end up very dead."

"That is a possibility, a risk that must be taken," said Palmer. "But US soldiers killing peacefully marching civilians would stir sympathy for the NCRA in every state! No, I do not think Barnes would dare authorize an unprovoked attack. Even so, I've told my friend that we'd not share our intentions with the marchers."

"Not even during the march. It's just a demonstration as far as they are concerned. At least until they get to the gates," said the major.

"That's right," replied Palmer. With growing impatience, he asked, "When will you tell me if you're in?"

"I'll meet you here in two weeks. If I do commit," said the major. "I need to meet with your friend as well, see if he's got the right stuff. He needs to know that it may end in disaster.

And, Mr. Palmer, don't kid yourself. If we do this, people will die."

I don't care how many die, if they're enemies of the NCRA," retorted Palmer.

Two weeks later, pastor Trevor McNally, a heavy-set man in his mid-fifties, greeted Major Benson when the officer knocked on his door. It was a cool day and McNally invited the officer in and offered him a cup of steaming coffee. Again wearing civilian clothes, Benson had no desire to be seen in uniform. Before handing the pastor the envelope he carried, he said, "I have had several meetings with Stanley Palmer, a friend of yours, and he tells me that you possess a strong adherence to the ideals and efforts of the NCRA. And he also says that you are the leader of people who are staunchly opposed to U.S. military facilities within the nation."

"That's correct. Stanley told me that you'd be coming. I'm not always in agreement with him, but yes, besides being a pastor, I'm also the leader of our local militia."

"Good! So you have some military order. Has Mr. Palmer told you why I've come?"

"He simply said a friend of his might be dropping by. He didn't care to reveal names or details over the phone. Others might be listening—you know how it can be."

"Yes, they're monitored. The information in this letter is for you, and you alone. I would like you to read it now and tell me if you're up to it."

McNally opened the envelope, read it carefully, then gave it back to the major. After a lengthy pause he said, "I like the concept of a demonstration, but I'm worried about consequences if it gets out of hand."

"All we want is for you to organize as many people as you can, including local militia, and march to the main gate. What happens within the fort is a matter for me and my men. If we meet you at the gate, all is well. If not, you can retire peaceably after giving your speech. That, sir, is the plan."

"This letter doesn't say anything about what you're going to do. Are you thinking of an armed uprising, a takeover?"

"That's under consideration, but whatever we do will be greatly assisted by the presence of your people."

"That's not terribly reassuring, Major. You're not telling me what measures you are prepared to take. You are aware of the fact that there is Fort Gillem and Moody Air Force Base in Valdosta near Atlanta. They can easily support Benning. We're talking real fire power."

"We can deal with them."

"You will have to. You must understand that my people are civilians. Yes, many of them have Kalashnikovs and ARs , and not just the members of the militias, but only a few have military training or have seen combat. Some, regretfully, are hot-heads who would love to see a lot of killing. That's downright dangerous. You are infantry, and so was I years ago. You know what killing is about."

"I do," said Benson, "But you won't be facing that."

McNally ran a hand over his round face and said, "I will talk to my people. I know for a fact that many will be avidly in favor of a march. But I need the assurance that there will be no violence against my folks."

"I hope that's the case. But there's always risk in any righteous endeavor."

"Uh-huh. I would feel better if I knew your ultimate goal, Major. I'm not a devious person and I don't favor bloodshed. If we decide to contribute to this, how do I get in touch?"

"You don't. I'll contact you. And Pastor, I was never here."

*****

One week later, the agreement was sealed. McNally said, "I met with my folks and told them that the march must be peaceful. They could bring signs, sing, and carry flags. They agreed. But many also insisted on carrying firearms. To be honest, that worries me."

"Pastor, you will be leading the march and will be in control," said the major.

"I pray that they follow my example. I have also arranged for TV coverage."

Benson appeared miffed and said, "That wasn't necessary. I didn't want there to be any publicity prior to the event."

"Then what good is the demonstration? If a tree falls on a house and nobody sees it, there's no story. Know what I mean?"

"Not if the wrong people see it," countered Benson. "Okay, call off *Freedom America* if you can," he said. "If they insist on coming, tell them to say or film nothing until the march reaches the fort. You and your people step off at 0600 Sunday morning. How many do you have?"

"Five or six hundred, give or take. But Sunday's church day."

"You tell them that it's all about patriotism and it is God's work. You have the glory of leading them into the annals of history."

At two in the morning, three men eased their Toyota pickup out of a shed and drove it into a thicket of trees near the assembly point. No one was about; there was no sound and the night was quite dark.

All had been arranged earlier, when a rust-stained cargo vessel anchored fifteen miles off Cuba. Money was exchanged and a heavy machine gun and several shoulder-fired missiles were lowered onto a low, slender craft. At thirty knots, the boat sped undetected toward an inlet known only to locals. From there, the weaponry proceeded to Chattahoochee County, Georgia.

"We don't join the march until it's begun," said a balding man with a sparse blond beard.

"What if the army in the fort doesn't do anything? I mean, doesn't come out fighting?"

"Then we slip back into the woods and wait. Something's bound to happen with the militia."

The man's compatriot smiled and said, "Maybe we can make a little scene, sort of draw a few of them out. Tat, tat, tat."

"We're gonna do more than that."

*****

Sergeant Major Griff Weller slammed open the door of the barracks and shouted, "On your feet! Ten hut! Dress right dress!"

The senior non-com was followed by Lieutenant Colonel Lewis Brand and three MPs with side arms. It was 0430 and still dark, but two platoons were already up and dressed in battle fatigues, not the "Class A" uniform usually worn on Sundays.

Though startled by the sudden intrusion of the brass, the MPs, and the no-nonsense sergeant major, the troops regained their composure and stared straight ahead. Sergeant Major Weller was thickly built, with a body fat index below 5%. He was also dark-skinned, and an officer of the Prince Hall Masons. He had a reputation for being, firm, fair, and by the book; this morning, he observed the platoons with barely contained fury. Two entire minutes passed as his eyes bored into them.

With a voice that terrified many a recruit, Weller addressed the men. "It has come to our attention that a number of you have contemplated sedition and insurrection with the intent of surrendering this fort to the NCRA. That is an act of treason."

Ramrod straight, some men nevertheless blinked as the sergeant major nodded to the lieutenant colonel. Brand held up a leather-bound volume, opened it to a book marker, and said, "Gentlemen, this is the Uniform Code of Military Justice. I wish to reacquaint you with Article 94, which addresses revolt, violence, or disturbance against lawful authority. It includes provisions against mutiny and the failure to suppress or provide information regarding mutiny, sedition or acts against persons or property of military establishments."

He closed the book and with eyes as sharp as pressure flaked stone, said, "Any individuals engaged in such behavior will be immediately court-martialed, as has been Major Randy Benson, who is now under arrest.

"In light of the fact that we are expecting a potentially violent demonstration this morning, all of you are restricted to quarters subject to the disposition of said event. Any who disobey that and attempt to join or engage with elements that approach this facility will be placed under arrest. Is that understood?"

He was answered by a chorus of "Yes, sir!"

"Very well. I remind you that the military forces of the United States are not a political entity. As active-duty members, you do not engage in the political sphere. And although we are based in a region that has seceded from the United States, we are in every respect loyal to the U.S. government and its Constitution. Any wavering, any act contrary to that, will be dealt with in the most severe manner."

He turned smartly and strode out the door, along with the military police. Sergeant Major Weller stood stock still, his eyes searching for any indication of disobedience. Finally, he said, "As you were," and followed the others outside.

A stunned silence pervaded the barracks. Few comments were exchanged, and there were looks of apprehension. There was an informer amongst them, and that alone muted conversation. But more than a few thought that a debacle had been prevented before they fell subject to the code and the charge of treason—and imprisonment for most of their lives.

CHAPTER 24

CHOPPER DOWN

The demonstrators milled about in the early dawn hours, congregating around two tables with donuts and several coffee urns. There was some laughter, and a thoroughly outfitted man, larger than most, offered a bawdy remark. But being Sunday, the Lord's Day, and with women about, others gave him a look of rebuke.

A considerable number of the militia carried their weaponry slung over their backs or held muzzle down. Small cliques gathered around those men showing off pieces altered so that they were capable of continuous fire. Those individuals had banana clips and dozens of rounds.

Pastor McNally drove his Land Rover to a vacant place off the road and looked to the assemblage. His son, seventeen-year-old Bastogne, said, "Do you think any active duty soldiers will be here?"

"No, I don't think so," said McNally, but he was concerned at seeing so many weapons.

He and his son stepped out of the Land Rover into the wet, foggy morning. Dampness pervaded everything; McNally wiped his bifocals. He turned to Bastogne, who had slung a .22 caliber rifle over his shoulder, and said, "That stays in the truck. In fact, I want you to stay here and keep watch. And I want you to phone me the moment you see any military surveillance. I can't imagine that they don't know we are here."

"Pa, this thing is really, really important. You gotta let me march."

"I said no!" Then putting a hand on his son's shoulder he said, "We got some people here that are itching for a fight. I don't know if I can control them if things get hot. This is not a military operation, not disciplined. Understand? There are people here all ginned up who may defy me."

"But you said it's just a march, real peaceful like."

"Look, I have a mind to call the whole thing off. There's something I don't like about it. If anything happens to you, your mother will never forgive me."

Bastogne said nothing as his father crossed the field and climbed onto a table. The pastor looked at the expectant faces, mostly resolute but some apprehensive. There was a smattering of applause.

He nodded and raised a hand in acknowledgement then somberly said, "Ladies and gentlemen, I welcome you. On this, God's holy day, we will show our commitment to our nation, our people, and the Christian values that guide us."

There were shouts of approval, but he raised a hand to silence them. "Now I see that many of you are armed, and like the Minute Men of ages ago, many of you are willing to shed blood in honor of this cause. But I ask you, in the name of the Lord, to respect this day by returning your weapons to your vehicles. There is absolutely nobody we want to fire upon. Indeed, no one we dare fire upon."

There were boos and derisive remarks, one shouting, "Take the fort! Take the fort!"

"You must understand," McNally beseeched over the tumult. "We will be approaching one of the most powerful military forts in the U.S. arsenal. Violence on our part can be, will be, met with unparalleled response. All we can do is conduct a peaceful demonstration indicating our commitment to the NCRA."

"It's time to march!" shouted one.

"Enough talk, let's get it done," enjoined another.

"Let us first pray," said the pastor, outstretching his arms. A few bowed their heads, but the march had already begun.

"You are still the leader," said a woman carrying a Confederate flag. "So, you better get in front. Just in case."

"I guess so," McNally replied. He had to scurry in an undignified manner to catch up and worm his way through to the foreground.

Fifteen minutes after their departure, a lanky, red-haired youth stopped in front of Bastogne, who was sitting on the driver's seat of the Land Rover, door open, radio blaring.

"How long they been gone?" asked the kid, hands on knees, breathless from running.

"Not long. You can catch up. What caliber is that?" Bastogne asked, looking curiously at the M14 rifle slung over the youth's shoulders.

"Fires a NATO cartridge, 7.62. But I left off the scope. Don't need it, I shoot pretty good," he said, unslinging the weapon.

"You really intend to shoot it? I mean kill someone, a soldier?" asked Bastogne, lighting a cigarette now that his father was away.

"If I have to. This is war, right? Why aren't you marching?"

"Pa told me to stay and keep watch."

"Hell man, this is like, um, Bull Run, or Shiloh. My great, great, great-grandaddy was at Dunker's Church at Shiloh, shootin' blue bellies. I recon he'll be proud of me today. You should go with me." He stopped and in a quieter voice said, "In case either of us get hurt."

"I'll ponder it. You go now, good luck."

"Yep, gonna see the elephant. That's what they said back in the War of Northern Aggression. Yessirree, gonna see the elephant!"

*****

Washington D.C.

"Madam President, it's on! The Cabinet is in the Situation Room waiting for you," said Iris.

"Okay, please turn it up," said Edith Barnes when she came in.

"There are two networks reporting," said Alexander Petrovich, Secretary of Homeland Security. "One is *Freedom America* and the other is CBN at Fort Benning. Von Hoffmann is with the march, and Tonia Bannister is inside. She should be on any second."

"Breaking News!" flashed on the screen, then there appeared the face of a young female reporter wearing a sweatshirt with the letters "CBN." Behind her was a flurry of military activity.

"I have just spoken with Captain Dennis Kellogg, the fort's information officer," said Bannister. "He has told me a sizable number of demonstrators are approaching the fort. A drone was sent aloft about an hour ago, and images indicate that hundreds, perhaps a thousands people, have begun the march and others have joined since it started. And although many, including children, are carrying flags and placards, others are armed."

"Do we know who authorized this?" asked Barnes.

"No, Madam President," replied General McRae. "I took the liberty of calling the NCRA spokeswoman, Janice Whitinghill, and she told me that it appeared completely spontaneous. However, somebody within the NCRA may have been in touch with people inside the fort. She claims that Lee and the top echelon had nothing to do with this, but I think she's hedging."

Edith Barnes turned her attention back to the screen as Bannister said, "Captain Kellogg has some important details to relate."

"Thank you, Miss Bannister," said the captain. "Apparently, there are a small number of troops who harbor NCRA sympathies on this post. Allegedly, they were attempting to foment a rebellion that would possibly have resulted in the surrender of this facility to the secessionist regime. That effort failed. Those who were involved are currently restricted to quarters pending an investigation. I will also report that Major Randy Benson, presumably the ring leader, is under arrest and everything within the post is operating as required."

"That's a goddamn relief!" said General McRae. "But we're going to throw the book at Benson and the others involved in this stunt."

Captain Kellogg handed the mic back to the CBN anchor. Turning toward a helicopter pad, she said, "At this time, we can see one of the army's Apache AH-64s lifting off. I have been informed that the crew's mission is to monitor the march and order it to disperse if it approaches within a quarter mile of the fort. We will keep you informed as the situation develops."

The President and Cabinet members turned toward another screen, in which Von Hoffmann was filming the march. People wearing red NCRA caps gleefully passed before the camera, many displaying weapons. One man carried an NCRA flag and another beat a tattoo on a drum while his companion blew on a fife, an obvious reference to the patriots of 1775.

Von Hoffmann approached one marcher and, thrusting a mic toward him, demanded, "What is your objective today?"

"Nothing less than the complete overthrow of the leadership of the fort and its rightful occupation by the NCRA!"

"That will require an enormous amount of support from within," replied Von Hoffmann. "Do you realistically think you have that?"

"I firmly believe that upon seeing us, the gates will be thrown open by the MPs themselves."

"But what happens if you run into opposition? After all, there are thousands of troops there."

The man pointed to the crowd marching behind him. "So what? They're gonna shoot into this group of patriots? I don't think so!"

The Toyota pickup crept along a dirt road parallel to the one beside the demonstrators. The heavy machine gun secured to its bed was covered with a tarp, both to make it invisible to aircraft as well as to dispel any alarm by those on the march.

The vehicle attracted little attention as the driver found a clearing beside a clump of trees. Two men slid out of the cab, while a third kept the engine running.

From a mile away, the chop, chop, chop of a helicopter was heard. The crowd turned their eyes skyward as the aircraft drew closer. At two hundred feet, it made a pass over the assemblage. From the ground, the demonstrators could see the faces of the crew.

Some halted and studied the Apache, which normally brandished a thirty-millimeter cannon as well as Hydra and Hellfire laser-guided missiles. But this chopper displayed none of that.

The craft hovered over the people below, flew away, then returned and remained in a nearly stationary hover position. A loud speaker came on and a crewman said, "We urge you to disband and not approach any closer to the fort. Those individuals who intended to assist you have been arrested. To avoid harm, please disperse now."

Numerous people looked at one another and someone said, "Who inside the fort was going to assist us? Nobody told us about that!"

While several dozen marchers wavered, others raised their fists in the air and boldly continued, some forming up in columns of four. One man with a bullhorn encouraged the marchers to ignore the threat. Others made a show of unslinging their weapons and waving them aloft.

Unseen by the crew of the circling chopper was the Toyota. As the helicopter banked away, the men pulled the tarp off the machine gun.

Turning again, the Apache was buzzing over the crowd when the .50 caliber erupted, its shells ripping into the cockpit. There was a burst of flame and black smoke as the craft began to spin out of control. It rose fifty feet, then plummeted into a field. Rotors tore into the ground, then there was an enormous explosion. Debris flew in all directions, some pieces pinwheeling into horrified marchers. Grass caught fire and a great pall of smoke rose in the morning sky.

People stared in disbelief. Some cheered, others screamed, while still others ran toward the wreck.

The driver of the Toyota revved the engine while the gunners stood proudly beside their weapon. One snatched a Confederate flag from the truck bed and waved it back and forth. A few people shouted, "Way to go! You brought down the bastards!" But others stared at the wreckage of the Apache in disbelief.

"Those goddamn sons of bitches!" roared General McRae. He pulled out his cell phone and looked for the number of the fort's commanding general.

Soon the other TV screen showed another Apache helicopter departing the fort at high speed.

All eyes were on the screen as Von Hoffmann, stunned by the crash, announced, "Oh my God! The chopper is fully engulfed. I doubt there are any survivors. This was supposed to be a peaceful. . ."

The camera panned upward as the second Apache pivoted, dipped its nose, and fired a Hydra missile at the Toyota as its driver attempted to speed down the dirt road. The ensuing explosion threw parts of the Toyota forty feet into the air. A huge smoking crater was all that was left of that part of the road, and the headless torso of one of the gunners was impaled on a tree branch nearby.

Pandemonium erupted as hundreds ran, most throwing down their placards and flags.

Skimming over an empty field beside the road, the Apache emitted a burst of machine gun fire. Clouds of dust rose then descended upon the crowd as they fled in panic. There was no longer need to instruct civilians. Those still retaining weapons quickly slung them over their shoulders. Many raised their hands in surrender as a third chopper menacingly approached.

An ambulance, fire engines, and three armed Humvees tore down the road. Sirens wailed and people ran for their lives.

Tonia Bannister had hitched a ride on one of the Humvees and was now on the screen again. Her camera crew panned over the fleeing crowd and focused on Von Hoffmann, who was vainly attempting to speak to several of the marchers. Frustrated by their unwillingness to stop, he began rounding up his people and stowing his equipment.

Tonia's camera then focused on one of the circling Apaches, which seemed to be monitoring the movement of frightened men and women.

The Humvees drew to within fifty yards of the flaming chopper. The CBN crew filmed foam dousing the flames and the ambulance closing on the wreck. A medical team emerged from one of the vehicles as black smoke rose into the morning sky.

"What a terrible tragedy," said the reporter. "We will attempt to get the names of the crew members once their families have been contacted by military authorities."

The camera panned the scorched field, then focused on a man coming toward them. He had been wearing a stained slouch hat which he'd removed. Observing the smoldering remains, he bowed his head and appeared to offer a prayer.

Tonia approached him, introduced herself and said, "Sir, were you a member of the demonstration?"

He nodded silently.

"Can you tell us how you got involved, what you saw?"

He stared into the camera, his face pallid. "I was the leader of the march. I told them that it was to be peaceful, a show of determination, an objection to U.S. forces on NCRA soil. But not this. I am so terribly sorry."

"Have you any idea of who did this? Murdered these American soldiers?"

He shook his head. "I never saw or spoke to the people responsible for this. I would have immediately banned them from the march. But I will find out who they were, so help me God. We believe our movement to be righteous, but it doesn't include this. This is murder."

Trevor McNally again bowed his head, mouthed a few words, and made the sign of the cross. He then turned and ponderously walked away.

The TV was turned off and the President leaned back in her chair. Iris entered and handed her a slip of paper. Edith thanked her and Iris left the room. Members of the Cabinet looked at their Commander in Chief.

"According to the speakers of the House and Senate, the matter we have just witnessed will be at the top of the list of on tomorrow's agenda. I will be meeting with them before I make an address to the nation, and I will insist that it be carried on all NCRA stations."

"Madam President," said Petrovich, "There will be many in both houses who will call for a military response."

Edith Barnes considered the suggestion then said, "I had previously ignored that possibility."

"And now?" asked General McRae.

"Nothing is off the table."

CHAPTER 25

A MATTER OF DIPLOMACY

Montgomery, Alabama

"Palmer, get your ass in here!" bellowed President Lee. Stanley Palmer entered Lee's office and was chagrinned to see Ralph Prescott, Goodwin, and Janice already there.

His face drawn and more dour than usual, he sat defiantly in a straight-backed chair. Ted Bender, Secretary of Transportation, came in and stood, arms crossed, against the wall.

"Pastor McNally called me ten minutes ago, apologizing for this fuck up and his role in it," said Lee. "He *told* me it was all your idea. You sure as hell didn't run it by me, and you know exactly what I would have said. Now we're really in the crapper. The entire world watched that chopper burn, the crew reduced to charred corpses."

"I knew nothing about the men in the Toyota! Neither did McNally, and Benson assured me that Benning was in the bag!" responded Palmer.

President Lee took a deep breath and said, "You actually thought that a handful of disaffected troops would take over the fort? Are you out of your mind? I should fire you this instant!"

Palmer glared at everyone in the room. "Go ahead, do it. Just do it! You're a fucking pansy. You make the pretty speeches, look presidential, but I'm the only one with balls! The people look to me for guidance, for true grit. I'm the one who makes things happen. So what if a chopper got creamed? They're the *enemy*, in case you forgot. What happened is only the beginning. I demand that we call up millions of our patriots! Run the bastards out of our country! We are supposed to be a sovereign nation, and we should damn well act like it!"

"You are really insane, aren't you?" said Janice somberly. Turning to Lee, she said, "Did you see the U.S. joint session on TV? Did you see what they're demanding? Palmer talks about an uprising of millions. Well, millions are on the verge of starvation. Their money is worthless. They're scared, Mr. President, and there are riots in the streets. You're reaping the whirlwind. All of you!"

"That's enough, babe," said Goodwin. "It's not going to do us any good to fracture. We still have a stake in the game."

"No! You find someone else to speak for this circus. I'm not making any more excuses for murder and stupidity. I'm out of here!"

Janice launched herself off the sofa, grabbed her purse and, turning to Goodwin said, "And mister, you have some explaining to do."

"You're still coming with me to D.C. for the meeting, aren't you?" asked Goodwin.

"I'll have to think about it," she said, slamming the door behind her.

Lee gave Goodwin a curious look. "Something I should know about?"

"Not a thing. Sometimes women can be a pain in the ass."

"I expect she'll probably come back when she remembers her place," said Lee.

Prescott simply shook his head and said, "Mr. President, you better start thinking of what to say to Edith Barnes before there's an air strike and a visit from the 82nd Airborne."

"Got that right," said Bender.

"So, what the hell am I supposed to do? What do I say to Barnes when she reads me the Riot Act? Do I say we're culpable and will pay damages? Will she accept anything less than total surrender? And what do I say to our nation?"

"Forget Barnes," said Goodwin. "There's nothing other than surrender that will appease her. Make an address to the nation. Say that we have no intention of challenging the U.S. or any of their forts and we regret the deaths of the troops. But look presidential. Say that we'll offer compensation for the families. Look strong, not contrite. Remember, you're talking to a hundred million of our people."

"A hundred million of devout and loyal citizens. That's firepower!" said Palmer.

"We can do nothing militarily, nothing!" shouted Lee, slamming his fist on his desk. "What you saw on TV, that Toyota being incinerated, is exactly what can happen to us! I was in the Army. I know what an armor division can do. Don't bullshit me, Palmer. We're living at the mercy of the United States. And that's the damn truth!"

"Besides that," said Prescott, "There are rumblings in some of our states, Mr. President."

"Yeah, we're taking on water. But it ain't over till the fat lady sings," said Lee. "And I sure as hell don't hear an operatic voice. At least not yet."

Grady Pratt, an aide and Lee's nephew, stuck his head in and said, "Mr. President, you might want to turn on the TV. The U.S. Congress is finishing its debate."

Lee reached for the remote and they all peered at the screen. CBN was on and the announcer said, "The senior senator of New Mexico, Peter Eagleclaw, is at the podium."

His deeply lined face tense, a thick braid of white hair falling over one shoulder, the Navajo, in a slightly accented cadence, began, "What we have witnessed is a travesty. Even though it might have been perpetrated by a few individuals, it represents a mentality that pervades the government of the NCRA. I ask, how many others in the secessionist states may be planning similar acts?"

He paused, looked into the camera, and said, "We have not yet heard a word of compassion or apology by that government. There are those in the United States who have expressed sympathy for NCRA citizens who have suffered hunger and other deprivations. But I have little sympathy for them now. What I do have is fury."

The anchor came on and said, "That appears to be the general attitude of every congressional member we have spoken to. But now we wish to turn our attention to a developing situation in Mobile, Alabama. Our reporter on the scene is Joshua Reems. Joshua, can you hear me over the disturbance?"

"Yes, Lisa. There is quite a commotion here. In fact, a riot, as hundreds are breaking into supermarkets in search of food and other necessities. Many are carrying signs demanding relief by the NCRA government, but others are calling for the end of the regime.

"Police are out in force, but we can see fires starting as the looting continues. This movement appears to have legs, and it may become a real threat to the government's leadership and longevity."

"Shit!" said Stanley Palmer. Looking for somebody else to take the heat, he turned to Ralph Prescott and said, "You're the agriculture guy. Why haven't you done anything about shortages?"

"I have begun food distribution, but we've been dealt a bad blow. You know that. I can't control the weather, and between the Godawful heat and floods, well. . ."

"Enough!" snapped Lee. "Prescott, find what supplies you can and send them to Mobile. Police batons are not going to stop hunger. Get it done!"

*****

Washington D.C.

Steven stood at the open door of the Oval Office and waited until President Barnes motioned him to enter. She pointed to the sofa and he sat. General McRae nodded, then said, "As we have seen, Madam President, Jeff Lee said nothing in his address that is at all conciliatory. Nothing has changed. What I have in mind is a fast, overwhelming attack."

"I have increased sanctions against the NCRA," said the President, thinking that the conversation was *déjà vu*. But McRae seemed determined and she decided to hear him out.

"A quick in and out decapitation and it's over."

Edith Barnes took a deep breath and said, "I hope this isn't in motion, General. I didn't and don't authorize it, and if it's begun you will abort it immediately."

The general leaned back in his chair, folded his hands and declined to use his John Wayne accent. "I will not allow a strike without your permission. You can be assured of that. And I realize your concerns, but let's take the historical view of what happens when dictators are not confronted. If somebody had eliminated Napoleon, Europe would have been spared twenty years of war. If Wilhelm of Germany had been assassinated, there would have been no World War I. The same with Hitler in 1936. Lee is a fascist and a dictator.

Eliminate him and the whole thing collapses. No need for more sanctions, it's as simple as that."

The President shook her head. "General, this nation does not engage in assassinations."

"I beg to differ with you, Madam President. It was common policy during Vietnam and, if you recall, General Soleimani of Iran was taken out by a drone. And surely you know that the U.S. overthrew numerous governments, starting with Hawaii in the 1890s. We're rather good at it."

"But can you demonstrate that good came from those interventions? Historically, most of our fiscal debt is a direct result of prioritizing military spending over any and all other considerations, including our responsibilities to citizens. My answer remains the same. No, remove Lee and others will take his place. The NCRA is a Medusa with many heads, starting with Goodwin."

McRae contemplated her remark then said, "We are at war. The nation has been split asunder, and we have the strongest military in the world. If I cannot use the forces at my command, I will tender my resignation."

It was Barnes' time to lean back in her chair. "We do not see things in the same way, General. I am attempting to bring down the secessionists as peacefully as possible. You are in favor of bloodshed. And that will not stop with a single assassination. Everybody in the world will know who killed Lee. He is a traitor, and eventually his government will fall. He and his ilk will be prosecuted in a court of law. I respect you and your service to the nation. So, if you will abide by my orders as Commander in Chief, I will decline your resignation."

"So what am I to do?"

"Let this play out, give it time. The NCRA is on its last leg. But if it raises arms, initiates an attack against the United

States, then I will remove your leash. Until then you will hang fire. I think that is the expression. That is all, General."

"Yes, Madam President. I'm at your command."

The general stood, made a short bow, and exited the office.

Edith Barnes took a deep breath and said, "I'm glad you came, Steven, we have to talk. I need your opinion on a number of matters. Was I right with McRae?"

"Yes, his attack would have resulted in a great deal of bloodshed. I believe you did the right thing."

"Thank you. What more do we know about terrorist actions?"

"There's a cell consisting of U.S. citizens. They're highly capable of creating mayhem. It's led by a graduate student and former soldier who has been studying at the University of Maryland. Unfortunately, I believe my daughter is with him."

"Oh no! I'm sorry to hear that. Do we have any idea where they are?"

"No. I've tried calling her, but I'm sure she's discarded her phone. She probably has a burner. They could be anywhere."

"What about Janice? I presume you can still get in touch with her."

"We have discussed our daughter, but she doesn't know any more than I do. It's all pretty worrisome. We have an APB out for them in the U.S., but we have no way of intercepting them in the NCRA."

"James Goodwin requested a meeting with me this afternoon. I gave him permission to come to Washington."

"What does he want?"

"He said he's an emissary for Mr. Lee. They suspect that we're planning a military operation, and they want reassurance that we're not. I told him that I will have somebody speak with him."

There was a knock on the door, and Iris entered. "That horrible man just called from the Hilton. He is insisting on having an audience with you."

Edith Barnes readjusted her oversize glasses and said, "Goodwin said that?"

Iris put her hands on her hips and said, "That's right. He sounds as agitated as if he just fell out of a plane. I think that Nazi man Palmer is with him, too."

"Phone Goodwin and tell him that I'm in a meeting with the Danish ambassador. I'll send someone to speak with him shortly."

Iris left the Oval Office. Barnes turned to Steven and said, "I have an unpleasant task for you. I have no desire to speak with him directly, nor do I want him to think that he can merely call and have a meeting with the President or even the Vice President of the United States."

"So, the pleasure becomes mine."

"Regrettably, yes. Hear him out, assure him that there is no attack immediately pending. But let him know that Congress is putting pressure on me, so any show of international violence by the NCRA will be met by answering force."

"Besides the fact that they have committed treason, is there anything else you want me to communicate?"

"No, but Director, do be diplomatic if you can."

"Of course. I am a very understanding person."

"Oh, do try."

She smiled sweetly, thought for a moment then said, "I gave permission for your wife to be with him so you might have a chance to speak with her in person. If so, ask her if she's learned anything about that cell and your daughter."

*****

The conference room was, to Goodwin's chagrin, small. It lacked the dignity of proportion that befitted his office. Nor did he expect to see the FBI director, along with Eli Barett, when they entered the room. Both men looked at Goodwin and Stanley Palmer but refused to offer their hands. The new arrivals remained standing while Steven and Eli sat at a round table, coffees in hand.

"I was expecting to be invited to the White House to meet with your president," said Goodwin stiffly.

"*The* president," corrected Steven.

"*My* president is Mr. Jefferson Calhoun Lee," replied Goodwin. "But regardless, we came here on official business regarding the NCRA military establishment."

"You don't have a military establishment," said Eli.

Palmer glared at him and said, "We want the truth. Our intelligence network has learned of a potential assassination of our highest leadership. I wish to warn you that—"

"That's enough," said Steven. "The United States is not considering any such action. Not now, not in the future."

"Well, that is reassuring," said Goodwin.

"On the other hand, any further actions against U.S. facilities will be met with extreme measures."

"That would not be a wise. . ."

The door opened and Janice walked in. "Oh, I didn't know that. . ."

She stared at Steven and said, "So sorry, I will leave you all to. . ."

"That's not necessary, my dear," said Goodwin. "Please do stay; we're nearly finished here."

"I don't think so," said Steven. Turning from Goodwin, Steven asked Janice, "Have you heard from Evelyn?"

"No, have you?"

"I haven't, and we don't know where she is."

"Is there something I'm missing, my dear?" said Goodwin, rising to his feet.

"Besides a situation concerning my daughter? Yes, the matter of you and my wife," interjected Steven.

"That hardly concerns you. She's with me and—"

The first blow to Goodwin's face was hard. Blood spurted as the second one slammed into his stomach. He bowled over as Steven's knee came up under his chin.

"Steven!" Janice screamed as Goodwin toppled against the wall.

Another blow was stopped when Eli said, "Enough Steven, enough," and pulled the director away.

"You've nearly killed him," said Janice, as she knelt beside Goodwin.

"Oh, he's far from dead," said her husband. He glared at her and said, "For a while, I thought there might be something between us, but I guess I'm wrong. You can fuck him all you want, lady, but he's going to prison. And so are you."

"You can't mean that! You told me—"

"I think we're done with diplomacy." He turned, slamming the door behind him.

CHAPTER 26

THIN ICE

Montgomery, Alabama

James Goodwin was still tending to his nose when he and Janice entered the mansion. He flopped down on the parlor sofa and dabbed at his nose with a fresh handkerchief.

"The bastard. The fucking bastard," he said, as Janice handed his bloody jacket to the maid.

"Victoria, please take this to the dry cleaners today. Make sure they remove all the stains."

"Yes, Mrs. Whitinghill," said Victoria, attempting to hide the smirk on her face.

"What time will I be seeing the doctor?" Goodwin asked.

"Tomorrow at ten. I told him that you had an auto accident and described the damage. He said there may be surgery involved."

"He can't see me today?"

"I asked the receptionist but she said he's booked."

"Damn, I can't go out in public like this. Get me a mirror, will you? I don't want to get off this couch."

He looked at his crooked nose and shook his head. "I'm going to get him. That's a given."

Janice sat down beside him and said, "We'll get your nose fixed. You don't want to tangle with him. He's younger, an excellent marksman and a black belt in karate. I've seen him in the dojo and he's relentless. He will kill you, James, and if he doesn't, Eli will."

"Not Eli."

"Why not?"

Goodwin just shook his head. "Because."

"Are you and Eli friends? Tell me."

"We went to school together; we're sort of chums."

"But he's Steven's best friend. He is my friend, too. Why hasn't he ever mentioned knowing you?"

Goodwin attempted to laugh, but it came out as a sneer. He moaned and laid the handkerchief gently upon his nose. She reached for his hand and he said, "Nothing's as it appears. You don't know him, neither does your husband. Only I do."

"It must be quite a secret."

"Mmm." He gave her a wink and said, "It is, darling. A very deep one, too."

"I see," she said, knowing that he wouldn't reveal any more.

There was a moment of silence. Finally, he said, "Have you heard any more about the divorce papers? It's been nearly a year; you should have heard from the attorney by now."

"I did. He told me that I could only serve papers in the United States. There's nothing I can do from here."

"How long have you known that?"

"A while."

"And you said nothing to me. I've tried to be good to you, Janice. You know how I feel about you, but now, well, I'm beginning to have my doubts. I think you and Steven are doing something behind my back."

"There's nothing happening."

"You've been talking to him, haven't you?"

"Only about Evelyn. She's gone missing."

"I think there's more."

Victoria returned and said, "I have to do grocery shopping. So, I'll be gone for a while."

"That's fine, Victoria. I thank you for your efforts."

"I'm thinking of getting rid of her," Goodwin said after the maid left. "She's getting too uppity. I like it when people know their place."

"What place is that?"

"She's a servant, a Mexican. Probably snuck across the Rio Grande. And she's been taking liberties, addressing me as 'James.' She calls you Mrs. Whitinghill."

"Should she call you Mr. Goodwin?"

"Damn right. And I don't like hearing 'Mrs. Whitinghill.'"

"I'm not Mrs. Goodwin, James."

"And never will be, huh?"

Janice remained silent then said, "Steven said that we're going to prison. Do you think we are?"

"We're not going to any prison, and he knows that. As a matter of fact, I might sue him in a U.S. court. He assaulted me, after all."

"They won't let you back in, James. You won't have a chance of getting to a court. He'll have you arrested and charged with treason."

"You're treading on thin ice, my dear. And thin ice can be very unstable."

*****

All the governors sat at a long rectangular table on the Capitol's second floor. There was none of the usual banter, no back slapping or jokes. Nor were there any of the alcoholic beverages so often in abundance at state gatherings.

President Lee, flanked by James Goodwin, started the meeting by asking a clergyman to offer a prayer. That was followed by the pledge of allegiance to the NCRA.

"You may be seated," he said with unaccustomed solemnity. "I welcome you all to this emergency meeting. Aside from the question of lawlessness, financial distress or a military invasion, the matter of extreme hunger is the most ominous disaster facing the NCRA. I am reluctant to attribute it on climate change, but the inability to get relief from the United States or Canada requires significant action on the part of our government."

"Climate change is affecting the United States, too," said the governor of Tennessee.

"Maybe," said Lee, "but not like the South. And any shortage on the east or west coasts can be supplanted with imports. We are at a great disadvantage. I know that some of our states are already rationing food, but we must be more judicious as to what communities receive it."

Glances shot across the room. Several governors stiffened while others nodded their heads.

"Think of triage, gentlemen," said Lee. "We are in a desperate situation, not unlike war. There are always casualties in combat, and the physicians must determine who will benefit most from life-saving efforts. And you know which communities must survive."

"Please correct me if I am misreading you," said Telly Bradshaw of North Carolina. "But are you implying that certain members of our citizenry should be provided with relief while others are denied?"

"Essentially, yes. Enumerated in our Constitution is that this nation is beholden to its white citizenry, since they are the ones whose ancestors founded a new nation independent of monarchies. By that I mean its Christian Anglo-Saxon citizenry. I'm not implying that others should outright starve, but in this nation our kind comes first. That concept is at the very core of our beliefs.”

There was dead silence around the room.

“So, exactly how are you going to implement this?” asked Bradshaw.

“It will be done with the utmost discretion. We cannot appear to show favoritism. The operating word is ‘appear,” said Lee. “TV coverage must show food being given to thankful minorities. But, actually, the bulk of the supplies will be ferried to core communities using the utmost secrecy.”

Governor Gordon looked around the room, then heaved a sigh. “Oh, come now, gentlemen,” he said, “don’t pretend we haven’t all been favoring our core constituents already, because we have. No virgins here, so stop acting like you have qualms.”

“Word will get out,” Bradshaw countered. “I have a very large black population in my state, and I have fears of what will happen if they are denied relief. My recommendation, Mr. President, is that we shame the United States into sending us relief. I cannot imagine that people in the U.S. with family here will allow our citizens to starve for lack of food. After all, are we not all Americans? We can also appeal to foreign aid.”

“In normal times, that would be reasonable thinking, Governor. But these are not normal times. There are shortages and droughts all over the world. And foreign aid will be discouraged by Edith Barnes. She’s a devil and will allow starvation if it will bring down our government. So, whether you agree or not, we will proceed. And I strongly suggest that you prepare for whatever opposition arises. In other words, arm your police and militias with everything you can find.”

*****

Four days later, Iris poked her head into the Oval Office and said, "Line four, Governor of North Carolina."

"Madam President," said Governor Bradshaw, "I'm sorry to intrude on your day, but I wish to convey something very significant in our relationship with the United States."

"I'm listening, Governor."

"I have been in close communication with my cabinet and legislature, as well as with Governor Stanford of Virginia. We have both polled a very large number of citizens in our respective states. And we have become increasingly concerned about rising tensions within the NCRA and some of the dangerous plans President Lee has recently instituted."

"We are aware of them. Is there something in particular you care to tell me?"

"There is. We wish to engage in exploratory talks regarding a return to the Union. Our states are facing a desperate situation, and we know that there will be no relief from your government as long as we are members of the NCRA. So, I and Governor Stanford wish to know what penalties we, that is, our citizens, will be facing? And, upon pledging our allegiance to the United States, how soon might assistance be forthcoming?"

"Governor, I can assure you that most people within your state and that of Virginia will not be prosecuted. However, it's a matter for the justice department to consider legal action against you, Governor Bradford, and any other officials who have committed treasonable actions. And Congress will likely require your resignation."

"For the sake of my citizens I will accede to that, and I will ask my cabinet to do the same."

"That is a wise decision. Regarding aid, I believe it will begin as soon as the majority of your population pledges its allegiance to the United States and the Constitution."

"Not ten percent, like after the Civil War?"

"Different times, Governor. Now women have the vote. "

"Yes, I guess so."

He paused, then said, "I hesitate to admit it, but the discord of the times, the excitement of creating a new nation, was intoxicating. Many of us were blinded by the rhetoric, the charisma of Mr. Lee, and the revisionist appeal of the old Confederacy. I and many of my colleagues failed to consider the scope and inequities of the NCRA's creed. In that regard, I am complicit and, in fact, terribly embarrassed."

"Sometimes people and societies, usually rational, can be persuaded to do irrational things, Governor. I encourage you to obtain the signatures of your citizens and then appeal to the Congress of the United States for readmission to the Union. I am pleased with your forthrightness and desire to restore the blessings of liberty to your people."

"Thank you. We will move with alacrity."

"I think we can issue a joint statement once the citizens of Virginia and North Carolina agree to rejoin the United States."

*****

"I don't believe it!" bellowed Lee upon seeing the two governors standing beside Edith Barnes during her speech before a joint session of Congress.

"It was food distribution that tipped the scale," said James Goodwin. "They were pretty worried; you could tell that they weren't with the program."

"Then why didn't they call me? We could have suspended the program in his state! They're hypocrites! How many other states are going to secede?" demanded Lee.

"I haven't heard anything about the others."

There was silence as Goodwin dwelt on the growing rift between himself and Janice.

"I want to be able to count on people," said Lee after several moments. "And that includes you, James. I know that you've got other irons in the fire, and I know that you're pretty lukewarm regarding the Christian values I believe in. So, you gonna bail?"

Picking at a hangnail, Goodwin glanced up, grinned, and said, "And go where?"

"Why, anywhere. You could take off to Jakarta, Argentina, Bali, anywhere you want."

"There might be a problem with the feds. Lots of countries have reciprocity treaties with the U.S. Of course, there are less conspicuous hideouts."

"So, what's your game plan, James? What are you up to? You and Palmer."

"I think that each of us are into things we'd rather not talk about."

"So you say. Just give me a heads-up if you decide on a long distance flight."

CHAPTER 27

THE PARTY

Washington, D.C.

The birthday party for Alexander Petrovich was supposed to be a low-key affair, but nothing about the flamboyant and corpulent secretary of Homeland Security was ever subdued. Over four hundred members of Congress, the CIA, FBI and Office of Management and Budget flooded the Hilton.

Unannounced, but anticipated, was President Barnes. Upon seeing her, Petrovich fairly danced toward her and was about to give her a bear hug when she said, "Alexander, all you get is a peck on the cheek."

He laughed uproariously. Iris put her hands on her hips and said, "Petro, you behave now in front of all these people."

Petrovich gasped, appearing seriously admonished.

"Now that we got through that, happy birthday, Alexander," said the president. "So, let's see who came to your party."

She accepted a glass of champagne from a waiter and said, "I feel absolutely devilish this evening."

"Why's that?" asked Petrovich, hoping that he and Edith Barnes might slip away from the Secret Service for a nightcap later. But that was highly unlikely, and of course there would be Iris, the ever-present sidekick.

"Why do you ask? After all, since FAX News reported the reuniting of Virginia and North Carolina, my ratings are off the charts. Even FAX News admitted that. Grudgingly."

"You ought to send them a bouquet of flowers," said Petrovich.

"What a splendid idea. You are such a charming and sagacious man. Who knows, Alexander, maybe we'll make a wonderful couple someday."

"Uh-huh," said Iris. "Three days before the world ends."

"Great party," said Eli, as he and Steven filled their plates with *hors d'oeuvres*. His eyes followed an attractive young lady holding a tray of champagne.

"See," said Eli, "lovely. Maybe you can talk her up. She smiled at you."

"She's required to smile at everyone. Besides, I'm not in the market," replied Steven, his eyes picking out others from the department interspersed throughout the crowd.

"Sure, you're happily married."

"Yeah, happily married," he said glumly. "Well, let's mingle. There's bound to be some lady here who will make gooey eyes at you."

A band struck up a few notes of "Hail to the Chief" before switching to a slow Frank Sinatra melody, and a few couples took to the dance floor.

From twenty feet away, a svelte woman of about forty said, "Eli, is that you?"

He turned and saw an astonishingly beautiful woman, who waved her hand and walked towards him. He offered a smile and a quick glance at Steven as if to say, "Who is she?"

"Eli Barett, it is you, isn't it?"

"Yes, I'm Eli. I . . ."

"Surely you recognize me."

He gazed at her blankly and she said, "Silly, it's Julie. Surely I don't look that different."

"Oh my God, of course! Please forgive me. It's been so long! But you look ravishing. How have you been? Are you visiting Washington?"

"I'm fine. Single again. I work for OMB and heard about the party. A lot of our people are here. Won't miss free food and champagne. You know, Eli, I often thought about all the wonderful times we had together."

"So have I. Yeah, they were great."

She gave him a long, appraising look, then said, "I tried phoning you a half dozen times. I didn't know what happened to you and I was terribly worried. But each time I called the message said 'no such number.'"

Embarrassed, he stared at the floor, then looked up at her. "I owe you an apology, Julie. I joined the FBI, was accepted, and was terribly focused on training. Regretfully, everything and everyone dropped from my life. And I was three thousand miles away. I know that's a lousy excuse, but at the time I was in a different galaxy. I did consider calling but really didn't know what to say. I guess I should have tried again, but work came up and. . ."

He gave a sad, lopsided grin and once again, mumbled the word, "Sorry."

She stared at him for an interminable moment. "Okay, if you say so. I would have understood, Eli. But we were pretty close."

"I know. But we move on, don't we?"

"Sure, but it would have been nice."

He nodded, not knowing what else he could possibly add. Julie gave the briefest of smiles, turned, found her old friend Iris, and melted into the crowd. Iris brought her to the President, and soon they were in an animated conversation.

"I can't believe you didn't recognize her," said Steven as they each picked up another glass of champagne.

"It's been twenty years, and she looks different. She really took me by surprise."

"The woman is a knockout, and she said she's single. That's an invitation if ever I heard one! Why didn't you go for it? Hell, if I were single, I wouldn't let her out of my sight."

"It would probably end up in marriage, and I'm not very good at that. The last one crashed, and I don't want to hurt a woman again. A roll in the hay, a date here and there, that's all I need."

"Sounds a bit thin, Eli. Maybe a few more apologies and she'll consent to seeing you. I mean, you two supposedly had such a great time."

Eli look dispirited, sighed and said, "Look, she kind of took the wind out of my sails. This is a nice party, but I don't care to stay. I'll grab a taxi. You stay. Lots of nice looking women
here. Maybe hit up Julie."

*****

Iris's phone rang at seven in the morning. "Hi, lady, it's Steven at the Bureau."

"Steven who? What Bureau?"

"Give me a break, Iris. I wouldn't disturb your beauty sleep if it wasn't important."

"I bet. Mr. Director, I haven't had my coffee and it's too damn early for anything serious. But what's on your mind? Anything the President needs to know? A thermo-nuclear blast in Vegas, a purse snatching?"

"Iris. . ."

"Uh-huh. You gonna sweet talk me now?"

"Won't get to first base. It's about last night."

"Oh, that bit with Eli and Julie. She told me about it. Weirder than my grandma's hair-do."

"I agree. I need Julie's last name and phone number. This is business, strictly business."

"Sure, sure. Got a pencil?"

"I'm putting it in my phone. We use phones now, Iris. Give it to me, will you?"

"You will tell me everything, won't you, dearest?"

"It may be classified."

"I've got a top-secret clearance. And I just love gossip."

*****

Julie met him at Cups and Company, a coffee shop on Delaware and C Street near the lower Senate Park. In a perfectly tailored business suit, she shook his hand and sat when he pulled the chair out for her.

"Iris gave me your last name and number," said Steven. "I'm glad you made time to see me."

"It was nice meeting you last night,' said Julie.

Steven ordered coffee and scones, then said, "And I saw that you met the President."

"A real honor. Of course, I was able to only because of Iris. A lot of people don't know that they've been pals since starting college."

"I never knew the details," said Steven, sipping his coffee.

"As freshmen they waited on tables together. Iris pretends to be a simple island girl, but she's sharp as a needle and can see nonsense three miles away."

"I've been on the receiving end—have the puncture marks, too."

Julia grinned then said, "And the President really amazed me. She was so charming, no airs, no egotism."

"Edith's a real human being, but she can be a loaded pistol when pissed off. Commander in Chief is a tough job."

"It must be. I wouldn't want it."

Julie paused and said, "Director, why did you want to meet? I don't know anything that can be of value to the FBI."

"In a way, you may have. It's about Special Agent Eli Barett."

Julia added some Splenda to her coffee and said, "That was the strangest encounter I've had in a very long time. It was as if he had no idea who I was. Surely I don't look so different. Maybe a few crow's feet and a pound or two more, but not the slightest recognition? Bizarre, absolutely bizarre."

"Eli doesn't speak much about women and has never mentioned you. How long were you two going together?"

"Over a year. We were damn near engaged. And that thing about calling? That... didn't jive. He was always so considerate, so caring. He would phone me two or three times a day, no matter what. He would say, 'Peach, did you like the movie last night?' Or, 'Peach, would you like pizza for lunch?'"

"He called you 'Peach'?"

"It was his favorite nickname for me. But last night Eli behaved as if he'd never seen me before. I'm really confused."

"That goes for both of us."

"Are you and Eli good friends?" asked Julie, stirring her coffee.

"We're great friends. He's a brave guy; he even saved my life once. In fact, he's a crackerjack agent and I trust him implicitly."

"But now you're questioning things?"

"I'm trying to put things in perspective. This is rather puzzling. Maybe everything he said last night is one hundred percent. But I've been in this business a long time, Julie, and I know that when my intuition waves a red flag, it does so for a reason. What I saw on Eli's face wasn't a matter of simply forgetting you. It was a matter of not knowing you to begin with."

She frowned and said, "I thought the Bureau knows everything about its employees. Surely he has been thoroughly vetted. I was, and I'm only a secretary at OMB. Of course, things, deeply personal things, may not be revealed if the right questions aren't asked."

"True. I could check his file, but I'm not sure I'd spot anything significant. Now you knew him back in the day, even though it was years ago. His family, excursions you both made, and all those things that are part of a relationship, even love, if I may say. So, since this involves an agent who knows almost every aspect of the Bureau, I'd like to ask some personal questions if you don't mind."

She nodded and said, "Intimate things?"

"Things the interviewer would not ask. If I do an investigation, I need to know things he doesn't think I know, like his relationship with you and his family."

"I assume this is a very serious matter."

"Extremely."

She paused, took a deep breath then said, "Okay. Eli was very close to his mother, and I liked her, too. But Tess had mental problems and was in and out of institutions. She's a lot better now and still lives in L.A. We correspond: Christmas and birthday cards. But back then, she was often very confused. I remember she couldn't tell Eli from his brother Tom. Okay, they were identical twins, but there were still differences. Eli eventually grew a beard so she could tell them apart."

"I didn't know Eli had a twin brother. He never mentioned him. Where does he live?"

"He doesn't, as far as anyone knows. Tom just disappeared. He used to go hiking, often alone. And one day he was suddenly gone. No one ever saw him again. In a way it was a mercy that their mother was so out of it. She barely noticed he wasn't visiting anymore."

"Was there a memorial, a family thing?"

"No, his mother was in no shape to organize anything. It was so sudden. Eli and Tom, both gone. As I said, none of my calls were ever answered."

"When did you learn that Eli was getting into the Academy?"

"Eli liked to surprise me, and he kept secrets. He didn't want to brag about things that might not pan out. So I really didn't know until Iris and I talked about old boyfriends. I mentioned Eli, and she surprised me by saying that he's in the FBI. That was about a year ago."

"And you and Eli didn't see each other again until last night?"

She nodded and said, "For years, I just thought he wanted to end our relationship and didn't know how to tell me. So he just went away. Ghosted."

"Strange. Tell me about trips together, things you both enjoyed."

"We went on a few vacations. One was to La Paz in Baja, Mexico; we spent three nights in a hotel." She grinned and said, "He told me it was the best sex he ever had. We drove around in his derelict VW and had a great time until the accident."

"What happened?"

"It started off as a great day. The water was beautiful—so clear. We went swimming, then decided to go back to the room. We had to climb onto an old dock. It was pretty dilapidated. I got up okay, but there were nails and he ripped himself pretty badly—tore his groin. Tetanus shots, stitches, and that was the end of the vacation. It was a month before he recovered."

"Can you get me his mother's address and phone number?" asked Steven, as an uncomfortable feeling welled up within him.

"I can give you the address, but she doesn't have a phone. She wouldn't know how to work a cell phone. But she is sometimes lucid, especially about things that happened a long time ago."

CHAPTER 28

THE BUREAU AND THE NOTEBOOK

Los Angeles, California

Steven got a car from the L.A. Bureau and pulled up to the curb in front of Tess's home. The sixty-year-old clapboard house was in the town of Rialto, some sixty miles from the city of Los Angeles. Turning to agent Leandra Sutter, he said, "I'm pleased that you came. This may be stressful for her, and I know you can smooth over rough edges."

"Do you want to take the lead?" Sutter asked.

"Not necessarily. You may have questions that I might not think of, so go ahead and ask. But she needn't know that Eli is in the FBI."

"That would raise a lot of questions."

"Right. And I don't want her to contact him, to let him know we've spoken to her."

There were a few potted geraniums on the porch. Weeds had grown unimpeded in the front yard, and a dog barked in the back as they mounted the steps.

"Mrs. Tess Barett?" Steven said, after the lady answered the door. He held up his I.D. and said, "FBI," and introduced himself and Agent Sutter. The woman put on her glasses, examined the badges, and said, "I guess you are who you say you are. There are so many scams these days, you don't know who to trust. But you two look official enough."

She invited them in and said, "Would you like some tea? I always have tea about this time of day."

"That would be nice," said Sutter with a sweet smile.

"Breaks the ice," she explained, when Mrs. Barett went into the kitchen.

Over tea, Steven said, "Your son Eli has come to the Bureau's attention — not in a bad way — but we do have some questions. As his mother, you might be able to answer them."

"Oh, I hope he's not in trouble," said Tess, a worried look on her face.

"No, ma'am," said Sutter. "On the contrary, he might be able to prove helpful to us."

"I'm glad to hear that. Well, I'll tell you whatever you want to know, but I haven't seen him in so many years."

"And he hasn't sent you any greeting cards or anything?" asked Steven.

The woman sadly shook her head. She let out a sigh and said, "Of course I was in the sanitarium for many months. In and out, you know. I did have a phone years ago and he might have called. But I really don't know. At least nobody told me."

"But he might have known where you were," said Sutter.

"Maybe. It's strange, because he was always so thoughtful. He did everything for me—groceries, hauling the trash, weeding the garden. I would surely like to see him again."

"May I ask," said Steven, "did he have a girlfriend?"

"Oh yes, Peach. That's what he called her. She's quite beautiful. I think they were in love. They were always together. She still sends me cards. I haven't seen her in a very long time."

"Did Peach ever ask you about him, where he might be and such?" said Sutter.

"I think she was quite worried about him. But there was nothing I could tell her. He just seemed to disappear."

"That's good to know, Tess, if I might call you that," said Sutter.

"Certainly, dear. It's nice to be able to talk to someone, especially such a nice young lady. I think you're going to do very well in the FBI."

Sutter smiled and patted Mrs. Barett on the hand.

Steven gave Sutter an "Oh, that's so sweet," look then said, "Tess, we heard that you had another son, Tom. What can you tell us about him?"

Tess sighed. "Oh, my Tommy. I don't want to besmirch his name, since he's no longer with us. He was a difficult child. He never said much, but I suspect he was sometimes in trouble with the law. Nothing serious, you understand, and he did manage to graduate from college. But he drove around in fancy cars. I never knew how he could afford them. He hung out with a young man I absolutely despised. I doubt that *he* ever got far in life." She sniffed.

"Do you remember that person's name?" asked Sutter.

The woman looked as if she were mentally flipping back pages of an old book then said, "Was it Jack? No, James. Yes, his name was James. He had a Southern accent and always bossed Tom around. I disapproved of that. Oh, I do miss Tom, none the less."

The house had the scent of having been lived in for a very long time. There was faded wallpaper and the curtains had stained over the years. All was still until Sutter said, "Is there anything here that once belonged to Eli or Tom?"

"Oh yes, indeed. I keep their room much as it was when they were little. Come, I'll show you."

They followed her into a tiny room crammed with model airplanes, cars, and framed photos.

"I even kept their cub scout uniforms," said Tess proudly as she opened a closet and removed two blue shirts and caps. "This shirt was Eli's, it has the merit badges, and this one is Tom's. Eli went on to be an eagle scout."

"How wonderful," said Sutter. Then, after showing appropriate admiration, she said, "May we borrow these caps? I promise you'll get them back. They might be quite helpful, Tess."

The woman shrugged and said, "I don't know how they might be useful, but if you promise to return them, I won't object."

The director and Sutter returned to the front room, thanked Mrs. Barett, and were about to leave when Steven asked, "What kind of car did Eli have?"

"Just an old VW. It was always breaking down, and he would take it to the garage on Tenth. That's where Tom would fix it up. He worked there, part time. I know because I used to get my hair done at a beauty shop in the nearby strip mall. I don't even know if it's still there."

They shook hands and thanked her for the tea and the cub scout caps.

"If you happen to see Eli, please have him write to me. I would like that very much."

Once back in the car, Steven said, "You did very well. Why did you ask for the caps?"

"I noticed hair inside. I don't think she washed them after they were last worn. And we know which each belonged to."

"DNA? Don't identical twins have the same DNA?"

"I read that there can be slight differences the way their sequences are expressed, and there can de detectable differences in folding. We could run a check on it. Get a sample of Eli's, too," said Sutter.

"You're damn smart," said Steven.

She grinned, fished in her purse for a lollipop and said, "Mama says I'm special."

*****

"Oh, no," said Janice, as her pen ran out of ink. She hunted through her purse and, finding no other, tossed the pen into a trash can. She then walked down the second-floor hallway to the open door of Goodwin's office.

He had told her that she was to stay out of his office, and, having no prior reason to enter, she never had. But that's where she would find pen and paper. It would take just a few seconds and she would be out. What harm could that do?

Finding a blank pad of paper and a pen, she was turning to leave when he walked in. He stood over her for a moment and said nothing. She took a step forward but he blocked her way. He stared at her with unwavering eyes and said, "Did you not hear me? Or did it not matter to you? You are never, never to enter my office! You have disappointed and disobeyed me, Janice."

"Disobeyed you? Just for getting a pen and paper?"

"It is my house. I make the rules. This room is private. I have things in here. . ."

"What things, James? Things I'm not supposed to know about? Pernicious, illicit things? Things that you whisper about to Tom in the middle of the night?"

"Whatever I do is my business, certainly not yours."

"Oh, tell me, James," she said tauntingly.

"Get out!" He grabbed the collar of her blouse and shoved her.

She looked up at him and said, "James, what's going on? Drugs? Submarines?"

His face reddened and he screamed, "Bitch!" She slapped her face hard, then flung her across the hall. Stunned, she sank to the carpet.

He stared down at her and said, "Yeah, I suspected you had your ear to the wall. You're nothing but a goddamn spy. I'm tired of your suspicions, your disdainful looks. Pack your stuff and get out of my house. We're done!"

He slammed and locked the door of his office, then gave her an icy glare. Pocketing the key, he turned and walked out.

She knew it would come to this. Tension had been building as she'd voiced her criticism of repressive policies. Goodwin's once confident and charming manner had begun to fracture. After one horrible argument she had considered leaving, but he'd warmed several degrees and she'd decided to stay. Comforting words had papered the chasm, and she had hoped that they could reestablish the rapport they once had.

But he had been on edge as the NCRA crises began to mount. With clever maneuvering, he could usually negotiate each as they occurred. *Yet*, thought Janice, *there was something more than matters of state that plagued him.* Increasingly he woke up with a start and a cold sweat. He would shake her off when she tried to calm him, saying that it was nothing. But she suspected that his terror was real. Very real indeed.

She'd considered having a serious discussion with him, but the time had never seemed right. And now she knew there would never be any discussion at all.

Janice had sold her car after the death of Shelley. It held too many bad memories, and Goodwin liked to drive her around in his luxury Lincoln. So she pulled her phone from her purse and googled. Hands shaking, she found a set of listings for taxi services. It took her several tries to find a company that was still in business; fuels shortages had hit the transportation companies hard. Then she searched again and found an address.

By the time the taxi driver arrived, she was anxious, angry, but resolute. She gave the driver the address and said, "Please give me your card. I might be needing another ride in a few minutes."

Looking into his rear mirror, the driver said, "You seem in some distress. I'll wait, no charge."

Janice thanked him. She got out of the back seat and walked towards her destination. Gold lettering on the door announced "Southern Security Investigations." Inside the foyer, a middle-aged woman sat behind a desk with a potted plant and a fish in a glass bowl.

"I need to talk to a detective. I presume you have one here," Janice said, her hands still shaking.

"We do, but he's expecting a client in about thirty minutes, and. . ."

"I can't wait. I must see someone now. It won't take long, and I can pay in U.S. currency."

Janice reached into her purse, pulled out five twenty-dollar bills, and thrust it into the hands of the receptionist.

"May I give him your name?"

"That's not necessary."

She was given a curious look, but the woman got up and opened a door behind her. A moment later, she returned and said, "Mr. Murphy will see you, Miss."

The detective stood, shook Janice's hand and offered her a chair.

"I understand that you don't want to reveal your name, though I think I have seen you before. Perhaps on TV. But I don't know if we can do any legal work unless I truly know who you are."

"I am not a criminal and my requirement is of vital importance. My life and that of others is in grave danger. You will not be involved beyond what I am asking for."

Murphy peered at her, saw her determination, then nodded.

Twenty minutes later, Janice thanked him, took the instruments he had given her, and asked the taxi driver to cruise by the mansion. Seeing that Goodwin's car was not in the drive, she paid the driver, asked him to wait a block away, and entered.

She went upstairs, fiddled with the tools to unlock the office door, and then opened the drawers of Goodwin's roll-top desk. In the second drawer were three leather-covered notebooks. She thumbed through each, and when satisfied, closed and locked the drawer but left the door open. *Something for James to ponder,* she thought.

The thought of leaving a note entered her mind, but she quickly dismissed it. Nervous, she hurried to where the taxi was parked.

"The Downtown Loft near the Capitol," she said.

"You okay?" he asked, seeing her touch the bruise on her cheek.

"I'm just fine, thank you," she replied, hoping that the swelling would not turn purple.

*****

Janice sat on the bed in the narrow hotel room. For the fifth time she read every notation in the notebooks she had taken from Goodwin's desk drawer. She rose and peered into the bathroom mirror. The bruise had swollen, and no makeup would cover it. Tears welled up as she contemplated the circumstances she found herself in.

Returning to the notebooks she had placed on the bed, she wondered how valuable the names, addresses and notations would be to the FBI. She had overheard the conversation between Goodwin and Tom and the reference to the trafficking of drugs. The notebooks contained a possible treasure of incriminating material which could conceivably lead to the trial and convictions of numerous felons—including Goodwin.

What immunity would be afforded her if she could deliver the notebooks into the hands of the FBI? she wondered. *What would Steven say?* What comfort could he give her, if any? She sat on the bed and gripped her cell. Dare she even call him after their last meeting? His threat of imprisonment, his bitterness, still felt like the thrust of an ice-cold spear.

There was no way that she could start a conversation with reasoned and pleasant words. That would be rejected with utter cynicism. She opened one of the notebooks to a page whose corner she had folded and called. As soon as he picked up, she spoke, not waiting for or offering hollow pleasantries.

"Steven, has Eli changed his phone number in the last month or two?"

There was a long moment of silence before he said, "No. He's had the same number for a long time. Why?"

"Because I don't think he's Eli. He's an imposter. Please listen," she said, hurrying on, her voice tense. "I was able to get hold of several of Goodwin's notebooks, secret ones. I saw the name 'Tom,' a name he used in a late-night call, and there was a phone number next to it. I didn't know who this Tom was, but I recognized the number. It's Eli's. I thought you would want to know."

"We had our suspicions, recently."

"I think the notebooks are valuable. There are lots of names in them, maybe even cartel people, because the conversations were about drugs and that submarine."

"I imagine they would be," Steven said dryly.

There was another pause. She hoped him would say that he was pleased to receive the information, but he remained silent. If he simply hung up there would be no reason for her to phone him again.

"James hit me. My face is swollen."

Silence. She plunged on. "I'm not with him anymore. I'm hiding, and I expect they'll be looking for me."

"Where are you?"

"In a hotel near the Capitol. But I only have enough U.S. currency for one more day. Hardly anybody is accepting NCRA script. Some people are bartering with food. It's getting really bad."

"We're aware of that. Who's looking for you?"

"Palmer, I bet. He hates me. And Goodwin. I saw an APB on TV showing my picture. There's a reward in U.S. dollars. I don't know what will happen if I'm caught. I'm really afraid."

"You have good reason to be."

"Can you help me? I mean, if I give you the notebooks?"

"If I can help you, and I don't know if I can, it won't be because of the notebooks."

"Really?"

He side-stepped the question and said, "Photograph every page and send it to my phone. That may be your ticket home. Where will you go after the hotel?"

"I'm not sure. I don't have enough money to go anywhere. Goodwin was giving me a salary, but I don't dare go to a bank."

"Do you know anybody who can hide you?"

"No. I only know people in the administration. And they'd turn me in."

"You have to go someplace they won't suspect."

"I know places in the Capitol."

"That might work for a few days. I assume you know it pretty well."

"Of course, every inch."

"Does it have a basement? A place people don't go?"

"There's a room that used to be an office. It has a bathroom, but it's now used for storage."

"Can you get in?"

"Yes."

"Get in, stay quiet."

"Steven, can one of your people come for me?"

"I'm not sure. Any rescue operation has to be approved by the president. I don't know if the life of one person is going to balance out an FBI or military action."

"I got myself into a real mess."

"Sure did. Keep your head down. Stay safe."

CHAPTER 29

INVESTIGATION

Washington, D.C.

"I don't have time for this!" bellowed Eli while heading toward Steven's office. He burst in, waving a memorandum. "Didn't we just do this?"

"A year ago. It's policy, a normal physical, no big deal unless you need a lobotomy. I know that might cut into your schedule. Do you need one?"

Fuming, Eli turned, mumbled, "Goddamn waste of time," and stormed out of the office.

Five minutes later, Steven placed the call. "That's right, Doc. I want a check on that specifically, and the results go to me, no one else. I need an answer ASAP."

Later that day, Leandra Sutter tapped on Steven's door. She gave him an impish smile. "Guess what I have, Mr. Director?"

"You're too happy to be an FBI special agent. We expect ultra-serious, dour appearances."

She gave him an even bigger smile and said, "Bingo. Or almost bingo. This is just so, so juicy." She slipped a thin file onto his desk.

"This is exact, no mix up?" said Steven, reading the one-page report.

"Absolutely, DNA doesn't lie."

She sat, the mirth gone. "In a way, I wish I hadn't gone to the house. Or at least hadn't asked for the cub scout caps."

"No, it's good you did. His game would have continued and we'd be fools. You asked the right questions, got the right evidence. This is sad on a personal as well as professional level, but better we know. And better now than later. I should mention, my wife called and told me that she found Goodwin's secret notebooks. Eli's phone number was in it with the name 'Tom.'"

"Interesting. Is she giving you the evidence?"

"Got it already. Sent it to my phone."

"Ticket home for the lady."

"Where did you get that?"

"I read minds."

"I don't believe it."

"I've done it since I was a child. Anyway, what's next with our buddy Eli? Or is it Tom?"

"To start with, he can tell us the truth. An admission of what actually happened to his brother and how he pulled off the switch. And then there's the alleged drug trafficking, and impersonation of an FBI special agent for twenty years. As for his fate, that's up to the courts. But he's not going anywhere."

Two days later, the doctor's report was on Steven's desk. He read it carefully, noting that there was no description of the injury Julie had mentioned weeks before. He leaned back in his chair and thought of how the matter should proceed. Should he really accuse Eli of lying and being an imposter? One thing he did know was that their twenty-year friendship was trashed. He contemplated it all, then walked down the hall to the office the agent shared with several others.

Leaning casually against the door, he watched as Eli concentrated on a report due at the end of the day.

"Hey, Tom, how's it coming?"

"Coming along. I'll have it ready in. . ."

His head jerked up. Turning to Steven he said, "What did you call me?"

"Tom. That's your real name, isn't it?"

"No. Where did you get that? I just answered because. . ."

"Because you're Tom, not your missing brother Eli. Or do those stitches, the ones in your groin, ever bother you? Peach mentioned how you got them on that vacation in Baja. Sometimes old wounds tend to itch. But we can talk about that later. And don't worry about finishing the report. I'll have someone else do it."

Theatrically, Steven put two fingers to his eyes then directed them at his former friend. He said, "My office, three minutes. And Tom, the truth, just the truth."

Steven returned to his office and waited. Exactly three minutes later, there was a soft knock on the door. The director waited ten long seconds before he said, "Enter," and pointed to a chair in front of his desk. He indicated two envelopes. Eli picked up one, glanced at the doctor's name, and handed it back.

With a deep sigh he said, "Yes, I am Tom. I admit it, for all the good it does. What's in this other one?"

"DNA, yours and Eli's. Hairs taken from cub scout caps— the ones kept by your mom."

"You were there? Does she know about. . ."

"You taking your brother's identity, lying to, and impersonating an FBI agent? No, but you can confess everything to her if you wish. Personally, I think it would only hurt her. But that's up to you."

"I'm glad you didn't tell her. I'm not sure what I would say after all these years."

"The truth might destroy her. But not us. So, talk," said Steven.

"What's this about stitches, Steven?"

"It's Director now."

"As you wish. So much for two decades of friendship, huh?"

Steven gave him a cool look then said, "Julie told me that when she and Eli were on vacation in Baja, he got his groin ripped while getting onto an old dock. It required stitches, and the marks would still be evident."

"Hence the physical exam. No stitch marks, right?"

Steven nodded, then placed a recorder on his desk, picked up his cell and said, "Sutter, please come in. Tom is here and I need a witness. And please have Mr. Bernard come with you."

"David Bernard, the attorney?" said Barett.

"Yes, you'll need one. Will he be satisfactory for you?"

"He's not independent and hardly unbiased. And he works for the Bureau."

"Yes, but he's fair and professional. He'll work for your defense, and time is of the essence."

The two men waited in silence until Sutter and Bernard arrived. The attorney, an elderly man wearing a grey three-piece suit, was surprised to see Eli. He frowned and looked at Steven.

"Sorry to burden you with this matter on such a short notice, Mr. Bernard, but our former agent requires an attorney and approves of your appointment."

"*Former* agent? Very well, but may I have a few minutes with my client? Has he been Mirandized?"

"Not yet, but we'll do it now."

Steven pulled a sheet of paper from his desk drawer with the exact wording and read the rights accorded a suspect. "Agent Sutter and I will give you five minutes alone with your client before we resume."

"I'd appreciate that," said the attorney.

"How much do you think he'll tell Bernard?" asked Sutter once they were in the hall.

"As little as possible. Probably stuff about being in the FBI but damn little about what happened to Eli."

"And we really don't know anything about that except that he suddenly disappeared," said Sutter.

"The only other person who would know is James Goodwin, and he wouldn't say anything even if we had him."

"But taking his brother's identity, joining the FBI under false pretenses and having access to highly secret information is still a felony."

"True. Still, I'd sure like to know the rest," said Steven. "Okay, we've given them enough time. I want to get Tom on tape."

"I'm really curious how he's going to play it out," said Sutter.

"Close to the chest with lots of reference to his work over the years," predicted Steven, as the two men reentered the office.

Sutter gave Tom a noncommittal glance and said, "Director, I know we're going to make a recording, but I'd like to take notes if you don't mind. Old school. It gets me thinking."

"That's fine. Mr. Bernard, is there anything you wish to ask us before we begin?"

"No, I think Mr. Barett gave me the all information he wishes to reveal."

"Very well, then I think we're ready," said Steven. He touched a button on the machine, gave the date, their names, and a few words regarding the topic then said, "Mr. Tom Barett, otherwise known as Eli Barett, you might start with the disappearance of the real Eli Barett, your brother, and your connection to it."

"Director," broke in Bernard, "Agent Barett did not discuss that with me. I suggest that the subject not be addressed unless it impinges upon his direct involvement with the FBI."

"In a very real sense, it does," said Steven. "Mr. Barett, under questionable circumstances, joined the FBI immediately following the disappearance of his brother Eli."

Steven, Sutter and the attorney gave each other a curious look when Barett said, "I want to clear this up right now. Eli was murdered, but not by me. He was killed by James Goodwin, a blow to the head with a wrench. Goodwin dumped his body in the ocean that very same night."

"Were you with Goodwin when he disposed of the body?" asked Sutter.

The attorney lifted a hand to stop the response, but Barett waved him off saying, "No, he wanted to do it alone. He didn't want me to know the details, where the body was dumped."

"Were you a witness to Eli's death?" asked Sutter.

"Yes. Goodwin was into drugs. A shipment came into the auto repair shop where he worked. Eli saw it and would have called the police. That's why Goodwin murdered him. I mourned my brother's passing, but we were never very close. He never confided in me, never even introduced me to Julie. That's why I didn't recognize her at the party."

"I think there's a gaping hole in your account," said Steven. "Janice told me that she overheard Goodwin talking to you on the phone about drugs. He called you Tom, but your phone number was in his notebook, which Janice located and recognized. It had your phone number next to the name 'Tom.' Janice sent me everything in that book. It's rather incriminating."

Barett looked blankly at Steven and declined to comment.

"Okay, we'll leave that for the court prosecutor. So, you decided to join the FBI. Why?" asked Steven.

"It was Goodwin's idea. He thought I might be a conduit of information. He said that he was into stuff and I could alert him to any danger from the bureau."

"But you just said that you were innocent of the crime," said Sutter.

"I was, but he insisted that by not reporting it I was an accessory and could be implicated. He was very persuasive, and I admit that I was easily influenced. He was always the leader. And he said that if ever accused, he would say that I was the one who murdered Eli."

"And you went along with it," said Sutter.

Barett nodded. "He could be very intimidating. I was in a state of panic with my brother suddenly dead. And then I found Eli's acceptance letter to the academy. He had already been vetted. The whole interview process, everything. And of course, we looked exactly alike. So, I took on his character and walked right in."

Leandra Sutter smirked. Tom was playing it well.

"Tell us about your friendship with Goodwin," she said.

"James? Not much to tell. We hung around together in California, then lost touch. He went into politics and joined the NCRA. I suspect he'll be taken down, pay for his treason. I would have liked to be in on that."

"And that's it?" said Steven.

The man shrugged. "What else can I say? You know me better than anybody else. We drank a lot together, confided on virtually everything. And we solved a hell of a lot of cases together. So, Director, what now? Am I under arrest?"

"Not at this moment, but there will be a full investigation," said Steven. He leaned forward on his desk and stared at his old friend. "You want to know what I really think? I think that most of what you told us is bullshit. I believe that you were in on the murder of your brother and the dumping of his body. Everything you did was about saving your ass. Back then, after the academy, you were as nervous as a mouse with a cobra. You were always looking over your shoulder. That's why you made every effort to befriend me. Stay close to power, see all the danger signs before they strike. I should have known, should have seen through it. And you were just unlucky when Julie came along and it all imploded."

"As I said, I had nothing to do with Eli's murder, and considering my commendable career, I doubt that I will spend a single day in prison. But, to avoid any embarrassment to the Bureau, I will tender my resignation now. To my mind, except for impersonating Eli, I haven't done anything illegal since
I've been here."

"Resigning is indicative of a voluntary action, as if you are the aggrieved party. In this case, you are not resigning. You are dismissed due to suspected criminal activity," said Steven. He stopped for a moment, then with a mixture of anger and resignation said, "I want your gun and your badge. Consider yourself under criminal investigation." The gun and badge were laid on the desk.

Barett looking glum said, "Look, I saved your life. That had nothing to do with whether I was Tom or Eli. I did it as your friend and an FBI agent. What about *quid pro quo*? For God's sake, why don't you just let me slip away? I'll forfeit my pension and disappear. No one besides us ever need know."

Steven listened, waited a few seconds, then shook his head. "Don't leave D.C. There won't be any fading away. Be here in the morning and bring your passport. You're dismissed."

"As you wish," said Tom, as he stepped out and gently closed the door.

"What do you think?" Steven said as Bernard collected his briefcase.

"All you have is circumstantial evidence regarding the real Eli, and that's pretty thin. Your real case is him impersonating an FBI agent. That is, unless you can connect him to drug trafficking with absolute and tangible evidence. Just a name in a notebook beside his phone number is not going to fly. Even if convicted, I doubt he will be serving more than two or three years. But if he doesn't show up tomorrow, then you have something to take to court."

"Very cool, almost casual," Sutter said, after Bernard left. "Tom had it all planned out; what to tell us, what not to. It was like, 'Okay, you found out a few things. What are you going to do about it?' It was flippant, as if he went to McDonald's, came back and said, 'Oh, I forgot the milkshakes. Damn!' No remorse, no apology for lying to the Bureau for twenty years. And no apology to you. He was smug, and I hate him for it," she said, with a rare show of anger.

"Janice said that Goodwin was angry with Tom. They may have had a falling out over the drugs. Money and drugs may be the evidence we need against both," said Steven.

"In which case Tom may turn state's evidence against Goodwin to avoid prosecution. Then, bingo, he's either in the protective program or free as a bird. And that will be his laugh at us. He's a bit short on character but not brains. The man's going to walk, of that we can be sure."

CHAPTER 30

CONFLICTED

Montgomery, Alabama

Peevish and glum, James Goodwin sat in President Lee's office, ignoring the usual recriminations between Prescott and Palmer. His mind replayed how, after the fight with Janice, he had returned to the mansion to find her gone. Of course, in his mindless rage he had told her to get out, to never return, and he had no legitimate reason to think that she would be sitting in the parlor, pouting with drink in hand.

He had hit her, an act that would have appalled him only days earlier. He cringed thinking of the stinging slap, the purple bruise that surely left its ugly mark. He sighed, for he had had a good thing going, but he knew that the end of their tryst had long been in sight. It was just a matter of time. Yet still. . .

He remembered treading tiredly upstairs toward his office when he came to an abrupt halt. The door was ajar. Frowning, he pushed it open and the word *"impossible"* assailed his mind as he stared at the open drawers, the papers strewn. *A robbery by a very skilled thief,* he first thought, *but there was never money in the drawers. Only statements and. . .*

They were gone, and only one person would have taken them. For a brief moment he'd been frozen in panic. The contacts, informants, cartels and shipment information, all gone. He'd torn through each drawer, his hands shaking, his breath labored.

He had pulled out his cell and was about to call Tom, then had thought better of it. That would wait. Tom was a member of the wrong camp.

Instead, he had slowly descended the ornate spiral stairs and poured himself a drink. So, she had the notebooks, but what the hell could she do with them? Blackmail him? With whom? Moreover, would she even be able to decipher much of its contents? He'd called Palmer and had him initiate a search. No sense letting her abscond with the stuff.

Dumb bitch. Beautiful dumb bitch, he thought. She must have gone to a lot of trouble, dangerous trouble, but she had nothing but scribbled, coded words and could never return, even if she wanted to. *What a waste,* he thought. *She had, after all, been real fine snatch.*

As if he had turned the sound up, he heard Prescott say, "So Mr. President, are you still going ahead with you plan? I'm not sure many people will cotton to it, considering what's happening."

"You're talking about the anniversary, the parade and cotillion? Damn right I'm going ahead with it. I need something to unite us, something grand that will bring in governors from every state. It's got to be even bigger than when I was inaugurated."

Turning to Goodwin, Lee said, "I want it to look ecumenical, a bright and godly face of the nation. Something that looks inclusive, loving, and caring. Prescott, you talk to the reverends of the black churches, have some of their congregation attend. And maybe we can find a few Hispanics, too."

"That's a tall order, Mr. President."

"Do it anyway. I want lots of those Civil War reenactors, cavalry, artillery, and women and children."

"Blacks don't appreciate Confederate flags," said Prescott.

"Mississippi has the stars and bars in its flag, and I don't see lots of blacks leaving that state. But we'll keep out the neo-Nazis. Yeah, none of that idiot fringe. We want it to look patriotic, civilized and historical, not a gathering of nut cases," said Lee.

"Those 'nut cases' are a large part of your base," said Palmer.

"I don't need a base, Stanley, I need a nation. Von Hoffmann is waiting in the hallway; go get him and his crew. And tell the others to come in, too. I want to give this speech."

"It better be damn good and conciliatory," said Ralph Prescott.

That's going to be a challenge, thought Goodwin.

*****

President Lee stood in his ornate office with several members of his Cabinet, along with the leaders of the Senate and the House. They all arranged themselves behind him while he shuffled a few pages on his podium and glanced at the teleprompter.

Von Hoffmann gave instructions to his crew as the lighting and sound equipment was given final adjustment. Lee appeared tense as the countdown was given. In what he hoped was an authoritative voice, he began, "Ladies and gentlemen, my fellow citizens, I want to start by saying that our government is well aware of the challenges it faces and is confident that each will be met with appropriate action. I particularly want to address. . . "

"You can't go in there," said Lee's nephew, to the furious woman approaching the closed doors.

"I can and I will!" she shouted.

"They're filming, it's a nationwide speech. The President is—" he yelped with surprise as the woman shoved him aside.

The door flew open and Lee gaped as Maria Estavo burst in. All heads turned toward her. She pointed to her husband and said, "Ralph, do you want a divorce? I will not be a party to this any longer. What they did to my people is outrageous!"

"This is not about you," remonstrated Prescott, as the camera turned toward them.

"But it is! I am your wife, and you're catering to a crazy bunch of idiots. I will not have people see me complicit. This is evil! The president of Mexico has thoroughly condemned the NCRA and—"

"Get her out of here!" shouted Palmer, advancing toward the Secretary of Agriculture.

With surprising speed, Prescott turned toward Palmer and slammed a fist into his face.

"Stop filming, for God's sake!" blurted Lee, but rarely had the camera man had such a delicious dust-up in the presence of power. He only glanced at Von Hoffmann, who was mesmerized by the sudden, close-up violence.

Palmer took a step back, tripped and fell in a disheveled heap. Blood gushed from his nose and he spit out two teeth. His eyes teared up, and between moans, he choked out, "Get out, you nigger bastard! Get out!"

Palmer attempted to stand, but Prescott drove a foot into his stomach. Again, Palmer fell, vomit spreading across the floor.

"I said turn off that damn camera!" shouted Lee, his jaw tight as he looked from Prescott to his wife.

"Ralph, take your wife home. You're finished here," said Goodwin.

Palmer rose and made a show of starting after Prescott but was stopped by Lee.

Heads shaking, lips compressed, the dignitaries exited the office, walked to their cars, and headed for the closest bar.

Lee reached into a cabinet of his desk and pulled out a bottle of Jack Daniels.

"The camera is off, Stanley," said Goodwin. "Go to the washroom and stop the bleeding before the carpet is ruined."

"The whole fucking world saw that," said Lee, downing the first tumbler and refilling it. "The whole fucking world," he repeated, his voice filled with despair and defeat as he filled a glass for Goodwin. "I thought it would be a good speech. A damn good speech. And then she came in."

"The thing with Prescott, his wife, and the NCRA has been building since he came aboard," said Goodwin.

"I don't know why he stayed, considering how opposed his wife is," said Lee. "She's the one that called the Mexican president about the camps. Damn near destroyed the hotel and restaurant business, not to speak of agriculture. Practically crippled us. Now we gotta pull things together. We're looking like the Three Stooges."

"I'm afraid so," said Goodwin.

"Well, the world can say what it wants, but we're not quitting. No! I want that anniversary parade more than ever, and the biggest audience we can muster. By God, I'm not a loser, I'm a winner. Always have been, always will be. So you tell everybody to get off their ass and get this thing rolling. I want it done. I want the whole damn world to see us shine."

*****

Lawrence had agreed to remain in the truck parked beneath a cluster of trees. It was a good place to watch for anybody approaching the barn.

"I think they know," said Evelyn as she and Devin lay together on a bed of straw covered with a blanket.

He traced his fingers over her bare breasts, kissed a nipple then said, "What gives you that impression?"

"I just have this feeling. The FBI looks for certain types of people, I mean terrorists."

"But we're not terrorists. We haven't done anything."

Evelyn sighed and said, "If we do something, something in which people die, what will become of us? Will they be hunting for us?"

"Not you."

"Why not?" she asked as he slid his hands between her thighs.

"Because you're not going to be anywhere around when it happens. I don't want you hurt."

"But I'm in it with you. I love you and always will. It's your honesty, determination, your. . . forcefulness. That's what attracted me."

He kissed her on the lips and said, "I understand that. I knew it from the beginning."

"Do you love me? You never said you do."

"I adore you. I wouldn't want to be with anybody else. You're brilliant, and the most beautiful woman I have ever known. But the word 'love' speaks of constancy, commitment. In good faith I can't promise that. I cannot guarantee you a future, especially not a happy one. People who go on crusade are always on crusade. If one peters out, they look for the next. It's an addiction, and a very dangerous one."

She propped herself on her elbow, and in the pale light of the morning looked into his eyes. "I want us to be together. I know we've planned this, but it's so. . . so lethal. Can't we just put it aside? The NCRA can't last much longer, and we don't have to kill a lot of people."

He kissed her again and said, "It can muddle on for years. You know that, and so do I. The system is evil. It's controlled by the type of people I've always fought against. The same people, the same interests I argued against in Rathmore's class. Someone's got to end it, and that someone will be me."

"I'm worried. For you, for me, for innocent people."

"None of those people are innocent, Evelyn."

"Do we really have to end their world?"

Devin gave her a long, sad look. "There are those amongst them who would gladly end ours. But you won't be ending anyone's. I have always trusted you," he said, drawing her closer. "And you have a secret you have never told me about, and I was taking a chance."

"You know?"

"I checked. Your father is the FBI director."

"Were you worried? I mean, about me spying for him?"

"No. I don't think you are cunning or devious. Had I thought so, I would have distanced myself from you a long time ago. Of course, I suspected that we were being watched. That's why we moved and left no forwarding address."

"She touched his cheek and said, "Devin, why did you want me?"

He gave her a thoughtful look and said, "Why wouldn't any man want you?"

"For sex?"

"No, because you are. . ."

He stopped then whispered the word, "Precious."

"But now you're sending me away."

"It's for your own good. And mine. You are conflicted."

"I guess. For a long time, it was all about upsetting the old order. It was so exciting. I had visions of *Les Miserables*.

In my head, I could hear the "Marseilles", I could see people at the barricades. But then it went from being an idealist, romantic vision to something else."

"So, everything I said was just a fantasy, a delicious theoretical adventure of the mind, is that so? And, of course, you never thought that it would really happen. Do I look like some silly teenager spouting radical notions, proclaiming idiotic Marxian dialectic?"

He peered into her eyes and said, "I was a soldier before and I'm a soldier now. Soldiers kill. That's what they do; that's what I trained for. And I'm very good at it. I will not shirk away from what I believe. Not now, not ever."

She sighed, looked at him and said, "So, there is no future for us, is there? But I do have a question. There are so many targets you could have chosen, both in the NCRA and the United States. I was even fearful that it might be the headquarters of the FBI. But you chose the NCRA. Why?"

He remained silent for a moment, as if weighing what he should reveal. Finally, he said, "Some years ago, a young black man named Antoine worked for a white woman in Mississippi. He did odd chores, planted trees, worked the garden, and tried to earn some money for school. She was pleasant, but Antoine stayed away from her husband, a man who was in the Klan."

Devin continued, "They had a daughter, Celine, about Antoine's age, and quite beautiful. Antoine and Celine fell in love, but her father learned about it. After seeing them together, he fired Antoine and told him to never come around again. After Antoine drove home, he realized that he hadn't been paid for his work. That night, he went back to the house and heard Celine screaming. Looking up to the second story window, he saw her father beating her. Antoine raced in and beat the man severely. Both young people fled and stayed together in an abandoned barn. They planned to run away, go to another state, but informants led Gordon and Klan members to Antoine. They killed him. Celine attended the funeral. She later had Antoine's child, a boy. I am their son. I grieve for both Antoine and Celine, and I will have revenge."

"Mississippi is part of the NCRA. People like those who murdered your father will be at the Capitol. And those are the people you intend to kill?" said Evelyn. "Yes, I understand revenge, but it's not going to change a system, to spur a revolution. And the man who murdered your father won't be there."

"The ones who would do the same will be there," replied Devin.

He rose from the bed and said, "It's time to get dressed. You have a future, perhaps a brilliant future, but not with me. You must leave me, go back to the life you had before we met."

She shook her head and said, "I want to stay with you no matter what."

He gently laid his hands on her shoulders and said, "We all want something. Some things we can have, can share, but there are some things we can't. There is such a thing as fate, even destiny."

"Then all I have is the memory of us, is that right?"

He reached around his neck and removed a chain and two small pieces of metal. He placed his dog tags in her hand, gave her a heartfelt hug and said, "Be safe, don't despair. Remember me, Evelyn. I'm doing what has to be done."

She was about to leave when she said, "I pray that you will survive. But isn't there anything I can do to help you? Anything at all?"

He pondered the question then said, "As a matter of fact, there is."

CHAPTER 31

A BLACK BALAKLAVA

"Please leave a message," was the answer when Steven called Tom's phone in the morning. He tried several more times over the course of an hour with similar results.

"Where do you think he is?" asked Sutter. "Or should I say, where do you think he's running to?"

She sat in Steven's office with two other agents and several attorneys, all of whom had downed numerous cups of coffee. They were becoming impatient when another agent entered, approached the director, and said, "We checked the manifests of all outgoing flights from Dulles. His name did not appear on any of them."

"He's either using a fictitious name and false I.D. or drove out of D.C. and arranged for a private plane," said Sutter. "There are small airports like Bundoran in Virginia. Of course, the pilot would have to file a flight plan."

"Unless they're flying below radar, under three hundred feet," said one of the attorneys.

"Damn dangerous," replied Sutter. "A pilot could lose his license, or worse. Not filing a flight plan is a violation in itself. But the question is, where would he go?"

"I've got a hunch he's meeting with Goodwin in Montgomery," said Steven. "With NCRA's multiple failures, maybe Goodwin will try to get out of Dodge. If so, Tom might be joining him."

"But an article in the local paper said that Lee is still having his parade and party. Surely Goodwin won't miss that," said Sutter.

"I don't think Goodwin gives a rat's ass about the NCRA anymore. He knows that if it falls he'll find himself in federal court on multiple charges. Getting out now makes sense. Who knows, maybe the parade is just a smokescreen. Maybe Lee's on the run, too. I wouldn't be surprised if they are all sharing one big secret," said Steven.

"According to Ben Franklin, three can keep a secret, but only if two are dead. I wonder who those two will be?" said Sutter.

"One of them won't be Tom," said Steven.

"So, if he's not flying out of Bundoran or Dulles, where could he be heading?" asked an attorney.

"I would put my money on the Montgomery Regional Airport. It's only ten miles from the Capitol. My guess is that's where he and Goodwin might meet," said Sutter.

"And then where?" said Steven.

"They could go anyplace in the world," said one of the agents.

"If I were them, I would fly to somewhere like Paraguay, completely change my appearance, then head for an African city like Kinshasa. They would probably have enough money to fly from there to a sweet spot like Bali and disappear," said Steven.

"I suggest that we head to the Montgomery airport. If we hurry, we might intercept them," said Sutter.

"Make arrangements," said Steven. "I want to be on a plane in thirty minutes."

He glanced at the other agents and said, "You two are coming with us. Get your gear, be ready to fly."

*****

Levi Grossman clicked on his remote and switched from the local station to CBN, then back again. *"It must be a slow news day,"* thought Grossman. The anchor was talking to "experts" about the attack on Fort Benning that had happened a week ago.

One commentator jokingly said that there should be a demonstration of U.S. airpower over various NCRA capitols. Others countered that such an effort would be counter-productive and unnecessarily intimidating.

"Afterburners twenty feet over them is what they should do," Grossman mumbled. Then, out of curiosity, he switched to Von Hoffmann's *Freedom America*. He loathed the reporter, but the station carried NCRA information before other stations.

Dressed in his usual silk suit and bow tie, Von Hoffmann stood in front of the Capitol explaining the seating arrangements of dignitaries who would be occupying the stands across the street from the nineteenth-century building. The details of the historic three-story building, with its fluted columns, cast-iron capitals and copper dome, were illuminated in the morning sun.

"The parade will be coming down Dexter Avenue and pass between the reviewing stands and the dais where President Lee, members of the cabinet, and select guests will be seated. Thousands upon thousands of NCRA supporters from all the states are expected to attend the review, and hundreds are invited to the evening cotillion. It should be the grandest Montgomery County affair in the last two hundred years," gushed Von Hoffmann.

The camera focused on twelve men, all wearing black bloused trousers, black protective gear, and side arms.

"I personally spoke with President Lee, who assured me that there will be excellent security for this historic occasion.

281

Expertly trained men such as those will certainly prevent any violence or intrusion during the next few days. In addition, numerous young men of the NCRA Christian Youth Security Force will be patrolling the neighborhoods."

Grossman shook his head and leaned back in his recliner. How many more of these bastards should he eliminate? How many for the sake of. . .

He felt tired, the old adrenalin that had sustained him had evaporated. He laid his head back and wondered if he should ever admit that he, an old soldier, had killed the neo-Nazis. *Now,* he mused, *the elimination of Jefferson Calhoun Lee, along with his advisors, James Goodwin and Palmer, would be a real story.* He glanced at his crossbow lying against the wall. Their demise would be cataclysmic, but their security needed be eliminated first. And just how could that possibly happen? Who could make it happen?

His push button phone rang and his nephew's voice was on the other line. "I think we should talk," Danny said. "But not on the phone. Can you meet me in the park? Near the fountain?"

"Give me twenty minutes."

The young man was sitting on a wrought iron bench when his uncle joined him. Danny looked around to make sure no one was around and said, "Something has been in my head for months, in fact since the crash. I keep thinking of my dad, my mom and all the others on that plane, before it went into that mountain. I swore to myself that I would bring vengeance upon the perpetrators, but I have done nothing. I am ashamed. People like Palmer and his Nazis were behind it."

"And what do you hope to do about it?"

"Kill them. Kill as many as I can. There will be things happening at the Capitol. I'm sure they will be there, and so will I."

"With what, Danny? How much experience do you have with assassinations? How many people have you killed?"

"Does that matter?"

"Yes, it does. There will be guards all around that place. You haven't been in the military. Killing isn't easy, never is. But those people will be dealt with, sooner or later."

"The neo-Nazis who were murdered, the ones with the notes on them. I always suspected it had to be you. Am I right?"

Levi stared into Danny's eyes but only gave the slightest nod. "Not a word. Never."

"Never," Danny repeated.

"I want you to go home. Say a Kaddish for your father and mother. Things may happen and I do not want you involved. I do not want to see you killed. What you want to happen will happen, but not by you. Promise me that, Danny. For the rabbi and your mother, promise me."

"I feel hollow. How can I let you do what I must?"

"Because I am an old man, a killer, and am willing to answer to the Lord. Promise me."

"I promise."

Levi thought about it for hours. *Who would take on such a suicidal venture with so little possibility of success? Certainly not somebody young with years of life ahead of him. It would require a person with certain skills learned over years of black ops. Somebody with a fever, an all-consuming sense of purpose. And a desire to righteously kill. Who other than he?*

The stress he had felt disappeared like tide going out, revealing God's word in the sand. A knowing smile came to his lips. A mission, and he was on point one more time.

He turned the TV back on to find Von Hoffmann was speaking again. "Despite the APB bulletin, Mrs. Whitinghill has not been located. Nobody seems to know if she is still in the NCRA, and there is concern that a secret mission by the FBI or U.S. military forces have taken her.

"There is further speculation that she and Mr. Goodwin have, after some rancor, gone their separate ways. Mrs. Whitinghill is the wife of the director of the FBI, and it's entirely possible that she may have gone back to Washington, D.C. The fact that she has knowledge vital to the security of the NCRA is, according to government insiders, compelling and possibly quite dangerous."

*****

At three in the morning, wearing a black Balaklava, dark clothing, and night vision glasses, Levi Grossman parked his car three blocks from the Montgomery Capitol. There was a slice of moon and lingering fog. The crossbow, now painted black, was lightly wrapped in a black trash bag.

He silently skirted the building, avoiding detection from two guards posted at its front entrance. He would deal with those later. Halting beside an ancient chestnut tree, he adjusted his glasses, stood stock still, and observed. There were three guards: one smoking a cigarette, lounging beside the back wall of the Capitol; the others, more diligent, patrolled the rear corners of the building with ARs slung over their backs.

The building had been extended with an addition in the rear, making it difficult for one guard to see the other.

A lone figure emerged briefly, then was hidden again by swirling fog. Grossman watched the ghostly image. Why anyone would be out an hour after the last bars had closed?

He removed the bow from the bag, knelt on the damp ground, and carefully appraised the readiness of the closest guard. Beside the man's AR, there was a holstered pistol and a dagger belted to his thigh.

Grossman picked up a stone and tossed it to the side. The guard looked about as it bounced on the pavement. The guard frowned, looked about, then, swinging around his AR to hold it at the ready, cautiously stepped forward. He opened his mouth but his scream stopped short—the arrow had pierced his heart. With a quivering movement, he collapsed, hand vainly gripping the shaft.

Grossman scrambled forward and dragged the guard behind the tree. Although he had no intention of using it on this night, he liberated the pistol and slid it into his belt. Then he removed the banana clip from the AR and tossed it, after which he placed a piece of paper on the man's chest and pierced it with the dagger. The note read, "You are replaced," a reference to the Charlottesville chant during the Trump administration.

A radio crackled on the dead man's collar. Grossman was about to ignore it, but then decided to touch the reply button and said, "Come here, by the tree. I need to talk. Important."

There were two of them, one three yards behind the other. *It would have to be done quickly,* thought Grossman. The guards, half hidden by mist, approached slowly.

"John? Where are you?" said the closest.

Grossman didn't answer.

"Show yourself. Are you hurt?"

An arrow struck the other guard between the eyes. The victim's cry of pain was cut short as his brain ceased to function. The guard in front turned in time to see his comrade drop to the ground, mouth open, staring sightlessly into the overcast sky.

The guard pivoted and spotted Grossman, who had stepped away from his cover. Infuriated, the guard raised his AR. But Levi already had the pistol leveled, and fired two rounds into the man's face.

The gunshot will have alerted the other guards, he thought, as he hurried toward the wall of the Capitol. He fully expected the arrival of more guards. Suddenly, there were two figures quickly approaching. One appeared to be the ghostly figure, possibly a woman, whom he had seen earlier. The other, twenty steps behind her, was a guard with an AR.

"No! Please don't!" The woman blurted, raising her hands, and backing against the wall.

The guard, mystified by the sight of the woman, slowed. He looked to her then to Grossman and shouted, "Drop it!" But it was too late.

The round from the pistol illuminated the night, and the guard crumpled at Janice's feet.

She peered at the elderly man, who stared back at her.

"I know you. I've seen you on TV. You're Mrs. Whitinghill, wife of the FBI director. Am I right?"

"Yes," she said shakily.

"What are you doing here?"

"I have to get into the building. I'm being hunted by people in the NCRA," she said.

"Yes, I saw the APB. How are you getting in?"

"I have a key. What is your name?"

"It doesn't matter."

"Why did you kill him?"

"Because he is evil. And there are others."

"Others?"

"The ones trying to kill you. I have to go. Stay safe."

CHAPTER 32

THE PARADE

Dressed from head to toe in black with an arm band proclaiming "NCRA Christian Youth Security Force" and a fascist style insignia on their shirts, six young men in helmets walked down Dexter Avenue, checking I.D. cards. They had been assigned to look for possible agitators and others intent on disrupting the parade and speeches. Each had rows of ribbons on their jackets. Arrogant and walking purposefully, three of them carried sidearms, while one had a rifle slung over his shoulder.

It was not a particularly difficult task early in the morning, since few citizens had yet found places to sit along the parade route. Those who encountered the youths presented their NCRA official Citizen's Card and smiled indulgently. They were then rewarded with a click of heels from Jack boots. But to the boys' chagrin, there were girls who snickered at them.

An occasional police car drifted by.

Evelyn had been told not to use her cell phone except in an emergency, and she assiduously avoided the neo-Nazi youths. As the morning progressed, a growing number of staunch NCRA supporters set up chairs and arranged their coolers and lunch baskets along the sidewalks. It was, they assumed, going to be a beautiful and exciting day.

Except for the taller buildings, it appeared to be the epitome of small-town America. Many stores were opening, and refreshment stands offering candy and shaved ice were already in place.

Evelyn, wearing a blue Antebellum dress with hoops and a small, stylish period hat, met with smiles and appreciative comments by passersby. A park several blocks from the Capitol was still a half mile away and that, Devin had told her, was to be her destination.

But that would likely be filled, she thought, *and what good would it do if she could see nothing from deep inside a crowd?* What truly bothered her, however, was the growing presence of police; that increased the difficulty Devin would have getting away. She began to feel terribly anxious.

*****

Devin Winfeld donned a slouch hat with its wide brim, the same commonly worn by Civil War soldiers both north and south. He buttoned up the short grey jacket and adjusted the pistol belt and holster. The Colt pistol, handle grip pointing forward, slipped easily into it. An eight-inch sheathed knife extended from the belt.

He had ordered the entire ensemble from a company that made uniforms for re-enactors. From a gun shop, he had purchased black powder and ball which filled all six cylinders of his revolver making it a lethal weapon. Re-enactors, he had read, rammed black powder into the cylinder, followed by Cream of Wheat. When the trigger was pulled, all that emerged was a puff of the combined powders resulting in nothing more than a bang and smoke. A simple bang and smoke did not appeal to Winfeld on this day. His plan did not involve the pistol, but the availability of it might be a very valuable thing.

288

He stopped and felt a strange sensation as he recalled the family story passed down over the generations regarding Sergeant Howard, an escaped slave. He was a direct ancestor who had served in the Union army—a man wearing the blue uniform who had survived the fatal attack on Fort Wagner in South Caroline with the 54th Massachusetts. *What,* thought Devin, *would he think of me wearing Confederate grey?* He'd heard that Howard was a bitter man who, along with other black soldiers, had not been allowed to march in the victory parade down Pennsylvania Avenue. *Well,* mused Devin, *I'll be in a parade. Damn right I will, Sergeant. I most assuredly will.*

The wagon was in the barn, loaded with bales of hay and festooned with Confederate and NCRA flags. The explosive device he had rigged was hidden under one of the uppermost bales; it was designed to be detonated with a hand-held device. He'd dispatched Lawrence with the pickup and a rented trailer to fetch the draft horses they'd hired from a farmer who lived a mile away.

Glen "Turkey" Madison, a slender man who wore blue overalls and a large straw hat, said, "Now, you be gentle with my animals. They're family to me. I'll be proud to see them go by in the parade. Being a childhood friend of President Lee, I'll be right up on the platform observing the whole shebang."

"Yes, sir, they'll look fine, pulling the wagon," Lawrence said, as he was about to lead them away.

"Wait a minute," said Madison, pulling out his cell phone. "Just stand by my horses for a sec. I always like to get a photo of people renting my animals. For my business purposes, you know."

"Uh, sure thing," said Lawrence, reluctant to be photographed, but not having any way to refuse that wouldn't raise suspicions. After securing the horses in the trailer, he slowly drove down the road and rendezvoused with Devin. Hitching up the horses, the two men drove the wagon to a secluded place near the staging area away from the milling crowd.

*****

"What the hell are you doing in Louisiana, Palmer?" President Lee shouted into his phone. "You're supposed to be here to coordinate security. You know damn well that four of your men were shot last night, and we have no idea who did it. The rest of the people you hired ran out of town."

"You've got the cops, Jeff," Palmer responded. "I've got business to tend to down here. A lot more important than watching a parade."

"More important?! The only protection I'll have are re-enactors and a few police!"

"Jeff, you, me, and Goodwin are all targets of whoever killed my guys. There's a serial killer out there."

"And that's why you're running?"

"That's part of it. If I were you, I'd get out now. Forget the goddamn parade."

"No, you run, go ahead. You're a coward, Palmer, always were. But whoever got your men will get you."

"Gotta find me first, buddy boy. And I ain't nowhere to be found."

Lee clicked off and placed a call to Kyle Ramsey, county sheriff.

"Palmer's gone, and his security team has vanished. You and your people are it."

"We're damn thin, patrolling the entire town and roads leading in. We'll do what we can."

"I want you and some of your people on the dais with me."

"Sure. I'll be along. A few of my men are already there."

President Lee fumed, looked out his office window and saw Von Hoffman and his crew arranging their equipment in front of the dais. In the distance, he could see hundreds of marching groups being directed to their positions. Enthusiasm and merriment seemed to permeate the crowd. Lee did not feel merry, and for a fleeting moment he wondered if Palmer was right. Perhaps he should call the whole thing off, send out a warning, tell people to go home.

But that could cause panic and irreparable damage to his regime. He sat back in his chair and consulted his watch. *Goodwin should have been here by now,* he thought.

Lee clicked James' name on his cell and said, "How far are you from the Capitol? Your speech writer has finished, and you should read it over a few times. We only have an hour before the whole shebang begins."

"Sorry to disappoint, Jeff, but I won't be there. In fact, I'm out of the NCRA. One way or another, Edith Barnes is going to fry your ass and you know it."

"Goddamn! First Palmer, now you!"

"Probably heading to the bayou, his old hangout. I knew he would."

"So what am I supposed to do? Beg for mercy at Edith's feet or fly to Antarctica? You could have told me weeks ago. We could have made plans together."

"It wouldn't have worked, Jeff. Too many fingers in the pie. And there's some stuff you don't want to be mixed up in."

"The pie, huh? I always suspected something. That's why you're skedaddling. Where are you going?"

"Classified."

"Well, the feds will be interested in that."

"Ratting on me isn't going to save your ass. The operative word, Jeff, is 'treason.'"

In a resigned voice, Lee said, "Where the hell can you possibly go where they won't find you?"

"Lots of places where they like money."

"Just out of curiosity, have you seen Janice, know where she is?"

"Nope. I don't give a damn about her anymore, but she's going to fry, too. She was the public face of the NCRA. Hey, Jeff, it was fun for a while. Now you enjoy the parade and the cotillion, and remember to duck when things go boom. Gotta go."

Lee could hear Goodwin laugh before he clicked off.

Apoplectic, and suddenly gripped by a raging inferno, he screamed, slammed his phone down on his desk, and shouted, "I made the NCRA, and I'm not going to fail! This is going to happen, and I don't give a shit how many die!"

*****

"Pull over here," James Goodwin said to his driver. The elderly black man edged the SUV with its police lights to the curb and kept the engine running. Goodwin slid out of the rear seat, entered the gun shop, and pointed to a Smith and Wesson .38. "I'll take that one, and two boxes of ammo," he said to the clerk while handing over hundred dollar bills in U.S. currency.

Pleased to make the early morning sale in U.S. currency, the clerk thanked Goodwin, who said, "Have a great day," and went out the door.

A half block away, six members of the Christian Youth Security Force were haranguing a young woman in an Antebellum dress. Goodwin had the car slowed and watched as the conversation became hostile, the young men demanding to see the lady's I.D.

"I don't have it with me," she protested. "These dresses don't have pockets, you know. I think you're being terribly rude, and you have no reason to question a patriotic woman. And for your information, I am a cousin of President Lee. He can surely attest to my honor."

"I don't care if you're related to Jesus himself," snarled one youth. "No I.D. and you don't get a step closer."

"Stop here," said Goodwin, recognizing the girl from a D.C. photoshoot. One of the boys turned and saw the imposing man and promptly snapped to attention.

"She comes with me," said Goodwin, clutching Evelyn's arm while displaying his government I.D.

"You young men did excellent work and will be rewarded for it." Then, seeing plastic zip ties edging from the corporal's back pocket, he said, "Give me a few of those. Now carry on."

There was a chorus of "Yes, sir!" as they saluted. Once Goodwin and Evelyn drove off, one of the privates jubilantly turned to the lieutenant and said, "We're going to get commendations, maybe be on TV!"

"I was the one that stopped her," said the corporal. "I should be promoted."

"I am making you a sergeant right now," said the lieutenant.

"The airport, hurry," Goodwin said, as Evelyn squirmed in the back seat, her hands zip tied behind her back.

*****

The spectator stands were filled with men in stylish suits and others wearing Confederate uniforms, all imitating ranking officers of the "Lost Cause." With sleeves adorned with gold striping, rows of shiny brass buttons and grey kepis, they sported officer's dress swords or cavalry sabers.

Beside them were their wives or girlfriends, attired in silks and brocades, complete with hooped skirts and pantaloons. They gaily waved NCRA flags as the parade began with the gallop of cavalry in front of the reviewing stand.

Clapping and hooting accompanied a fife and drum contingent. Mounted figures attired as Robert E. Lee and "Stonewall" Jackson rode by the dais, smartly rendering their salutes.

President Lee, a distant relative of his namesake, rose and returned the honor. Sitting beside him was County Sheriff Kyle Ramsey, who said, "Isn't that grand? I can just imagine them, the real ones, looking down on this now with pride and admiration."

"Indeed," replied Jeff Lee. Then leaning toward Ramsey, he said, "You've got this all buttoned up? I don't see very many of your men."

"As I told you, we're spread pretty thin, but we're doing surveillance. My people are trained professionals. And you know what I think of those strutting, ridiculous kids."

"A little extra help can't hurt."

"As long as they don't become a problem. Law enforcement is a serious thing and requires responsible people."

"I won't argue with that, Sheriff, It's just that. . ."

"What?"

"Not sure. Just got this feeling," said Lee as he waved to another passing unit.

Behind the equestrians came three dozen members of the Daughters of the Confederacy. They were followed by a high school marching band led by short-skirted girls with the requisite pompoms.

In their wake came a brass band leading two hundred Confederate infantry re-enactors. Held aloft were many original battle flags, some singed or torn, others with bullet or shrapnel holes.

That group was followed by six large Napoleonic era black powder artillery pieces, complete with ammunition caissons, pulled by jack mules. The deep rumble of iron wheels, the cheers of the audience and the intermittent singing of "Dixie" resounded in a cacophony of joyous sound.

Devin's contingent was the thirteenth major unit that would be passing the reviewing stand. The group consisted of supply wagons, all decked out in flags and banners. Accompanying them were re-enactors, including women and boys, all in period dress, representing medical personnel and camp followers.

Lawrence, holding the reins, sat nervously erect, his eyes glancing right and left for NCRA security that would pull them out of line. But none appeared, and his wagon flying the stars and bars was just another unremarkable unit amongst many.

*****

Glen "Turkey" Madison's phone rang as did several others on the dais. He slid his finger over the screen and read the words, *"U.S. Homeland Security Alert. Be advised that it is likely that suspected terrorist Devin Winfeld and his accomplices have infiltrated the NCRA anniversary parade, attired as Confederate soldiers. It is also possible that they have planted a bomb within the NCRA Capitol. They are considered armed and dangerous."*

Madison jumped up when Lawrence's photo appeared on the screen. "Oh no! Oh my God!" he shouted. Spotting the sheriff sitting beside President Lee, Madison squeezed past others on the dais, leaned over and pointed to his cell. "Did you see this? This man?"

The sheriff frowned and glanced at Madison's phone.

"I rented my horses to him this morning! They're supposed to be hooked up to a wagon somewhere in the parade! See, he's wearing a Confederate uniform. He may have a bomb!" Madison exclaimed.

"Shit!" said Lee, staring at the phone. "Why didn't we know about this?"

"Investigation was Palmer's job. But once again he's proven to be unreliable, a loose cannon," said Ramsey.

"So, what do we do?"

"I'll alert every one of my deputies. But if I were you, I'd stop the parade right here and now. If they have a bomb, you know damn well what their target is."

*****

A car skidded to a stop and Tom Barett stepped out. The engines of a nearby Cessna were powering up, and Tom strode towards it.

"I didn't think you'd make it," Goodwin shouted over the roar of a Learjet that was coming in for a landing at the far end of the field.

"It was close. Had to take a lot of back roads to get around the crowds. I brought all the cash I could get my hands on. The FBI took my gun. Do you have one? Perhaps two?"

"No, only one. I just bought a .38 and I'm itching to use it," said Goodwin.

Evelyn, hands tied behind her, stood by the door of the plane, staring at Tom.

"What the fuck is she doing here?" Tom blurted.

"Insurance, pal. Her daddy will give anything to get her back. And if he doesn't care, she's pretty and. . ."

"Oh, no. She's not coming with us. Steven will kill both of us. And she's my friend, dammit!"

Hearing this, Evelyn started walking down the steps towards Tom, but Goodwin grabbed her.

"Shit!" Tom yelled. He took three steps toward Goodwin, but two rounds shot from the .38 knocked him to the tarmac.

Evelyn wrenched her arm away from Goodwin and knelt over Tom. A round had penetrated his chest, another his thigh. Blood began to pool on the ground as she tried to stem the flow.

"Run, kid," Tom urged, but Goodwin lunged forward, grabbing her again. He thrust Evelyn towards the steps of the aircraft. She stumbled, then tried to run away. Goodwin grabbed her arm and dragged her towards the Cessna.

The Lear, its door already open, came to a halt twenty feet from the Cessna, and Steven jumped to the ground, followed by and five agents. Sutter stepped in front of the Cessna and pointed her weapon at the pilot, who immediately cut the engine.

By now Goodwin had one arm around Evelyn's neck, his pistol's muzzle pressed against her head.

Steven, never taking his eyes off his daughter and Goodwin, edged closer to Tom, who was gurgling up blood.

"Shoot him, Steven, shoot him," Tom said, choking on the words.

"This plane flies or she dies right now," snarled Goodwin.

"Release her, and we'll talk," said Steven, as two agents stationed themselves on either side of the steps.

"Not a chance," retorted Goodwin, his eyes darting to an agent, who fired three rounds into the starboard tire. Another round struck the front wheel, causing an immediate deflation and rocking the Cessna. Thrown off balance, Goodwin reached out to grab one of the struts.

Wrenching herself free, Evelyn twisted away, dropped to the ground and rolled under the plane. Goodwin attempted to steady himself while aiming the pistol, but Steven fired five rounds and Goodwin collapsed against the side of the plane. Blood from multiple exist wounds smeared the side.

Steven holstered his weapon, helped Evelyn to her feet, and cut the bindings. She threw her arms around him.

"He was going to take me. . ."

"I know," said her father.

They knelt before Tom; Evelyn said, "Dad, Eli tried to save me, he really did."

Trembling, she looked at Steven and said, "Can we save him? We have to get an ambulance."

Steven didn't reply, but opened the former agent's jacket to inspect the wound. "Tom, can you hear me?"

Evelyn gave her father a curious look and said, "Tom?"

"All's well that ends well," said Tom, his breath rasping. "Glad it's over. Took you a long time to find out, huh?"

He gave a wan smile, feebly pointed to Evelyn and said, "Wouldn't let him take her. Couldn't let that happen."

"You did good. I thank you," said Steven quietly. The grim-faced agents looked on.

"We were friends once, right?" said Barett, "Weren't we?"

"Yeah, we were, Tom."

Tom took a breath, coughed, then became still. Evelyn touched the blood on the man's lips. "Eli?"

"He's gone," said Steven, "but your mom's at the Capitol. I have to get her out."

"The Capitol? Oh my God," said Evelyn. "That's where Devin's heading. He's in the parade and he has a bomb."

"There was that warning from Homeland Security," said Sutter. "They identified Devin and Lawrence — and included Evelyn in the description."

"What's his plan?" Steven asked his daughter.

"He didn't say exactly. He and Lawrence were going in a wagon."

"I bet they're going to blow up the Capitol, along with Jeff Lee," said Sutter.

"Everyone get in Goodwin's car!" Steven yelled, as he took his daughter's hand and sprinted toward Goodwin's SUV.

"What about Eli?" asked Evelyn.

"An agent just called for an ambulance."

Goodwin's driver, shaken by the death of his employer, stared at the agents charging toward the car.

"FBI," said Steven. "You're taking us to the Capitol. Go!"

With siren screaming and lights flashing, the SUV tore down the highway as vehicles hastily pulled to the side of the road.

"What were you doing before Goodwin found you?" asked Steven.

"I was supposed to warn Devin if he was about to be caught."

"Then he would still have his cell phone, wouldn't he?" said Sutter.

"Yes, I'm sure he does," replied Evelyn.

"Call him," said Steven, "Tell him that we know what he's intending. Tell him that he must pull out of the parade."

"But—"

"Evelyn, your mother is hiding in the Capitol, She'll be killed if that explosion goes off."

Frantically she placed the call, but it went to voicemail. She tried Lawrence's phone with the same result.

"I don't think he's going to pick up. He must be close enough to think he's safe."

"Keep trying," said Steven, as the car careened down the road.

CHAPTER 33

THE SEARCH

Agitated, President Lee surveyed the crowd along the parade route. Many were on their cell phones and already dozens were streaming for their cars.

"They're running," he said to Ramsey. "They must have seen the Homeland Security message. But it could be a hoax, just to disrupt the parade."

"I wouldn't put money on that, Mr. President."

Lee's phone rang. "Who's this? It better be important. Make it quick."

"Sir, this is Deputy Alvin Stokes. I was trying to get the sheriff but hit your number by mistake. It's pretty serious."

"Go on."

"I was summoned to the airport by the tower crew. There's been a shooting and we have two bodies on the tarmac. One is James Goodwin."

"Goodwin? Are you sure?"

"Yes, sir, got his I.D. and I've seen him dozens of times on TV."

"Who's the other one?"

"No I.D. on him. And there's a Learjet here, too. I asked the pilot where he's from and he said D.C., but he wouldn't give me any more details. I also spoke with the pilot of the Cessna, Goodwin's plane."

"The pilot told me that he was confronted by FBI agents. One of them shot Goodwin. Then they drove off in his car. They were in a hurry."

"You know where?"

"No. Can you tell the sheriff that I need backup here?"

"He can't spare anyone right now. Call the morgue, get the coroner. We'll deal with the rest later."

Lee turned to Ramsey and said, "FBI was at the airport. Your deputy says one of them shot Goodwin."

"Then they must be coming this way."

"Lord, I hope not. They're the last people I want to see. Unless. . ." Lee snapped his phone shut and sat stone still.

Masses of people began to fill the streets. Adding to the tumult were cars unable to proceed and cavalry pushing through the crowd.

*****

"We can't go any further," said the chauffeur.

"Then we'll get out, and Evelyn stay here and try calling Devin again," ordered Steven, as he and the agents bolted from the car.

"I can find him. Let me go with you," pleaded Evelyn.

"I don't want you anywhere near him. If he has a bomb, he'll detonate it even if it kills him. And he won't care if it kills you, too."

Followed by Sutter and the other four agents, Steven pushed his way through the crowd until they approached the Capitol. Pulling his cell from his jacket, he phoned Janice.

"Are you still in the basement?" he asked when she picked up.

"Yes, but there's a lot of activity around here. I've locked the door. Where are you?"

"About three hundred yards from the Capitol. We think it's going to be bombed."

"Oh my God! Stay away. I'll be okay. Do you know anything about Evelyn? Is she with Devin?"

"No, she's in a car a half mile from the Capitol. She's all right. I'm coming."

"No! It's too dangerous," said Janice, anxiety in her voice.

Abruptly ending the conversation, Steven and the team struggled on. A team of horses pulling a wagon burst through the crowd as pedestrians scrambled out of the way. Several were struck by the wagon and knocked to the ground as the heavily laden wagon careened by. A number of pedestrians were run over or trampled.

Evelyn tried twice more to reach Devin; receiving no response, she got out of the car. In desperation, she struggled past re-enactors, terrified children, and their frightened parents. It became apparent that reaching Devin would be difficult, and stopping him would be impossible. Exhausted by the day's events, she stopped, and the crowd streamed passed her.

A woman carrying a screaming child, his body shattered, pushed past Evelyn. "What sort of monsters would do a thing like this?" she wailed. In the distance were shouts of "Doctor, we need a doctor!"

"Monsters." The word assailed Evelyn. Tears came to her eyes as she watched the pandemonium. She knew that she could have prevented it, could have alerted her father weeks before. She was culpable, a co-conspirator and a terrorist. She felt sick, struggled toward a tree, gagged and vomited.

The Capitol. *That's where mother is, that's where Devin was headed,* she thought, wiping her mouth. And bomb or no bomb, that's where she should be.

She began to walk toward the stately building, hearing words over a PA system exhorting the crowd to proceed in an orderly manner. The plea was ignored; the panicked crowd surged and scattered like an ant hill stomped on by a boot.

*****

"That message from Homeland Security, didn't it say that the bomb could be inside the Capitol?"

"I can't answer that," replied the sheriff, "but my men did a thorough search of it two days ago. And I've had people in there. I don't see how anybody could have gotten past them."

"I think it's all a ruse," said Lee stubbornly. "Just a ruse, you hear?"

He was interrupted when the governor of Mississippi nervously approached him and said, "Sir, I'm taking my wife home."

"It's not over!" shouted Lee. "I'm not going anywhere and I demand that you remain here!"

"No, sir, that wouldn't be wise. We'll talk later. If you're still alive."

Ramsey found three deputies and sent them into the building. To people still in the Capitol, the police shouted, "Get out, everybody out!" Scrambling up spiral staircases, they peered into offices, mostly deserted.

"There's a basement, and a storage room—check it," said a sergeant.

"I was just down there yesterday," replied a deputy. "It's locked. Nobody goes down there."

"Do it anyway. Somebody might have broken in."

*****

Most of the employees had fled out the front and side doors of the Capitol when Steven and his agents burst in through the back.

"Who the hell are you people?" asked one of Ramsey's deputies, startled by their appearance.

"FBI!" shouted Steven, as he and Sutter rushed down the stairs to the basement. The door had been kicked in and there was nobody inside. Rushing back up, Steven confronted the deputy and said, "There was a woman in there. Where is she? Where did your people take her?"

"I have no idea. I sure didn't see her. Is she the terrorist?"

"No, she's my wife. We're going to find her, and you're going to help."

"Bullshit! If she was in here before, she's not now. And you have no authority over me."

Furious with the man's intransigence, Steven pulled his Glock and said, "This is my authority. Move!"

"Find anything?" Ramsey demanded into his phone.

"Not yet, but the FBI's here and they're searching for a woman. They must know the bomb's in here. It's got to be for real," said his sergeant. "Have Lee call off the event. Better do it now!"

"The whole shebang is breaking up anyway. Crowd control is the best we can do. I'll tell the President."

When Ramsey mounted the steps of the dais, Lee seemed in a daze, his eyes flicking from one panicky group to the next.

"We can reschedule the parade in a few weeks, Mr. President. If you don't address the crowd, I will. We've got to get order."

Deflated and resigned, Lee reluctantly went to his podium, turned on the mic and said, "Ladies and gentlemen, we have not confirmed that there is an explosive device anywhere in our proximity, but for the sake of safety, we are temporarily suspending the current activities. I request that everybody evacuate the area. If no threat is found, these proceedings will begin again at a future date. Please leave in an orderly manner."

But it was far from orderly. The panic spread from those viewing the parade to the marchers and drivers of wagons who attempted to turn their vehicles away from the Capitol. Surrounded by pushing, shouting people, frightened animals balked, kicked in their traces, or bolted. Charging out of line, uncontrolled animals pulled wagons through spectators, over fences and onto crowded roads.

Devin was only fifteen yards from the dais when the mules pulling the wagon just ahead of theirs panicked and charged toward a reviewing stand.

"Now!" shouted Devin. Lawrence slapped hard with the reins, urging the horses toward the dais. When they balked, Devin whipped them savagely until they broke into a run.

Assembled before the dais were a dozen infantry re-enactors attempting to escort people from the stage. They looked about in terror as the horses, eyes wild with fear, charged, hoofs and wagon wheels tearing into those surrounding the President.

Screams erupted. Eyes turned to Devin and Lawrence when one private shouted, "It's them! They've got a bomb!"

"Kill them! Kill them!" rose from the throats of grey clad men, holding weapons with fixed bayonets.

"Jump!" shouted Devin, as he sprang off the wagon, but Lawrence, trying to manage the horses, was struck by a rifle butt, then impaled by a bayonet. Screaming, he toppled to the ground.

The horses reared up, flipping the wagon and launching Devin into the air. He tried to scramble out of the way, but hay bales tumbled, pinning him to the pavement. He glanced up as a rifle butt was raised above his head. His eyes widened, he shouted and thumbed the device still in his hand. He didn't see the rifle butt descend because it never did.

The explosion incinerated those within a sixty feet of the wagon. The lives of the re-enactors, all those around the dais, as well as dozens of spectators still in nearby stands were agonizingly terminated. The imposing columns supporting the front of the building split and collapsed into a pile of rubble. That was followed by an avalanche of brick and mortar as the structure's ancient front toppled onto twisted corpses.

From hundreds of yards away, people heard an enormous roar and saw a cloud of smoke and debris rise into the air. The copper dome, now unsupported, fell and splintered into metal shards. Smoke and ash rained down upon the heaps of stone, brick, and jagged metal. One of the FBI agents lay crushed by a stone pedestal; two others were attempting to rise, their suits, hands and faces the color of ash.

Steven, Sutter, and the deputy slowly rose to their feet. They coughed and wheezed, tripping over stone and broken furnishings.

Stunned, and choking Steven shouted, "Janice? Where are you?"

Sutter put her hand on his shoulder and shook her head as dust continued to descend.

"We need to get out of here," she said, between spasms of coughing.

He knew she was right. Several fires had started, sending more smoke through the roofless building. They were standing under a section of flooring held up by twisted metal beams. Scorched draperies hung from above and floated, ghostly, over the void below. A remaining section of the floor above tilted precariously, and a swivel chair rolled off and crashed by their feet.

They stood still as dust and ash settled over a moonscape of debris. Then Steven took a half dozen steps, knelt beside the dead agent, and said, "Help me get this pillar off Jason."

That done, Steven, Sutter and the deputy went to each of the prostrate forms to determine if any were still alive. None were.

They then stepped over sections of the dome and stared out to what had been the dais and viewing stands.

Bodies and parts of bodies lay amongst remains of the stands, wagons, and pillars. Shredded bunting was draped over unmoving figures. There was no sign of Lee or any of his cabinet, only a large blackened space and the smoldering remnants of the dais.

"We best pick up Jason and get out of here," said Sutter, staring up at one sliver of the dome that had not yet collapsed.

"Good idea," said Steven, as sirens wailed from blocks away.

"You hear that?" said the deputy.

"I hear sirens," said Steven.

"No, a man's voice. From over there," said the officer.

They scrambled toward a void left by a collapsed wall. Tunnel-like, the space beyond was cluttered with rubble.

"He's in there," said Sutter, spying an extended arm.

Tearing away stone and splintered wood, they dragged a man out. He was elderly, and wearing a period frock coat. "I think my leg's broken," he said, then pointed back at where he had been trapped and said, "A woman's inside. Still alive, I think."

With frantic exertion, the agents and deputy shifted debris until the deputy said, "There she is. Yes, she's alive."

Face down, covered in dust, they pulled her from the wreckage and turned her over. Steven knelt beside the woman.

Gazing up, she gave a tremulous smile and weakly said, "Thank you. I thought I was going to die."

"What's your name?" asked Sutter.

"Clara. Clara Brighton. I was up there," she said, pointing vaguely to what had been the second floor. President Lee wanted his other set of glasses. Is he. . ."

"They're gone," said Steven. "They're all gone. Was there anybody else with you?"

The woman shook her head. "No, just me. Will you take me out of here?"

"Best we go out the back way," said Sutter. "This place is unstable."

They carried Clara and Jason over the tumbled brick onto the littered lawn. Figures began to emerge through the pall of smoke.

Steven peered back at the ruins. He felt drained and defeated.

"You did everything you could," said Sutter.

"Not enough," he said, shaking his head.

"Daddy?"

He turned, blinked. "Evelyn?" he said, reaching out and pulling her toward him. "Your mom, she's. . ."

"Over there. She's lying down by that tree," said Evelyn.

Janice painfully rose on an elbow, smiled faintly, then lay back down. She closed her eyes and felt his hand holding hers.

"Steven," she said, as he lifted her off the grass.

CHAPTER 34

A BETTER DAY

Washington D.C.

In thousands of cities and towns, people peered at their screens as news programs flashed "Breaking News."

Never had there been such a large audience for news coverage since the moon landing in July of 1969. Presidents, chancellors, dictators, allies, and antagonists watched as President Edith Barnes stood before the podium in the Brady Press Briefing Room.

Standing alone, peering through her oversized glasses, she said, "I wish to express my condolences and that of the people of the United States for the tragic loss of life in Montgomery, Alabama. The terrorist attack was carried out by a few individuals. They were in no respect aligned with or directed by the government of the United States.

"The entity calling itself the Nationalist Christian Republic of America is no longer a political entity. Investigators report that the detonation resulted in the loss of the NCRA leadership, as well as many bystanders. The Constitution and apartheid practices it represented are null and void.

"The U.S. legislature is in the process of returning the secessionist states to the Union. This may be a lengthy effort, and will entail requirements such as school textbooks being rewritten and the eradication of racist rhetoric and non-scientific mythology.

"In addition, we require that adult citizens of the seceding states pledge their allegiance to the Constitution of the United States. The speakers in the House and Senate have indicated that the former U.S. senators, representatives and governors of those states must resign from office and new elections take place. The question of treasonous actions is a matter for the courts.

"There will be no martial law declared in any of the states. Food and medical supplies are already en route."

She stopped, removed her glasses, and solemnly looked into the camera. After several long seconds she said, "The NCRA and the catastrophe it brought on is over, but we are a long way from harmonious unity. There has been a vile, racist mindset in this land for decades that has led to this disaster. And there are numerous people who still hold those views. Hopefully, in time, and with a new generation schooled in the value of all people, this stigma upon our nation will fade into oblivion.

"Dear citizens, I trust that the wisdom of our people will persevere and lead us forward. This nation will have a new birth of freedom—restored, and enhanced by the better angels of our nature."

*****

In Maryland, Doctor Bhavna Sanvi and her class of biology students watched the president's address. She smiled at the remarks about textbooks and scientific content.

The angst that had besieged her when hounded out of Montgomery had slowly dissipated as she was welcomed into a new community. But she wondered about Wendel Talbert and how he would react to new guidelines and the banning of the books he'd demanded she teach from.

Later that day, she received a call from Jerry Rabinowitz, who had gained admission to the University of Maryland.

"Hey Prof, one of my old friends, Tommy, called from Manassas. Some of the kids and faculty are wondering if you and others might consider coming back."

"Not if Talbert's still there and prayers have to be said every day."

"Well, Tommy said that Talbert resigned, and there's a new school board, new administration. Some of the teachers who left have gotten invitations to return."

Bhavna sighed and said, "I haven't received one yet, Jerry, A lot of people there were glad to see me leave. I doubt that they will be very welcoming. No, I'm pleased that my replacement can now teach facts, not myth, but racist attitudes don't change overnight. I'm quite happy here, actually. Come on by and we'll have lunch."

"Sounds good."

The invitation to return to her former teaching post was in her mailbox the next day. She read it, and pondered her options. *All those years*, she thought, *and they want me back. Something to think about, but not today.*

*****

"I had a rather somber meeting with your daughter, Director. Based on your statements, I gave her an incomplete for the last semester, which means she has a chance at a do over," Rathmore said.

"That's very generous of you, Professor," Steven responded. "Are you readmitting her to your class?"

"I already have. I must say, she's rather subdued. Maybe contrite is a better word. She has indicated an interest in law enforcement."

"Oh, Lord."

"And I might also mention that she has met my nephew, Ronald Cal, and they seem to be taken with each other. He's a pretty sharp guy. I suspect marriage is in the offing. You and I might be in-laws."

"Dear, dear. Need I investigate him?"

"Oh no, he's hoping to join the FBI after graduation. That's in a few months. Should I give him your number?"

"That might show favoritism. But hell, why not?"

"You know, he asked me a lot about Evelyn."

"What did you tell him?"

"Just that she's extremely bright."

"You are quite devious, Professor. Have you considered politics?"

A laugh came through the phone. "Heavens, no. I'm just a dotty old professor."

It was Steven's turn to laugh as they ended the call.

*****

Steven, with Sutter's help, was arranging files in his office when his cell phone rang.

"Would you be interested in lunch?" asked Janice.

"I might consider it, Mrs. Whitinghill," replied Steven. Sutter grinned.

"I think we might have things to discuss, if you're interested."

"Perhaps."

Sutter raised her eyebrows and gave him a "Told you so" look.

"I would really like to see you again. Evelyn thinks I should, too."

He was quiet for a minute.

"Steven, are you there?"

"I'm here. Maybe we can pick up the pieces. I have missed you; I think you know that."

"I do. I just rented a furnished apartment outside D.C. How about dinner?"

"Sure. Is this formal? What should I wear?"

"Anything you want; you could come naked for all I care."

"Maybe after dinner, Mrs. Whitinghill."

"That was nice," said Leandra Sutter, fishing for a lollipop in the depths of her purse.

"I promoted you and you're still sucking on lollipops," said Steven. "Hardly professional."

"They're my favorite. Do you want one?"

Steven shook his head.

"You know, mama said I'm special."

"You already mentioned that. I'm going to have a long talk with mama, young lady."

She simply smiled, got up and walked to the door. "You are a real sweetie," she said.

"Phone number. Your mama," said Steven as the door closed behind her.

*****

There was no official celebration after the fall of the NCRA, but it was announced that there would be a fly-over, a sort of closure as the media termed it. Levi Grossman walked down Pennsylvania Avenue on the sunny winter day. It was amazingly quiet in Washington for a Saturday. Only a few cars ventured onto the streets and everything seemed subdued. But there seemed to be an assumption that a corner had been turned, that the nation was coming back together.

The sound came from miles away as people began to look skyward. Horns began honking and people cheered as the first of fifty tactical fighters, each representing a state of the

Union, flew over the Capitol. Plumes of red, white and blue spewed out of the aircraft and their wings glinted in the sun.

Levi watched the last of them wheel about until they disappeared behind distant clouds.

He smiled, let the sun warm his face, and walked on, passing a man carrying a bouquet of flowers. He nodded and said, "Good morning, Director."

Steven smiled and said, "Good morning. It is a nice day."

"It certainly is. A very nice day indeed."

EPILOGUE

Stanley Palmer was enormously pleased with himself. Reclining in his chaise lounge, he surveyed the mango swamp with its lush vegetation and reached for another beer. It was his third one that morning, and its icy tang was all the more refreshing as the sun climbed high overhead.

"Got out just in time," he said, as if others were listening. "Could have been tiny bits of protoplasm if I was on that dais. Wonder what was the last thought of Jefferson Calhoun Lee?"

Palmer laughed and considered his prospects. He pointed to an imaginary person that might have sat across from him.

"Yes, sir, got my money, but gotta make it last; no cartel sub coming this way, not with the navy out there. I have my contacts still, but that all might be just too much of a hassle. I'll just hang out here for a year or two until all the fuss dies down. Then I'll sidle into New Orleans, find a woman. Could sure use one about now. I can start a radio station under a *nom de plume,* as the French call it. Maybe talk about life in the bayou—snakes, gators, pirates and injuns."

The only thing he intended to do later that day was wash some laundry and hang it out to dry. He had fished around for a clean shirt and found one that he hadn't worn for months. He'd been pleased to find a pack of cigarettes in the pocket. He had so few left.

As he extracted the pack from the pocket a folded piece of paper fell to the sandy ground. Unconcerned, he reached down and was about to toss it when curiosity got the best of him. He opened and peered at a note.

Dearest Daddy,

I am going away and will probably never see you again. I tried to make you like me, tried to please you, but I know that I never could, so I couldn't stay. You would always condemn me, and I would live in fear for as long as you live. But I hope you find happiness someday, though I wonder if that will ever be. Don't try to find me. I have nothing more to say to you. But I still wish you well.

Your daughter,

Shelley

Palmer had built a little fire the night before; its embers still emitted a whiff of smoke. For a moment, he considered balling up the paper and tossing it into pit. But he refolded it and slipped it back into his pocket. He wasn't exactly sure why, but somehow it seemed that burning her last words to him would somehow be wrong. He wished he hadn't found the shirt, hadn't found the note. He had tried hard to ignore the memory of her. But he could not.

"Killed her," he said to himself. He took his church key and pried off the bottle cap, but the beer seemed to have a sour taste.

"Goddammit, I killed her," he said out loud.

The pleasure of the day evaporated and a pall came over him. He spilled out the beer, rose, and went into his aging trailer for the laundry and walked down to the water's edge. It was hot, and he removed his shirt and laid it on the bank. Gathering his laundry, he waded in.

He did not notice the creature lurking yards away, only its eyes protruding above the murky water. He barely heard the swish of its tail or saw the rows of yellowed teeth before he felt them rip into his flesh.

He screamed, flaying his arms as the gator rolled over and over, dragging him farther from the bank. The splashing water floated away the shirt and sent it into the murky depth of the swamp. The paper slid from the pocket and slowly began to float away.

The last thing he saw was the note. The last image in his mind was that of his daughter. *"Shelley!"* his brain screamed as blackness descended. The scream was silenced as the gator consumed him.

THE END

ABOUT THE AUTHOR

RON SINGERTON

After graduating from California State University at Long Beach in 1965 Ron Singerton joined the U.S. Army Security Agency and spent his overseas time in Asia.

The subsequent twenty-five years were devoted to teaching history and art in Southern California High schools, where he developed a particular love for writing and historical research.

During the early 1980s, he authored a series, *Moments in History*, of some thirty mini books on famous people and events ranging from Columbus to the moon landing. The books were adopted as supplementary teaching material for the State of California and approved by the Los Angeles School board as a teaching aid. Published by Santillana Publishing Company, the original ones are considered collector's items.

An avid horseman and saber fencer with a special interest in the American Civil War, he "heard the bugle and the sound of the drums" and became a re-enactor, riding with the Union cavalry in dozens of engagements from California to Gettysburg, Pennsylvania.

Always interested in an exciting but obscure story, his historical research meandered from the nineteenth and twentieth centuries back to the ancient world. Singerton once said, "Technology of the past often appears elementary to us; the emotions do not." For a writer, the thoughts of peoples long past, as well as civilizations now little more than sand-pitted ruins, still evolve into a pageant of love, intrigue and dire conflict. "It is nothing less than a shadowed mirror of our own world."

Through the writings of Plutarch, Pliny and Julius Caesar he uncovered an epic event that would take him from Rome in the last days of Republic to the Great Wall of China. After years of research the tale became the gist of a two-volume novel: *The Villa of Deceit* and *The Silk and the Sword*.

In his third historical novel, *A Cherry Blossom in Winter*, Singerton turns to the tumultuous opening years of the Twentieth Century with a stirring novel of the Russo Japanese war of 1904.

Ron is also an award winning artist, with artwork in glass, stone, paint and bronze sold and displayed online, in galleries, and numerous art shows.

If You Enjoyed This Book

Please write a review.
This is important to the author and helps to get the word
out to others
Visit

PENMORE PRESS
www.penmorepress.com

All Penmore Press books are available directly through our
website, and internationally.

Villa of Deceit
BY

Ron Singerton

Action Adventure, Crime, Mystery,

Rome, 70 B.C.E.

A house in turmoil: a controlling father, an adulterous mother, and an angry son made reckless by a forbidden love. Young Gaius defies his father Toronius, fleeing with a slave girl whom he marries, only to see her die in childbirth. Disinherited and grieving, Gaius leaves his infant son Tacitus behind with a trusted aunt and devotes his life to the sword.

On the battle field Gaius is trained and tempered into a hardened veteran of war. His leadership and bravery in campaigns earn him respect and the rank of Senior Centurion. But his greatest challenge is returning home to face his son Tacitus, now grown to a wild, undisciplined youth. Gaius forces the errant boy against his wishes into the army that he may be molded into a man.

Like Gaius before him, Tacitus must fight to become his own man in defiance of his father. But together as Legionnaires, they must survive an invasion mired by betrayal and confront the fury of war.

PENMORE PRESS
www.penmorepress.com

Silk and The Sword
BY

Ron Singerton

Action Adventure, Crime, Mystery,
Roman History

Young Tacitus, torn from the girl he loves and accused of defiling his late mother's temple, is dragooned into the Roman army by his father Gaius, a bitter and unbending Centurion. With his father and seven legions, he joins General Marcus Crassus in an ill-fated attack on the sprawling Parthian Empire. After the Roman forces are decimated at the Battle of Carrhae, Tacitus, Gaius, and four hundred survivors venture eastward on the fabled Silk Road to find a river beyond a wall that will lead them back to Rome.Tacitus becomes the soldier he never wanted to be while battling bandits, trekking through frozen mountain passes, and dealing with a formidable foe on the other side of the world. But his greatest challenge is a personal quandary: should he return to Rome for his long-lost love or seek the hand of a princess in the mysterious land beside the Great Wall?

"A tour de force of Roman military survival across a long and arduous trek through the Parthian empire, the silk road, and into the celestial kingdom

PENMORE PRESS
www.penmorepress.com

A CHERRY BLOSSOM IN WINTER
BY
RON SINGERTON

As the 20th century dawns, Japan is a rising power at odds with determinedly expanding Russia. In Moscow and St. Petersburg, aristocrats advance their political interests and have affairs as factory workers starve. Young Alexei Brusilov, son of an ambassador, accompanies his father to Japan and there falls in love with the daughter of a Japanese war hero. Despite threats and warnings, he pursues this forbidden romance, delighted to discover that Kimi-san returns his affection, until disaster overtakes them.

Amid the rising storm of revolution at home, Alexei returns to St. Petersburg to become a naval officer. A deadly rivalry with another cadet, a dangerous family secret, and friendships with revolutionaries imperil his career – and his life. Years later, Alexei finds himself aboard ship as the rusting and badly out of date Russian fleet is sent half way around the world to fight a modern and determined Japanese Navy. Will Alexei live to see his love again, or die under the blazing guns of the fast moving enemy cruisers?

"This is a sweeping work about the clash between Western and Eastern cultures, pretended morality, and grand passions struggling against heavily ritualized matrimony.... The author's observations about Russian society and his grasp of its good and bad points would likely have gained an approving nod from Tolstoy. This is first-rate storytelling!" —John Danielski, author of The King's Scarlet and Blue Water Scarlet Tide

PENMORE PRESS
www.penmorepress.com

Blossom In The
Ashes
By
Ron Singerton

1941: Two Brothers, One Woman, One War

Tad, elder son of Russian-born political refugee Alexei and Japanese-born Kimi, flies planes for the U.S. Navy; his brother, Koizumi, is a fighter pilot in the Imperial Navy of Japan. When Koizumi visits his family in Hawaii, he is accompanied by the beautiful Sayuri. To Koizumi's dismay, she and Tad begin a passionate romance, only to be torn apart when she and Koizumi are ordered back to Tokyo.

All too soon, Tad discovers that, if being estranged from a brother for 25 years is bad, seeing him in your gun sights is worse. And as American bombs fall on Japan, Tad fears that he will never see Sayuri again.

Commitment, terror, compassion and unswerving loyalty comprise *A Blossom in the Ashes*, a story of unyielding nations in a world gone mad.

"A riveting novel that is a new twist on family relationships during World War II. Singeron's characters are interesting, the story engrossing and fast-paced. It's a must read for those who like this genre." — Marc Liebman, author of award-winning novels *Forgotten* and *Inner Look*, and *Big Mother 40*, a top 50 war novel.

The sequel to award-winning *A Cherry Blossom in Winter*

REFUSED

BY

RON SINGERTON

Paris! 1861, City of light, art, scandal and great expectations, where extreme wealth rubs against raging poverty, with insurrection roiling beneath the surface.

In the United States, the war of 1861-65 destroys families and communities. Three survivors decide to leave behind the ruins of their former lives. Union cavalryman and aspiring artist Jack Volant, a survivor of Gettysburg, sails to Paris to pursue his artistic vision. Charlotte Stuart, herself a talented sculptress, and her half-brother Jerome turn their backs on a scorched plantation and intractable prejudice.

Charlotte becomes a favorite of Empress Eugenie, wife of Emperor Louie Napoleon and a renowned patron of artists, while Jerome joins forces with revolutionaries. Eventually, Charlotte is able to introduce Jack to Les Refusés—the French Impressionists whose avant garde styles are deemed unacceptable by French jurists. For a little while, Jack is able to forget the horrors of war, painting alongside Monet, Pissarro, Cézanne, Degas, and Manet. Elsewhere in the city, Jack's disreputable brother Marcel profits from the sale of Egyptian artifacts of dubious origin.

But in 1870, everything changes. A spirit of revolution sweeps through the city like a wild fire, and the disastrous Franco-Prussian war reduces Paris to a city under siege where starvation rules.

En Plein Air

by

Mary Sharnick

It is summer of 2001, and renowned American painter Orla Castleberry is in Naples, Italy, as part of a project to call attention to human trafficking perpetrated by the Camorra, a notorious criminal organization. With the help of friends in unusual places, she is able to meet the lawyer who fiercely prosecutes the Camorristi on the rare occasions when any of them are brought to trial for justice, as well as the lawyer who defends them — and usually succeeds in winning their acquittals: Orla's realistic depictions of the abuse of young women, and of the nuns who labor to rescue them, are intended to increase public awareness and aid, but they also provoke the Camorristi into menacing Orla and her family.

PENMORE PRESS
www.penmorepress.com

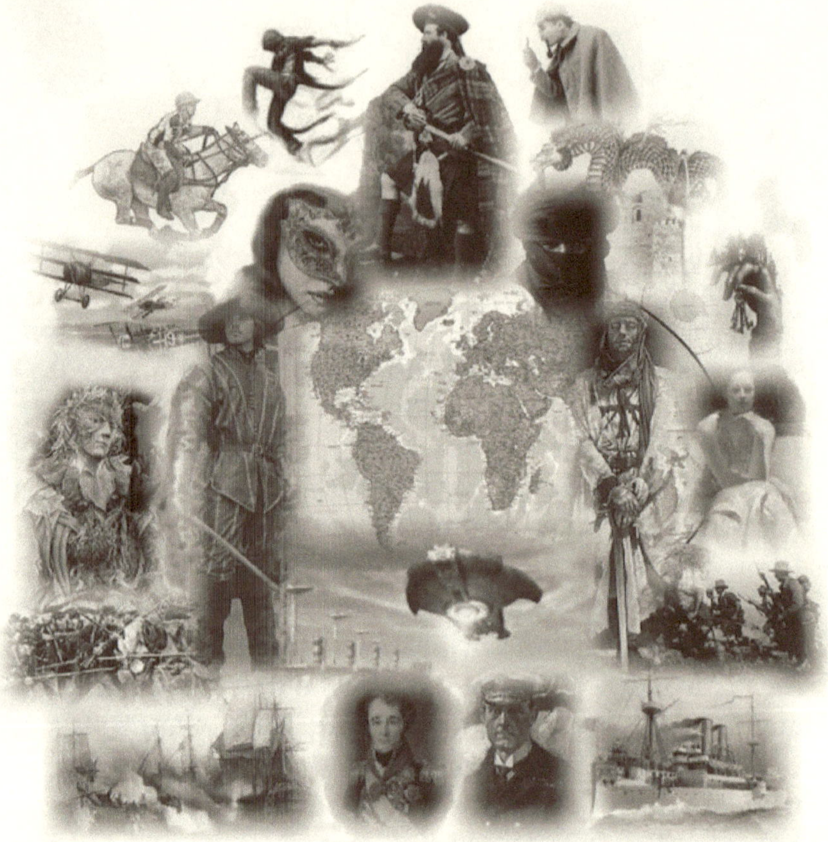

Penmore Press

Challenging, Intriguing, Adventurous, Historical and Imaginative

www.penmorepress.com

9 781957 851389